# PART ONE
# RIVALS

Lovers and madmen have such seething brains,
Such shaping fantasies, that apprehend
More than cool reason ever comprehends.

*William Shakespeare*

# THE NEW BOY

'**S**ub-Lieutenant Calman is here, sir,' said Second Officer Dunning.

Captain Fitzsimmons looked up. A little man, he bristled all the time, no matter what humour he happened to be in. Emma Dunning was an extremely good-looking young woman, trim in her Wren uniform, but he had never seemed aware of it, or even that she was a woman. 'Then you'd better show him in,' he snapped. 'And get hold of Mr Linton, will you. He should be standing by.'

'Aye-aye, sir.' The Wren stepped back. 'Captain Fitzsimmons will see you now, Mr Calman.'

Richard Calman hesitated in the doorway, uncertain whether he should address the young woman as ma'am, or not. Although technically they were of the same rank, he could not doubt that she had seniority. Then he braced himself and entered the room, stood to attention, and saluted. 'Sub-Lieutenant Richard Calman reporting for duty, sir.'

A tall, slender and very obviously young man, he possessed regular features, and a good voice, although his accent was unplaceable.

'What are you?' Fitzsimmons inquired.

'Sir?'

'Calman is not a Scottish name.'

'Yes, sir. I am not Scottish.'

'It's not Welsh or Irish, either.'

'No, sir. I am English.'

'With an accent like that?'

'The accent is West Indian, sir.'

'What?'

'Well, part British Guianese and part Barbadian.'

'Good God! But you're not black.' Fitzsimmons peered at him. 'You're not, are you?'

'No, sir. My father manages a sugar estate in British Guiana.'

'But you said you came from Barbados.'

'No, sir,' Richard said patiently. 'I come from British Guiana. But I went to school in Barbados. I went to Harrison College for two years before Dartmouth.' His tone was proud. 'The Barbadian accent is very strong. It sticks with one. Like the Australian.'

He hesitated, wondering if he had committed a gaffe, although there was no suggestion that Fitzsimmons might be Australian.

'Hm,' the captain said, and looked at the door. 'Yes?'

'Lieutenant Linton is here, sir,' Miss Dunning said.

'Ah. Yes. Mr Linton, I'd like you to meet Sub-Lieutenant Calman.'

'Calman.' Linton returned the salute, then shook hands. 'Welcome aboard.' He was a stocky young man with fresh features, who wore the dark-blue, white, dark-blue ribbon of the Distinguished Service Cross.

'It's an honour to be here, sir.'

Linton looked sceptical, as if wondering for how long the new boy would feel that way.

'Mr Calman,' Fitzsimmons said, 'will join your flotilla and take command of *433*. Goring is still there, isn't he?'

'Oh, indeed, sir.'

'And the boat is back in the water?'

'Yesterday, sir.'

The captain nodded, and looked at the open file on his desk. 'It doesn't say here whether or not you have experience of torpedo boats.'

'I don't, sir'

'Ah.'

'I've been with *Warspite*, sir. As a snotty.'

'Good God! What on earth persuaded you to leave a battleship for an MTB?'

'They asked for volunteers, sir. And –' he hesitated – 'it meant a leg up.'

'That's honest, at any rate. I hope you don't regret it. Still, Goring will show you how it's done. And he began life as an engineer. There is nothing about these boats he doesn't know.'

'Thank you, sir. Would that be Engine-Artificer James Goring? The VC?'

'I see you keep up with the news. He's a petty officer, now. And as I said, what he doesn't know about MTBs isn't worth knowing. Thank you, gentlemen. Carry on.'

The two officers saluted and left the office, Richard picking up his kitbag from where he had left it, beside Miss Dunning's desk. She smiled at him, encouragingly.

'I have a feeling I upset the old man,' he suggested, as they went down the stairs.

'I doubt it,' Linton said. 'He's always like that.'

'I got the impression that he thinks MTBs are a bit difficult.'

'They are.'

'Oh. I'm sorry. I—'

'Forget it. Learning to handle the boats is just a matter of practice. And as the old man said, you couldn't have a better teacher than Goring. The ambience, now, that may take a little longer to get used to. An MTB is a very small world. You'll be the captain, and you'll need to make sure that everyone remembers that. But at the same time, you'll be one of seventeen men confined to a very small space and serving under sometimes highly dangerous conditions. Every man will be fulfilling a vital role when you're in action. You have to trust them, but even more important, you have to make them trust you. Savvy?'

'Yes, sir. Would that be why Crabtree left?'

'Sub-Lieutenant Crabtree is in hospital,' Linton said. 'And is likely to remain there for some time. He stopped several bullets in an action last month, as did the boat, which is why it has been out of the water undergoing repairs.'

Richard gulped. 'I apologize, sir. My day for putting my foot in my mouth.'

'Natural error.'

They emerged from the Command Building on to the dockside, bathed in the August sunshine. Above their heads half a dozen barrage balloons floated lazily, and in front of them the blue of the inner harbour sparkled, even intersected as it was with pontoons and small craft, some moored alongside, others carving white swathes as they made their way in or out into Portsmouth proper and the bigger ships lying

at anchor in Spithead, with the solid mass of the Isle of
Wight in the background. The breeze was no more than
gentle.

'Hard to believe there's a war on,' Linton remarked, as he
led the way to the ramp leading down to one of the pontoons.

'Or that we're winning it,' Richard commented.

Linton ignored the remark; he had already worked out that
his new subordinate was inclined to speak without too much
interest in how his opinions might be received. So he merely
asked, 'Were you with *Warspite* long?'

'I joined February 1940.'

'Two and a half years? Then you saw action in the North
Sea during the Norwegian campaign.'

'Yes, sir. Not that there was a lot of it. We exchanged fire
with some German units, and we did some bombarding of
shore installations, but it was mostly dodging aircraft. It was
more exciting in the Med.'

'Of course,' Linton agreed. 'You were at Punto Stilo. And
took a hit, if I remember rightly.'

'From aircraft, yes. More than one. But we scored a big
hit on *Giulio Casare*.'

'And you were at Cape Matapan as well.'

'Yes, sir. That was bloody murder. Those three Eyetie
cruisers found themselves right under our guns. Well, what
were we to do? I've never seen anything like it. I had no
idea fifteen-inch guns could be so destructive, and it was
point-blank range.'

'As you say, they were the enemy,' Linton pointed out.
'And there had been a battle. I've never served on a
battleship.'

'But you must have seen endless action,' Richard
suggested, as they descended the sloping gangway, their
shoes clumping dully on the swaying wooden boards beneath
them. 'I mean, you served in the Med yourself, didn't you?
You were part of the flotilla that sank *Napoli*.' He glanced
at the medal ribbon on Linton's tunic. 'Was that where you
got the DSC?'

'I got this one for the raid up the Gironde last year. They
tell me I'm to have a bar, but there hasn't been an investiture
since.'

'And that will be for the attack on *Napoli*?'

'My boat was the only survivor,' Linton said sombrely. 'And we didn't sink *Napoli*. There was no way four MTBs were going to sink a super-battleship. But we damaged her, so that she was stuck in port for a while, and as you may know, last month the RAF finished the job.'

'Must have been some show. That was where Petty Officer Goring got his VC, wasn't it?'

'Yes. He saved the life of his CO. You may have heard of him. Lord Eversham?'

'I suppose everyone has heard of Lord Eversham. He got pretty badly shot up, didn't he?'

'Actually, he broke his leg in several places. But in the circumstance he would have died, but for Goring. His boat got hit, and he, Goring and the cook, Wilson, were the only survivors. With the ship sinking under him, Goring managed to get her ashore on the Yugoslav coast and make contact with the guerrillas.'

'And the other two boats were also lost?'

'With all hands.'

'So where is Lord Eversham now?'

'Convalescing. A shattered leg takes a lot of time. But he'll be back.' They had reached the last arm of the pontoon, and Linton indicated the twelve boats moored there. 'Those three are my flotilla. And that one is your command, Mr Calman.' Richard surveyed the little ships. 'They look sleek.'

'Depending on when last they were overhauled, they'll do better than forty knots at full speed.'

'But I see what you mean about size. Forty knots! Can they shoot with any accuracy at that speed?'

'Depends on sea conditions. You'll learn about battle tactics over the next couple of weeks.' Linton went to the nearest boat. '*432* is mine. *433* is just outboard. Petty Officer.'

'Sir!' The petty officer stood to attention, as did the other sailors busily washing down the decks and attending to various duties.

'Carry on,' Linton said. 'We're just passing through. Sub-Lieutenant Calman is commanding *433*.'

'Welcome to the flotilla, sir.'

'Thank you, Petty Officer.' Richard entered through the open gangway; the hull moved beneath his weight.

'Plywood,' Linton reminded him. 'They're tender.'

Richard followed him round the stern deck to the boat moored alongside, where another petty officer stood to attention.

'Petty Officer Goring,' Linton announced. 'Sub-Lieutenant Calman is your new CO.'

'Sir! Welcome aboard.'

Richard studied the young man, and he was remarkably young, certainly when compared with the rather grizzled veteran on *432*; he did not think this man was greatly older than himself, but of course, he had to be. He was tall and lean, but with powerful shoulders and strong hands; it was his smoothly rounded features that gave the impression of youth. And whatever his age, he wore the crimson, dark blue, crimson of the Distinguished Conduct Medal on his blue tunic, even if the distinctive crimson of the Victoria Cross had not yet been added; as Linton had pointed out, the action with the Italian battleship that had brought him so much honour had taken place only six months before: there had not yet been time for an investiture. Although the lesser medal indicated an already noteworthy career. 'I'm glad to be here, Mr Goring,' he said, and extended his hand.

A moment's hesitation, then Jamie Goring clasped the fingers.

'Well, I'll leave you to it,' Linton said. 'We're not on patrol today, so I suggest you take her out for a spin this afternoon. The sooner you get the hang of her the better. Goring will show you the ropes.'

He returned to his own boat, and Jamie again stood to attention, blowing a short blast on his whistle. 'Crew will stand by for inspection,' he called.

Men appeared from all over the place, lining up on the foredeck between the two torpedo tubes. Richard unslung his kitbag and placed it on the deck, and Jamie carefully moved it to one side to allow him to pass along the narrow side decking, which he did somewhat precariously; it was considerably narrower than anything he had previously encountered. Jamie followed and walked beside him down the row of men.

'Leading Seaman Wellard; Able Seaman Bright. Able Seaman Walker. Able Seaman Smith. Ordinary Seaman . . .' The names whirled around Richard's head. There was no way he was going to remember all fifteen of them, until he reached the last. 'Cook Wilson.'

A somewhat cadaverous-looking man with a weather-beaten face. 'Cook Wilson has been with this command,' Jamie explained, 'from the start.'

'Of course. He was with you in the Adriatic. But it couldn't have been on this boat.'

'Well, no, sir. This is our fourth boat together. I mean, he and I both served under Commander Lord Eversham from the beginning of the war. We are the only two survivors of the original crew.'

'Lord Eversham,' Richard said, half to himself. An almost legendary figure, the man who had not only led the raid into the Adriatic to attack *Napoli*, but the hardly less famous raid up the Gironde last year. It was probably a good thing only two of these men had served with him on those occasions; he was clearly going to be a hard act to follow. 'Thank you,' he said. 'Carry on.'

The crew went about their duties, and Jamie signalled the obviously youngest member of the ordinary seamen. 'Put Lieutenant Calman's gear in his cabin, Lewis.'

'Aye-aye, Petty Officer.' The boy hurried off.

'Now, sir,' Jamie said, 'where would you like to start? At the top and work down, or at the bottom and work up?'

'As we're here, Mr Goring, let's start here.'

'Very good, sir. Dimensions. We are seventy-one feet, nine inches overall length, twenty feet seven inches beam, four foot six inches draft. That's aft, and on full load, as we are now. You'll understand there is not a lot in the water and so at displacement speed she can be tender. On the plane, now, she's a dream.'

'Lieutenant Linton suggested we could do forty knots.'

'We have touched forty, sir, but that does depend on sea conditions and load. Deep loaded, again as we are now, we displace fifty tons, and so a more realistic full speed would be thirty-eight.'

'You are an engineer, I believe.'

'Yes, sir. I was a motor mechanic before the war. That's why his lordship recruited me for his crew.'

'You know his lordship well, do you?'

'My father serviced his cars, and those of his mother. And I crewed on his lordship's yacht, before the war.'

'Did you now? His mother . . . I assume that would be the Dowager Lady Eversham.'

'Yes, sir.' Jamie's face remained impassive. 'There is of course a current Lady Eversham. She was a Wren.'

'Hm. This mother, would her name be Kirsten, or something peculiar like that?'

'Kristin, sir. Her mother was Swedish.'

'Oh? I understood that she was Spanish.'

'She is Spanish, sir. By birth and upbringing: her father was Spanish. But she has lived most of her adult life in England.'

'And, I believe, has quite a reputation.'

Jamie kept his face expressionless. 'I wouldn't know about that, sir.'

'You only service her cars, eh?'

This man is going to be difficult, Jamie thought. He decided to hurry on. 'Now, armament, sir.' He rested his hand on the shield for the gun, which was situated on the foredeck immediately beneath the bridge. 'This is our pride and joy. It's a quick-firing six-pounder. I know it doesn't look very big, and of course its shell would bounce off the sides of a battleship, but when we're engaging something our own size, like an S-boat, or a sub, for that matter, it can be deadly.'

'And you have done that? Engaged an S-boat?'

'Yes, sir. Several times.'

'Ever sunk one?'

'A few, sir.'

Richard regarded him for several seconds to make sure he wasn't taking the mickey, then he said, 'And I suppose you've engaged a sub, as well. Presumably on the surface.'

'And submerged, sir. Our earlier boats were designed for anti-submarine warfare.'

Richard looked along the deck. 'I don't see any charges.'

'We don't carry any, sir. Our current prime duty is convoy protection and offensive action against enemy shipping.' He gestured at the two tubes situated one on each side of the bow. 'Eighteen-inch. Then there are the two twenty-millimetre pom-poms . . .' He indicated the guns pointed at the sky immediately aft of the bridge. 'They are primarily anti-aircraft, but they can be used as surface to surface, as can the two machine guns. They are three-oh-three.'

'And the crew all know their stuff?'

'The crew is composed of specialists, sir. In action, I command the gun, with three men, Leading Seaman Wellard commands the tubes, and the machine guns are each taken by its own ratings. Cook Wilson is trained as a medic and copes with the wounded until we can return to base.'

'And who helms the boat?'

'Why, sir, you do.'

'Now, the bridge.' Jamie led the way up the two steps to the steering platform. 'May I ask, sir, on which ship you served before joining us?'

*'Warspite.'*

'Were you, sir? That must have been quite an experience. We were moored close to *Warspite* when we were stationed at Scapa Flow, over the winter of 1939–40.'

'I remember. And Lord Eversham covered himself in glory, as usual, by attacking a German fleet on its way to invade Norway. I suppose you were in that show as well?'

'Yes, sir, I was. And we didn't actually attack a German fleet. We had been laying mines, at night, and the Germans were steaming without lights, as you say, on their way to invade Norway. We found ourselves in the middle of them before we knew it.'

'And Lord Eversham attacked.'

'He had not yet inherited the title, sir. He was plain Sub-Lieutenant Duncan Morant. And he followed the lead of our flotilla commander, Lieutenant Leeming. We were lucky to get away with it; both the other two boats in the flotilla blew up.'

'You seem to have had a pretty full war, Mr Goring.'

'Goes with the job, sir. What I wanted to ask was, do these instruments mean anything to you?'

'Not a lot.'

'But if you were a watch-keeping officer . . .'

'Down to a few weeks ago, Mr Goring, I was a midshipman, who ran orders from the bridge and provided the captain with anything he wished. So tell me, how old are you?'

'Today is my twenty-first birthday, sir.'

'Good lord! Twenty-one! And a petty officer? I hope you're going to celebrate?'

'Well, sir, as we're not on patrol again until tomorrow, I have been given liberty for the afternoon and night, and had intended to, ah, spend the time with my family. But as we're required to go out—'

'That's nonsense. On your twenty-first birthday? You can show me how to handle her when we're on patrol tomorrow.'

'Mr Linton gave us a command, sir. He will expect it to be obeyed.'

'Well . . . you'll have tonight off. There's my word.'

'Thank you, sir. We can familiarize you with the instruments when we go out this afternoon. Now, sir, if you'll come with me.' There was a hatch at the rear of the bridge deck, and he led the way down this ladder into a large cabin, the centre of which was occupied by a long table. 'This is the mess deck, although as you can see it also contains a lower steering position just in case the bridge becomes untenable. Here is also the radio station.' He indicated the two sets, MF and VHF mounted on the forward bulkhead.

'Who is our radio operator?'

'We do not maintain a continuous watch, sir, although of course at sea the sets are always on. Every member of the crew is trained in their use; it's a part of the qualifications for joining.'

'I see,' Richard commented, uncomfortably aware that in their haste to replace the wounded Crabtree the admirals had not made it a necessary qualification for him.

'But in the main, sir,' Jamie said, 'this cabin is used for the mess. I'm afraid we all mess together.'

'So I understand,' Richard said, somewhat grimly. He had no real objection to eating with his crew, but he was aware of a growing suspicion that whatever he did on board this boat, and that included eating, was going to be in the shadow of the famous Lord Eversham.

'Down here, sir –' Jamie went down the short forward companionway – 'is the galley . . .' – from which attractive smells were emanating as Wilson fussed over his pots – 'and then the fo'castle.'

Richard peered at the twin rows of bunks, each three-tiered. 'There's hardly space to turn over. You don't use hammocks?'

'There's not sufficient headroom for that, sir. It's not as uncomfortable as it seems; most nights we're in harbour, and can use the mess ashore, while if we're not on call those of us living in the neighbourhood can even go home.'

'And that includes you.'

'Well, yes, sir. Lymington is only a longish bus ride away. Providing they're running.'

'I see.' Another uncomfortable awareness, that he lacked any sort of home, in England, apart from this boat or the officer's mess. 'So where is the engine room?'

'Under the mess deck. We'll go there now.' Jamie led him back up the companion, and then down the aft ladder to a small lobby, in the forward bulkhead of which the door to the engine room stood open. 'Engine-Artificer Brewster.'

A little man who Richard had just met on deck. 'Brewster.'

'Mind your head, sir. The deck's a little low.'

Richard ducked and entered the confined space. 'That's an impressive piece of machinery.'

Brewster looked at Jamie, and Richard remembered that down to a few months ago this would have been his engine. But the petty officer gave a quick nod, and Brewster spoke enthusiastically. 'It is a three-shaft Packard, sir, capable of developing four thousand brake horsepower. And with these –' he gestured at the two side bulkheads which Richard now realized were huge fuel tanks, on which the sight gauges showed just under full – 'holding over thirteen hundred gallons each, we have a range of over two thousand miles, cruising speed.'

Richard inhaled, sharply. 'Is it petrol?'

'Yes, sir. It's a petrol engine.'

'But –' he looked at Jamie – 'isn't that highly inflammable?'

'It can be, sir,' Jamie acknowledged. 'That is why these boats do tend to explode if they receive a direct hit.' He watched his officer's expression. 'Didn't they tell you that when you volunteered, sir?'

'They told me they could be vulnerable,' Richard agreed. 'I suppose it didn't register that I would be sitting on top of damn near three thousand gallons of the stuff. Thank you, Brewster. Now, Petty Officer, you said something about a cabin.'

'Just along here, sir.' Jamie showed him to the aft end of the lobby, and into one of two small sleeping cabins, in which in addition to the bunk, on which his kitbag waited, there was a small desk and bookcase. 'Your heads are through there.'

'Thank you, Petty Officer. It looks very comfortable. Who uses the other cabin?'

'At the moment, no one, sir. The boats are designed to carry, in addition to the skipper, an executive officer, where the skipper is also a flotilla leader.'

'And thus I do not qualify.'

'I'm sure you will, in the course of time, sir.'

'Thank you for those kind words, Petty Officer. And now . . .' He half turned his head as the sound of a tannoy blared across the afternoon.

'All commanders report to flagship.'

'Well, sir,' Jamie commented. 'It looks as if the CO wants to welcome you.'

'What do you reckon?' Wilson asked, when Jamie joined him in the galley. The pair, having served together for more than two years, and especially as the only survivors – with Duncan Eversham – of the wrecked *412*, had become good friends.

'He's out of his depth, and only just realizing that,' Jamie said. 'And he feels he's walking in the skipper's shadow.'

'Well, he is doing that. But will he measure up?'

'We'll have to see. But as he's what we've got, we had better see that he does.'

'When do you think the skipper will be coming back?'

'With a leg that badly broken? Not for a good while yet. And when he does, it won't be to us. He's to get his next stripe.'

'Captain? How do you know that? Of course, you're a friend of the family.'

Jamie grinned. 'Chance would be a fine thing. But her ladyship still uses Dad's garage. Both their ladyships, in fact.'

'And they chat up your old man?'

'Her ladyship, the older one, chats up anybody, when she's in the mood.'

'You had something going for her, didn't you?'

'Eh? What do you mean?' Jamie's voice was suddenly sharp; had he been that careless?

'Well . . . when we pulled her out of Guernsey, back in '40, didn't you spend a fair time in the skipper's cabin with her?'

'She happened to have a chunk of broken glass embedded in her foot. I had to take it out and dress the wound.'

'And as I remember, she had virtually nothing on at the time. Lucky for some. She's a real looker. And I'm supposed to be the medical orderly.'

'And if I remember rightly, Joe, you were busy at the time with the really wounded. Anyway, you have got to be joking. She's a Lady, and old enough to be my mother. You'd better hope the skipper is soon back: that stew smells good enough to eat.'

Jamie went up to the bridge. Old enough to be my mother, he thought. But she wasn't his mother. And it was quite impossible to consider Kristin Eversham merely as his mistress, even if he knew that she had spent a lifetime in that role for various men, beginning with Duncan's father, before he had married her. When they had first got together, she had told him that when the late Douglas Lord Eversham had decided to divorce her, ten cases of adultery, each with a different partner, had been proven against her. Not that this had bothered her; she had found the whole thing a huge joke. But then, as the sole heiress of her Spanish multi-millionaire father, Kristin could afford to treat all life as a joke, and did so.

Except . . . he did not feel she treated him as a joke. Perhaps that supposition was merely an aspect of his masculine pride, but he felt it was evident in their relationship. When, out of the blue, at least as far as he was concerned, she had let him know that she wanted to sleep with him, he had supposed he had to be dreaming. He had been eighteen years old, and she had been forty-two. When he had come down to earth, guiltily, because her son was the man he most admired and respected in all the world, he had assumed she was a randy older woman in search of a one-night stand. But that had been more than two years ago. And her passion still seemed unfulfilled. So where he had begun by telling himself never to look a gift horse in the mouth, he now knew that he was desperately in love with her. Or at least with her body; but then, he had never known any other female body, save for one very forgettable night in Gibraltar. And she . . . he wasn't sure that Kristin Eversham knew any more than he did what love was. But he had the evidence of his senses that she wanted him as urgently as he wanted her.

So where was it going to end? Where could it possibly end? He supposed the only good thing about being at war was that considering an end, to anything, was a waste of time until the war itself ended, and right now there was no sign of that happening in the near future. So, he lived only for the present, taking each day as it came. Like today. As he had obtained liberty, he had telephoned her last night, and they had been going to meet at their private hideaway – her son's yacht – this afternoon. And now he was required to wet-nurse his new officer. She would be furious at being stood up. But she had been connected with the Navy long enough to know that these things happened, and in time of war more often than not. And there was always this evening, supposing she could get away – and Kristin could always do anything she really wanted to.

'Gentlemen!' Commander Webster surveyed his eleven skippers, assembled in the mess cabin of 444. A powerfully built, stocky man with a pronounced chin, he was normally good-humoured but today he was distinctly agitated, and frowned as he regarded the new face. 'Who are you?'

'Sub-Lieutenant Calman, sir,' Linton explained. 'Replacing Mr Crabtree on *433*.'

'Ah! Welcome, Mr Calman. You've arrived at an opportune moment. How long have you been in MTBs?'

'Today is my first, sir.'

'What?' The commander looked flabbergasted.

'Mr Calman has come to us from *Warspite*, sir,' Linton said. 'On which he has seen considerable action.'

'A battleship,' Webster remarked, his tone disparaging. 'Who's his PO?'

'He has Goring, sir.'

'Hm. Well, I suppose that's something.'

'I am going out this afternoon, sir,' Richard ventured, 'to receive instruction. From Goring,' he felt it prudent to add.

Webster did not look mollified. 'Yes, Mr Calman. You will be going out this afternoon. But any instruction you may receive will have to be by the by.' Again he surveyed the faces in front of him. 'I have just been given these orders from Rear-Admiral Lonsdale personally. They are verbal and top secret. The squadron, that is the entire squadron, will put to sea at 1700. This is not to be a raid, apparently. We are to proceed along the coast as far as Eastbourne, take station there, and await further orders. I have no idea for how long we are required to wait in that position, and I am aware that there is no harbour at Eastbourne, but this should not be a problem. The weather is utterly settled, the sea is like a millpond. We will therefore anchor, and as I say, await further orders. Now, I was not allowed to inquire into the nature of these somewhat unusual instructions, and so neither are you. It wouldn't do you any good, anyway, as I am not in a position to answer any questions. As I said, this operation appears to be top secret, and must remain so until we are stood down. There will therefore be no liberty, as of now, and absolute radio silence, although you will maintain a listening watch in the case of orders requiring immediate action. Thank you, gentlemen. I will wish you good fortune in, well, whatever task we are told to perform. Dismissed.'

'What do you reckon is up?' Sub-Lieutenant Owen wondered as they returned along the pontoon. His *437* was moored immediately astern of *432*, and was the third boat in C Flotilla.

'If not even the old man knows, how do you expect me to?' Linton countered.

'You're straight from a battleship, Calman,' Lieutenant Matthews commented; he commanded D Flotilla, and his *438* was outside *437*. He was the only other surviving officer of the Mediterranean campaign earlier that year, but had not taken part in the Adriatic operation; his boat had been bombed and sunk while alongside in Valetta just previously and as there was no replacement available, he had been awaiting repatriation to England when his comrades had gone to their doom. 'Ever had orders like these before?'

'Probably, sir. But on a battleship any orders very seldom filter through to the midshipman's mess.'

'Well,' Owen declared, 'I reckon we're being mobilized for the invasion.'

'What?'

'This Second Front everyone is talking about.'

'You have got to be joking,' Linton said, 'Second Front? With twelve MTBs?'

'Of course not. But don't you see, old man, it's part of the general mobilization. What's the nearest French port to Eastbourne?'

'Dieppe,' Richard said.

'There you go.'

'And you reckon,' Linton said, 'that we're about to invade France via Dieppe. You think there are at least half a million men concentrated in Sussex waiting to go? And the whole fleet? All poised to go, without anyone knowing anything about it, and leaving from the one place on the south coast where there is no harbour?'

'To carry out an invasion across sixty miles of open water?' Matthews put in. 'How are the troops going to be sustained? If we're going to invade anywhere, it has to be out of Dover, twenty miles from Calais.'

'Anyway,' Linton said, 'we don't have half a million fully armed troops in England.'

'Then you tell me what we're doing,' Owen said.

'I have absolutely no idea,' Linton replied. 'We'll find out when someone is ready to tell us.' He accompanied Richard to *432*. 'You going to be all right?' he asked, as they stepped on board.

'I'll have to be.'

Linton glanced at him. 'You can rely on Goring.'

'You've sailed with him before? I mean, before the Adriatic?'

'I've been on MTBs for eighteen months, always serving under Eversham, until he got hurt in February.' He gave a wry smile. 'I lost my boat on that raid up the Gironde, following him.'

'But you got out. And picked up a gong.'

'We all got gongs for that one. And Eversham picked me up. And my crew. His lordship never lets his people down.'

'He seems to be pretty well hero-worshipped around here.'

'Well, let's say that when he saw an enemy he went for it.'

'And Goring served with him all that time.'

'Goring was with him long before I ever knew either of them. Wherever Eversham was, Goring would be right behind him. A strange relationship, really. Eversham, Eton and Cambridge, millionaire yachtsman and playboy, son of the most notorious woman in the country, and Goring, village school and his father's garage. And yet . . . well, friends. Close friends.'

'I hope you're not telling me something I don't want to know.'

Linton laughed. 'Good lord, no. I don't know about Goring, but his lordship was one of the aristocracy's most famous studs, at least until he got together with that pretty little Wren lieutenant up at Scapa Flow, and shocked everyone by marrying her.'

'*Warspite* was up there at the same time,' Richard said thoughtfully. 'I remember Eversham, just about. And you say he married someone on the base? Good lord! You wouldn't remember her name?'

'Well, I know it's Alison. Alison . . . ah . . .'

'Not Brunel? A signals officer.'

Linton snapped his fingers. 'That's it. Don't tell me you knew her?'

'Yes, I did.'

'Oh, yes?'

'Oh, nothing like that. I was a snotty and she was a second

officer. I don't think she knew I existed. I do remember that
she was very good-looking.'

'She still is.'

'But I'm surprised Eversham's family allowed him to
marry her. I mean, she wasn't exactly aristocracy. And she
left Scapa very suddenly and somewhat mysteriously. There
was some talk of a scandal.'

Linton grinned. 'The scandal, my boy, was her taking off
with Eversham. As for his family agreeing, you've never met
Kristin. She organized the whole thing. Well, good luck.'

Richard had hoped for an enlargement on that cryptic
explanation, but as there obviously was not going to be one,
he said, 'Thank you. There's just one thing more: what do
I tell my people?'

'Everything that you know. Some of them will be down
for the night off. That is of course cancelled.' Another grin.
'Don't worry about it; they're used to it.'

'Hm. It won't do much for my popularity. First day on
the job, and I cancel all liberty.'

'You're not here to seek popularity, old man. As I told
you this morning, you're here to command your boat
and your crew. Do that without fear, favour, or hesitation, and
your men will follow you, without hesitation, to hell
and back.'

'You're telling me to be a Second Lord Eversham.'

'That,' Linton said, 'May be out of your range. But if you
make it your goal, you can't go too far wrong.'

Richard surveyed his crew as they ate lunch. Conversation
was limited, as they were obviously sizing him up just as he
was doing for them. There was also an element of curiosity,
as they all knew he had just returned from an officers'
conference at which he would certainly have received orders
in some direction or another.

He swallowed his last mouthful and wiped his lips with
his napkin. 'That was excellent, Wilson. My compliments.'

'Thank you, sir.'

He looked around their expectant faces. 'Now, I'm sorry
to say that all liberty has been cancelled, as of this
afternoon.'

There was a rustle, and a certain stiffening of expressions; even Jamie looked concerned.

'We, the entire squadron, have been ordered to sea. I can tell you nothing more than that, because I do not know anything more than that. We are to take up a position at a point on the south coast and await further orders. Until we receive those orders, it is impossible to say for how long this exercise will continue. As the exercise is top secret, it will, sadly, be impossible even for those of you who may have made arrangements for tonight to cancel them. I am sure your loved ones will accept that this is a concomitant of being at war. Thank you.'

He stood up, and the crew stood also. Then he went down to his cabin, took off his tunic – the August heat was extreme – and sat at his desk to write up his personal log.

Was he apprehensive? He had always believed in being honest with himself, therefore . . . more curious, he thought, as to what was going to happen, and how he would react. He had volunteered for this posting mainly because of the leg up, the moving out of the waiting world of the midshipman . . . as well as the romantic suggestion of rushing about the Channel in a small boat; he had always dreamed of one day owning a yacht without any real expectation of being able to realize the dream.

As for commanding men . . . it had been drilled into him at Dartmouth that he would have to do this, the moment he was commissioned. But on a battleship, the only actual commanding he had been required to do was when in charge of one of the boats, and never under fire; on the bridge of a battleship, surrounded by senior officers calmly going about their business, one had had a tremendous sense of invulner-ability. Nor had there ever been any intimacy with the lower deck; the very idea would have shocked *Warspite*'s officers. In this tiny piece of plywood the only place he would not be intimate with his crew was here in this cabin, and he was intelligent enough to understand that if he ever got around to regarding his cabin as a refuge from his crew, he was on the way to a nervous breakdown.

His business, as pointed out by Linton, was to command, consciously, confidently, and hopefully, successfully. To follow in the footsteps of the great Lord Eversham. Who, for all his renown, had only survived due to the devotion of the man Goring. He wondered if he would ever elicit such loyalty himself, and had a sudden urge to meet the famous commander, find out what made him tick. Perhaps Goring would know how that could be arranged, when they came back from whatever they were about to undertake.

# BAPTISM OF FIRE

Jamie Goring knocked on his captain's door. 'Excuse me, sir. I think the commander is coming over.'

'Eh?' Richard sat up, reached for his tunic and cap, was still fastening his buttons when he reached the deck, only then realizing that it was past four. Webster, having exchanged a few words with Linton, who was on his bridge, was at that moment coming through the open gangway on to *433*. 'Sir!' Richard and all the crew members on deck stood to attention.

'At ease,' the commander said, and came up to the bridge. 'All set?'

'Ah . . . I think so, sir.'

'You need to be sure about it, Mr Calman.'

'We're ready, sir.'

'Very good. Now, I appreciate that you are being thrown into the deep end without first having learned to swim. But you have Goring, and he is worth three of any normal men.'

Jamie had remained on the main deck so as not to hinder the officers' conversation.

'So I have been told, sir.' Repeatedly, he thought.

'However, in all the circumstances, you will take station at the rear of the line. I have instructed Mr Linton to do the same, just to make sure you do not get into trouble. Mr Linton is the most experienced officer the squadron has.'

'Yes, sir.'

'Just follow his example in all things, and do as Goring recommends, and you won't go wrong. I will see you at the rendezvous.'

Richard couldn't suppress a suspicion that he didn't really believe that. 'I will be there, sir.'

'Very good.' Webster looked at his watch. 'Fifteen minutes. Good luck.' He went down the ladder to where Jamie waited. 'And to you, Mr Goring.'

'Thank you, sir.'

The commander regained the pontoon, and Jamie joined Richard on the bridge.

'Do we start her up?' Richard asked. Despite his determination to take what was coming in his stride, he was both excited and apprehensive of the next few minutes.

'Not right now, sir; we wait for the commander to start first. However, we must be ready.' He flicked the switch on the intercom. 'All set down there, Billy?'

'Aye-aye, Petty Officer.'

'Bilges clean?'

'I'll check them now.'

'Who's Billy?' Richard asked.

'The engineer, sir. Brewster.'

'Aren't we all now on duty?'

'Ah. Yes, sir. I do apologize. It was Lord Eversham's habit, to have us address each other by our Christian names, even on duty. He felt it bonded, if you know what I mean. If you prefer otherwise, it won't happen again.'

'Who am I?' Richard asked, somewhat grimly, 'to change Lord Eversham's arrangements. Petty Officer, I am really sorry about your birthday celebration.'

'Our business is to obey orders, sir.'

'Will your girl be upset?'

My 'girl', Jamie thought, will be hopping mad, knowing my girl. But he answered as truthfully as he could: 'I'm sure she'll get over it, sir.'

'Hm. What's that noise?'

'The bilge pump, sir.'

'You mean we make water? I do not hear anything coming out.'

'The bilges are normally dry, sir. Except for condensation. Brewster is making sure there are no fumes down there.'

'Fumes?'

'Petrol gives off vapour, sir. You can't see it, and as a rule you can't smell it, at least above the ordinary engine room odours, including the petrol itself. But it's heavier than air, so it accumulates in the bilges, and is highly inflammable. If we allow accumulation down there, and there is a stray spark when you turn the ignition key, well . . . we'd all be sitting on a cloud.'

'Hm,' Richard commented, not sure how seriously to take him.

'I think the commander is ready to leave, sir.'

Richard looked along the row of boats to the flagship, whose deck was certainly a hive of activity, at the same time as the afternoon became filled with blaring tannoys. 'So what do we do first?' As far as he could see, Webster had not yet started his engine.

'You assemble all hands for casting off, sir.'

'Ah.' Richard thumbed the switch on his own tannoy, took a deep breath, and said. 'All hands will prepare for casting off.'

Instantly everyone appeared on deck, saving only Brewster and Wilson, lining the inboard rail against *432* each man to a warp or a fender. The noise of the various tannoys became submerged in the roar of the engines starting up. Richard looked across at Linton standing with his executive officer – as he was a Flotilla Leader – someone he had not yet met, and received a brief thumbs-up sign; as his was the inner boat, *433* would have to cast off first.

'Time, sir,' Jamie said.

Richard was starting to get the hang of the drill. He thumbed the intercom. 'Starting up, now. Brewster.'

'Aye-aye, sir. Standing by.'

Another deep breath, and he reached for the switch.

'Gear should be in neutral, sir.' Jamie spoke quietly enough, but there was a suggestion of urgency.

'Oh. Right. Ah . . . ?'

'You just pull the throttle lever sideways, sir, and it'll slip out.'

Almost to Richard's surprise it did so. He turned the key and the engine burst into life and then settled into a low rumble. He reached back for the lever, and was again checked by the quiet voice. 'We need to cast off, sir.'

'Quite.' Back to the tannoy. 'Cast off forward. Cast off aft. Bear away.'

This was the drill he remembered from handling the pinnaces. Linton's men released the warps, and two hands reeled them in and cheesed them down; two more used boathooks to push *433* away.

'Now, sir,' Jamie said. 'Just a touch.'

Richard clicked the lever back in, and the rumble became a purr. *433* moved smoothly away from the pontoon. The other ten boats were already streaming out of the inner harbour, the entrance to which lay on the starboard hand.

'Now, sir,' Jamie said. 'A bit more.'

Richard thrust the throttle forward.

'No, no,' Jamie said, as the boat seemed to leap out of the water, causing those of the crew still on the foredeck to grab supports to avoid being tossed overboard. Richard hastily brought the throttle back to the ticking over position. 'She's very sensitive,' Jamie explained. 'But you will need a little more speed to turn her for the entrance.'

Richard felt very inclined to tell him to take the helm, but he knew that would be fatal, so he gritted his teeth and very carefully moved the throttle a quarter of an inch. The purr became a low growl.

'Now, sir,' Jamie said. 'Equally easy on the helm.'

The entrance, through which all of the other boats had passed, save for *432*, and Linton was prudently hanging well back, was now widening to starboard. Richard rotated the wheel.

'Too much, sir,' Jamie said, as the boat nearly turned in her own length.

Richard brought it back, equally violently, and *433* went off in the other direction. For a few moments he sawed the helm to and fro and then got the boat under control and heading between the pier heads. 'Whew!' he commented. 'That was a bit of a mess.'

'You'll get the hang of it, sir,' Jamie said.

Actually, proceeding across the outer harbour, still travelling at no more than five knots to avoid putting up a wake which might damage other craft, was relatively simple, and a few minutes later they were in Spithead, with the other boats strung out in front of them, passing between the two forts that guarded the eastern entrance to the Solent. 'A thousand revs is permissible here, sir,' Jamie suggested.

Richard eased the throttle forward, and the growl of the engine increased while the wake spread away to either side, but handling her at this speed, something just above fifteen knots, he estimated, was relatively simple. 'Do you know, Petty Officer, I'm dripping sweat.'

'I know, sir. Lord Eversham once told me that his first time out was an absolute shambles.'

Richard glanced at him.

'That is a fact, sir.'

'Then I have to say it is the most reassuring news I have heard all day.'

Once out of the Solent, the flotilla increased speed to twenty knots, continuing in single file and taking the inshore passage through the reef south of Selsey Bill. It was a perfectly beautiful afternoon, with not a cloud in the sky and hardly a ripple on the surface of the sea. Richard found he was thoroughly enjoying himself; it could have been a pleasure cruise.

It was just past eight, and the first suggestion of dusk, when they rounded Beachy Head and closed the town of Eastbourne. This was of course blacked out but before the light finally faded they could make out the beach defences and the patrols along the front. By then they were anchored in an orderly line, flags lowered and stowed, riding to the tide and bobbing gently on the still small waves.

'What do you reckon the drill is now?' Richard asked.

'I think we could have dinner, sir. And then we may as well turn in, keeping an anchor and a radio watch, of course.'

'Very good, Petty Officer. Carry on.'

Wilson had the meal waiting, and it was a far more convivial affair than lunch; Richard concluded that his men were perhaps preparing to accept him. When they were finished he went back up to the bridge to enjoy the evening for a few minutes, and also to savour his immediate surroundings. My kingdom, he thought, resting his hand on the wheel; it was a peculiarly exhilarating sensation.

He looked across the water at the other boats, but although it remained a clear night, with the stars appearing to be just above his head, the moon had not yet risen, and the other craft were just dark shapes; all ports were of course blacked out and they were not even showing any riding lights.

Jamie emerged. 'Oh, I beg your pardon, sir. I didn't mean to intrude.'

'You're welcome, Petty Officer. I suppose you've done this sort of thing often before. I mean, waited for something to happen.'

'There have been one or two occasions, sir, yes.'

'And what do you feel?'

'Well, sir, it's best not to feel at all.'

'Explain how you do that?'

'You keep your mind on other things.'

'What other things?'

'That's up to you, sir. It has to be something that completely absorbs the mind, but at the same time can be switched off, just as completely, when the time comes. That means, you shouldn't allow yourself to drift into emotions or worries. They're inclined to stay with you and be distracting.'

'How about an example.'

'Well, sir, my favourite is to go through all the kings and queens of England, giving little mental sketches of each one and what happened to them. It's actually pretty stimulating stuff; they were a pretty wild bunch.'

'You mean you go all the way back to William the Conqueror.'

'Oh, good lord, no, sir. That's kid's stuff. I go back to Cerdic.'

'Who?'

'An Anglo-Saxon king of Wessex at the turn of the fifth century. He is generally regarded as the founder of the present royal house.'

'Good heavens! I never knew that. You read a lot of history, do you?'

'And biography. There's nothing else worth reading, because it's all real.'

'Interesting point. And when things do start to happen?'

'Then you can drop the subject, instantly. In a small boat like this, things usually happen very quickly, and before you know it, it's over and you're out the other side.'

'Suppose you don't? Come out the other side, I mean.'

'In that case, sir, you don't know it, do you?'

'It's a philosophy. Have you never had the desire to move on? To something bigger? Perhaps safer?'

'Oh, no, sir. I've sailed small boats all of my life. I wouldn't want to do anything else.'

'You mean you've sailed with Lord Eversham all of your life?'

'No, sir. When I was a kid I sailed with my dad. He had – still has, in fact – a Bristol pilot cutter. You know boats, sir?'

'I'm afraid I don't. I've always wanted to own one, but there has never been the opportunity. Or the money, to be honest. I suppose that's why I volunteered for the Navy.'

'Your time will come after the war, sir. A pilot cutter is an old design, quite deep draft, with a big main and a couple of foresails out on a bowsprit, and a gaff-rigged staysail. Not fast, but very good in a sea.'

'And you cruised around the Solent?'

'Well, yes, sir. But a bit more than that. My dad took a couple of months off every summer, and we cruised the whole west coast of Europe. Even down to Biscay.'

'Good heavens! And his lordship?'

'Ah, now, *Kristin* would go anywhere.'

'Eh? I hope you're not talking about the Dowager Lady Eversham?'

'Good lord, no, sir,' Jamie protested. Although I could be, he reflected. 'His lordship named his boat after his mother. She's a forty-five-foot schooner. An absolute dream.'

'Where is she now?'

'In a boatyard in Lymington.' Where I should have been this afternoon, he thought, with Kristin. And he hadn't even been able to phone her tonight.

'Well,' Richard said. 'I'm going to turn in. You've arranged the watches?'

'Yes, sir. There will be two men on duty at all times: one on deck and one on the radio.'

'Very good. What time do you have me down for?'

'Oh, good lord, sir. There's no necessity for you to take a watch. If we were at sea, now, it would be a different matter. But in this snug anchorage—'

'You wouldn't be trying to mollycoddle me, I hope, Petty Officer.'

'I wouldn't dream of it, sir.'

Richard couldn't see his face clearly in the darkness, but in any event decided to let it go; after an unaccustomed three hours on the helm he was feeling exhausted.

Unused to the constant motion of a small boat at anchor, even in a calm sea, Richard slept fitfully, and was awakened by a loud noise. There had been no alarm, but he got up anyway, pulled on his clothes, and went on deck, where most of the crew appeared to be gathered. 'Aircraft, sir,' Leading Seaman Wellard explained. 'A whole lot of them.'

'Jerry?'

'I don't think so, sir. They're flying south.'

'And look there, sir,' said somebody else.

Richard looked to the south. The eastern sky was streaked with pink, to suggest that dawn was not very far away. But to the south there were also glows of red, appearing and then fading, almost like pulses.

'Holy shit!' Wellard commented. 'Begging your pardon, sir. That's gunfire.'

Richard went up to the bridge, where Jamie was studying the flashes through binoculars. 'Shouldn't we be over there, Petty Officer?'

'We haven't received any orders, sir.'

Richard looked at his watch. Four o'clock. Then he looked along the line of anchored vessels, but it was still too dark to make out what, if anything, was happening on their decks. 'Damnation,' he muttered.

'Here we go, sir,' Jamie said. The VHF radio was crackling.

Both men went down the ladder and into the cabin. 'This is the squadron commander speaking,' Webster's voice said. 'All boats will weigh anchor and proceed at full speed to the south. Our task is to engage enemy E-boats and S-boats which are attacking Allied troops and transports outside the port of Dieppe. I will give you our dispositions when I see what is happening. Good hunting and good luck.'

'Hallelujah,' Jamie said. 'Shall I sound action stations, sir?'

'Yes, Mr Goring, please do that.' Richard's head was spinning. It was Dieppe. And Allied troops and transports, not just shipping. Was it possible that Owen had been right? He returned to the bridge while Jamie rang the bell, thumbed the intercom. 'Are you there, Brewster?'

'Yes, sir.'

'Very good. We are putting to sea now, and I shall be using full speed for the next couple of hours.'

'Aye-aye, sir.' Almost before Richard had stopped talking the bilge pump was whirring. He allowed it two minutes before turning the switch. Around him the entire morning had burst into sound as every engine came to life. And his crew were all on deck, wearing steel helmets and pulling on their life jackets.

Jamie joined him, carrying their gear. 'Ship ready for sea, sir.'

'Thank you, Mr Goring. Weigh anchor,' he said into the tannoy, pressing the switch to activate the electric winch, and used the few seconds while the anchor was bedded against the bow to pull on his own life jacket and don his helmet, dropping his cap to the deck beside his feet, then engaging gear. The boat moved forward, and glancing to his left he noticed that *433* was actually the fourth boat to be under way. 'We shall be using full speed,' he said into the tannoy, and watched his crew hurrying back along the deck to the shelter of the cabin or go right aft.

He waited the few seconds to allow Linton to overtake him and assume the lead, and as soon as *432* began to surge away eased his own throttle forward. The growl became a roar and the MTB seemed to stand on her stern as she rose on the plane and cut her way across the calm sea. Clouds of spray rose from the bows and some splattered across the windshield and on to his helmet, although most flew to either side, while astern of him the wake spread into the still dark morning. It was the first time he had been on the plane, and all his apprehensions were overtaken by an immense exhilaration.

Now they were into the wakes of the other vessels in front of them, and the sudden turbulence made her harder to hold. Richard reminded himself that if it was only sixty miles to Dieppe, and they were making well over thirty knots, they should be there in under two hours; already the muscles in his arms were aching and his shoulders were feeling heavy.

Jamie was at his shoulder. 'All right, sir?'

'So far.'

The day in front of them was steadily brightening. As according to the almanac the official dawn had arrived, Jamie set the ensign, which streamed above them in the breeze, then braced himself against the mast and levelled the binoculars. 'It's some do. Crikey! Look at that?'

The land was still not visible to the naked eye, but Richard saw a huge plume of smoke rising out of the horizon, and now there came into view a mini-armada of ships, transports, destroyers, small craft weaving to and fro, punctuated by flashes of red and smaller plumes of smoke, while in the sky, but much further off, there were great vapour trails as dozens of aircraft wheeled and engaged in a scene reminiscent of those over England during the Battle of Britain.

'Shit!' Jamie commented. 'I beg your pardon, sir. One of the destroyers seems to have bought it.'

A ship was certainly on fire in front of them.

Wellard emerged from the hatch, carrying his note pad. 'Signal from squadron commander, sir. C Flotilla will bear left and get behind enemy. D Flotilla will bear right to pick up survivors from stricken vessels. B Flotilla will follow me. Acknowledge. I have done that, sir.'

'Thank you, Leading Seaman.' It was now broad daylight. Richard looked around and found *432* on his port quarter. Linton raised his hand and pointed east of south. Richard raised his hand in turn, and made the alteration of course. Owen was outside Linton.

Wellard had returned to the wireless station, and now he emerged again, pad in hand. 'Signal from Flotilla Leader, sir. On approach, reduce speed to fifteen hundred revolutions for accuracy. This is a melee, so you will use your judgement as to selecting a target. Only use your torpedoes when you have a definite target; remember that if you miss, your fish will continue on course and may well hit one of ours. Good hunting and good luck. I have acknowledged, sir.'

'Thank you, Leading Seaman,' Richard said again. He was aware that his heart was pounding, but to his relief it was with anticipation rather than apprehension. 'When do we sound battle stations, Petty Officer?'

'When we come off the plane, sir, otherwise we could lose someone overboard.'

'Good thinking.' Richard stared ahead as he tried to judge the distance. They were within ten miles of the action now, and thus the shore was only about twenty miles off; the houses of Dieppe could be seen, coming and going through clouds of drifting smoke. There was a considerable battle going on over there, although what the objective of it was he couldn't determine. Presumably it was possible for an Allied force to seize the port, but he didn't see how they could possibly hope to hold on to it, any more than the force in 1940 had been able to hold on to Narvik in Norway . . . and they had been supported by major naval units such as *Warspite*.

Meanwhile, there was an equally ferocious battle going on closer at hand, where the destroyers were endeavouring to protect the transports from the attacks of the swarm of German MTBs. He had never seen a Schnell-boat before, but he had read about them, and knew that they were about a third bigger than anything possessed by the Royal Navy, a hundred feet long and powered by MAN diesel engines, which earned them their name: Quick-boats. But however quick they were, they couldn't match the smaller English boats for manoeuvrability, and the MTBs carried the heavier armament, the six-pounder gun, where the Germans were still relying on the twenty-millimetre. They had two of these, but the six-pounder had far the heavier weight of shot.

Webster had led A and B Flotillas into the heart of the action. D Flotilla was lost to sight on the other side. And C was now only five miles off, and well to the east. Richard glanced to his left and saw Linton's arm raised and swinging to his right, while at the same time *432* came off the plane.

Hastily he throttled back, and the roar diminished while the spray ceased to fly. 'Sound battle stations, if you will, Petty Officer.'

'Aye-aye, sir.' Jamie rang the bell, and the crew came on deck. 'We'll need to keep on eye on those chaps.'

'Eh?'

Jamie pointed skywards, and Richard saw some planes detaching themselves from the fight over the land and sweeping towards the ships. 'Pom-pom crews!' he said into the tannoy, and two of the seamen hurried to the bridge to man the anti-aircraft machine guns.

'Good luck, sir,' Jamie said.

'And to you,' Richard said. 'I'm going to mix it. You'll fire as you bear.'

'Aye-aye, sir.' Jamie slid down the ladder and went to the six-pounder, where the three gun-crew were already waiting with the first of the shells. Further forward four men and Wellard were standing by the torpedo tubes, and the other two were manning the two standard machine guns. The only men not on deck were Brewster and Wilson, but the cook was positioned in the hatch, ready, if necessary, to undertake his subsidiary duty as medical orderly, and now he was joined by Brewster as was customary as long as all was well in the engine room; anyone below in the event of a hit would not stand a chance.

Now they were very close, and the German commander had spotted their approach. Two of the little ships detached themselves from the melee and turned towards them, and Richard observed to his relief that their torpedo tubes were no longer manned, to suggest that they had already fired both their missives.

He stared at them, resisting the temptation to look to his left and discover what Linton and Owen were doing. An even greater temptation was to give the order to fire his own tubes: the boat racing at him was no more than two miles away. But it was coming bow on, and presenting a very small target. And now the German guns opened fire. There were flashes of red and plumes of water leapt skyward to either side; the thought of one of those shells striking his plywood was horrifying. 'Reply when you are ready, Mr Goring,' he said into the tannoy, delighted with the calmness of his voice.

Jamie did not waste his time acknowledging the order; he knew his voice would not be heard above the screaming of the engines and the sound of the explosions, to which was now added the chatter of the pom-poms as a couple of aircraft swooped low over them, machine guns belching flame, but with little hope of hitting anything travelling at their speed, even if they were down to twenty-odd knots.

The two boats were now hurtling directly at each other at a combined speed of over fifty miles an hour. Jamie glanced back at the bridge and saw Richard's face, rigid with concentration, his whole body seeming to be frozen. Christ! He thought. I hope he doesn't mean to ram. He stared along the range finder and pulled the lanyard. The gun exploded and recoiled beside him. The breech swung wide, the cartridge case was ejected and another shell thrust into the aperture.

Now at last *433* turned away. Jamie swung the gun with it as they passed the German, no more than a hundred yards apart. He knew his first shot had missed, and he tried to line up more accurately, aware as he did so that a hail of machine gun bullets were whistling about him. He knew from experience that accurate shooting when two vessels were passing at speed was impossible, but now he heard a gasp from behind him, and turning his head saw that Ordinary Seaman Bloom was on the deck, blood pouring from his chest. At the same moment there was a thud on his own body, the force of the blow turning him away from the range finder.

Shit! He'd never been hit before. 'Wilson,' he bellowed. 'Mr Wilson.' Then he turned his attention back to the gun. The two boats were now past each other and for a moment *433* was in open water.

'You're bleeding, Petty Officer,' Able Seaman Bright said. 'You should stand down.'

'Fuck that!' Jamie said. Actually, apart from a slight difficulty in breathing, which he put down to the impact, he was feeling no discomfort . . . as yet.

'Stand by!' Richard said, his voice still calm although a trifle hoarse. 'I'm going about.'

Because now that they were past the S-boat, it was isolated. *433* heeled violently as Richard brought her round in such a tight circle that for a moment Jamie thought they were going over, but then they were on an even keel again.

'Stand by tubes,' Richard said.

The torpedo crew had also been thrown off balance by the abrupt manoeuvre, but now Wellard brought them back as Richard lined his boat up: in front of him the S-boat was also turning to resume the fight, but far more slowly.

'Fire one,' he called. 'Fire two.'

*433* gave a little leap as the torpedoes were released and sped towards the enemy. The German skipper saw the streaks and took evasive action, twisting away from the first. But as the MTB had continued on her straight course, Jamie had also been able to line up a shot, and at that moment his six-pounder shell burst on the S-boat's foredeck. There was a plume of wood and metal and flame, and the German lost control, turning directly into the path of the second torpedo. This time there was an ear-shattering explosion, and where the S-boat had been was replaced by a cloud of black smoke.

Richard stared at his victim in disbelief. If he had been at Matapan and seen the destruction of *Pola*, even *Warspite*'s fifteen-inch guns had taken a few minutes to reduce the enemy cruiser to a blazing hulk, and it had not actually blown up, but had been finished off by torpedoes from destroyers. Now he pulled the throttle back to bring the engine into neutral, and *433* glided to a halt some two hundred yards away from the drifting smoke.

Wilson was on deck and with the help of Brewster was lifting the stricken Bloom into the cabin. Jamie left the gun to go with them. 'He's dead,' Wilson said. 'Lucky you all weren't killed.'

'Yes,' Jamie agreed. 'But we seem to have found ourselves a skipper.'

'And what about you? You realize you're pouring blood? Aren't you in pain?'

'A twinge. I'll survive.' He went up the hatch to the bridge. 'Nice shooting, sir.'

'We wouldn't have hit but for your shot, Petty Officer.'

'Lucky, sir.'

Richard regarded him for a moment, frowning. 'You've been hit. You should get Wilson to look at you.'

'A flesh wound, sir. I'll get him to patch me up as soon as this is over.'

Richard hesitated again, then said, 'Think there'll be any survivors?'

'I doubt it, sir. But I suppose we should have a look.'

'Well, you take her for a moment. I wish to speak with the crew. Did someone else get hit?'

'Yes, sir. Ordinary Seaman Bloom. I'm afraid he's dead.'

'Damnation. Carry on, Petty Officer. I'll be back in a moment.'

'Aye-aye, sir. Shall I close the casualty?'

'If you would.' Richard went down the ladder to the main deck. He felt that he had to move, to do something to negate the awful intimacy of this small-boat conflict, which was so much more intense than on the battleship, where everything was remote, and the enemy even more remote. Now he had a dead man on his hands, and the living? 'That was good work, Wellard. I congratulate you all.'

'Thank you, sir. You handled the boat like a veteran.'

Richard waited for what he felt would be the inevitable comparison, but it did not come; perhaps Wellard had never served with Eversham. 'Thank you. Pity about Bloom.'

'Yes, sir. He was a good bloke.'

'Now, stand by to pick up survivors, if there are any. And then, there is still a battle to be fought.'

For although the action with the S-boat had carried them a couple of miles away from the conflict, it still raged behind them, even if he was not sure how much they could contribute without torpedoes.

*433* was now moving slowly through the water. Richard joined Jamie on the bridge. 'See anything?'

'Wreckage, sir. And a couple of bodies. But they are definitely dead.'

'We'll have a closer look. Will you organize a recovery squad, just in case someone is still floating about.'

'Aye-aye, sir.' Jamie released the wheel and Richard grasped the spokes.

'Aircraft attack,' shouted Ordinary Seaman Lewis, manning the starboard pom-pom, at the same time opening fire.

Richard gave a hasty glance at the sky, and saw the Messerschmitt coming directly at them, low, its wings already spitting red. Violently he thrust the throttle forward, at the same time twisting the helm hard to port. *433* gave one of her leaps, but this was in the nature of a corkscrew, as she seemed to turn on her stern. Men tumbled about the fore-deck, although miraculously no one went overboard, and Jamie, just beginning his descent of the ladder gave a startled exclamation as he fell off the bridge, and crashed on to the deck.

The aircraft shot overhead and away, and Richard was able to regain control and bring the boat on to an even keel. 'Mr Goring,' he snapped.

'He's down, sir,' Lewis said.

'Take the helm.' Richard went down the ladder himself, stood above Jamie's body. But Jamie was totally inert.

The telephone jangled, and Harry the butler picked it up. 'Eversham House.'

'Harry!' the voice said. 'Let me speak with Lord Eversham. It's Rear-Admiral Lonsdale.'

'Sir!' Harry was an ex-Navy man himself, before retiring to become Duncan Eversham's valet. As that was no longer a practical post in a war, and he was too old to be called up himself, he had gravitated to being Lady Eversham's butler, a confusing business as there were now two Ladies Eversham resident in the house. But as both were a trifle unpredictable, life was at least exhilarating. However . . . 'I'm sorry, but Lord Eversham is not at home.'

'Not at home? How can he be not at home in his condition?'

'Well, sir—'

'Never mind. Is Lady Eversham there?'

'No, sir. Lady Eversham is out with his lordship.'

'Ah.' The admiral's voice took on a note of uneasiness.

'But the Dowager Lady Eversham is at home, sir. In fact, she's here now. Would you like me to put her on the line?'

'Ah,' Lonsdale said again. Kristin Eversham had always been one of his two favourite women, and they had been friends, for a while close friends, for several years; he was one of the few people who had not dropped her when the facts behind her divorce had been made glaringly and embarrassingly public – not that they had ever embarrassed Kristin.

But he had early recognized that any man who allowed himself to get too close to her was on a hiding to nothing, at the very least liable to have his personality and ambitions submerged beneath that overwhelming charisma, that flowing beauty. And then, last Christmas, he had at last proposed to her. It had been an act of madness, brought on by a typical Eversham lunch, when the wine had been flowing like water.

The amazing thing was that she had said yes. It had taken him a couple of months to realize that her acceptance of his proposal had had absolutely nothing to do with him: she had been in the grip of some secret emotion of which he knew nothing, and when the emotional crisis had ended she had realized that she did not want to marry him after all.

That had actually been rather a relief, as by then he had also realized that being engaged did not mean that she intended to change her lifestyle in the slightest, would still do whatever she felt like doing whenever she felt like doing it. Nor had he been able to believe she would change her habits even as his wife, which could have been intensely embarrassing for an admiral. But they had only spoken once since she had broken the engagement, when after that near fatal mission to the Adriatic, she had been at the railway station to greet her badly injured son on his return.

On that occasion she had exuded all the warmth that could so dominate those around her. But again he had quickly realized that he had merely been one of those included in the glow of relief at having Duncan home, if not in one piece, at least capable of being put back together. So . . . but his hesitation had been fatal.

'Who is that, Harry?' The soft voice with the delightful Spanish accent drifted down the line.

'Admiral Lonsdale, milady.'

'Jimmy!' She had taken the phone. 'I thought you had forgotten my existence.'

'Ah! Well. I wasn't sure—'

'Silly man! You must come to lunch. Tomorrow. Duncan would love to see you. He gets so frustrated.'

'Does he? Harry said he's gone out.'

'He and Alison are walking the baby.'

'Walking? With a badly broken leg?'

'He's on crutches. And the physiotherapist says he must walk every day. Anyway, I said, Alison is with him.'

Lonsdale reflected that as the current Lady Eversham was less than half the size of her husband, it was difficult to see what she could do if he fell over. But he said, 'I hope they haven't taken that man-eating monster of yours.'

Kristin refused to take offence; her dog was her fourth most important love. 'Lucifer is not a man-eating monster. He cannot help being large. All Pyrenean dogs are large. And he is boisterous by nature. But he would never harm Duncan. In any event, he did not go with them. He's right here. Would you like to speak to him? He loves telephones.'

'Well . . . as it happens, I would like a word with Duncan. Would you ask him to call me as soon as he returns? I have some news that will interest him.'

'What news?' Kristin's voice was suddenly alert.

'It's top secret.'

'Oh, really, Jimmy. Who am I likely to tell it to. Except Duncan?'

'Well, as I say, it hasn't been released yet, and I'm not sure that it will be released, at least until after the war is over. A couple of nights ago we carried out a raid on France.'

'Oh, good lord! Not another fiasco like St Nazaire?'

'The raid on St Nazaire,' Lonsdale said, mildly, 'achieved its objective, no matter how severe the casualties, which was the destruction of the U-boat pens, at least for a few months. The raid on Dieppe was on a much larger scale, something like five thousand troops, and this was, I'm sorry to say, a fiasco. The Germans seem to have known we were coming, and more than half of the force, mainly Canadians, were either killed or captured. We also suffered severe casualties both in the air and on the sea.'

'I can see why you don't want this made public. Are you saying that some of your boats were involved?' A sudden note of anxiety entered her voice, but Lonsdale did not notice it.

'A squadron, yes. Covering themselves with glory, as always.'

So that's why Jamie didn't show, she thought, and tried to control her breathing. 'Well, all I can say is, thank God Duncan wasn't there. Don't tell me you lost some?' Now her voice was trembling.

'Only one. But there were some other casualties.'

'Would you explain that?' Kristin spoke very quietly.

'Well, I thought that Duncan might like to know that that boy, Goring . . . you may remember him. He saved Duncan's life in the Adriatic. He's to get the VC.'

'Of course I remember him.' Kristin's voice continued to be low. 'Are you saying that Jamie Goring is dead?'

'No, no. But he took a hit and then suffered a severe fall, dislocated his left shoulder and broke his left arm.'

Breath rushed through Kristin's nostrils. 'Is he going to be all right?'

'I think so. Given time. It's a bad break. And of course, because his wound wasn't dressed immediately, he lost a great deal of blood.'

'Where is he?'

'In Southampton General. They have an intensive care unit there.'

There was a moment's silence. Then she asked, 'Why is he in intensive care, with a broken arm?'

'Well . . . because of the bullet wound, mainly. It smashed a couple of ribs and there was that blood loss. By the time they returned here he was in a pretty bad way, needing a massive transfusion and that sort of thing. So I thought Duncan might like to know about it.'

'Thank you, Jimmy. I'm sure he will.' Now she was under full control, at least externally.

'Well, then . . . I'll see you tomorrow.'

'What's happening tomorrow?'

'Kristin, you have just invited me to lunch. Tomorrow.'

'Did I? Well, then, I'll see you tomorrow, won't I? Thanks for calling.'

The phone went dead, and the admiral remained staring at it for some seconds before replacing it. Was it possible, he wondered, that Kristin was suffering from some kind of premature senility?

'Not bad news, I hope, milady?' Harry asked, solicitously. In the three years since all her normal staff had been required to join up, leaving her with just her Spanish maid, Lucia, and himself, they had become very close.

'Is there ever any good news, nowadays? I am going out for a while, Harry. Tell his lordship I will see him later.'

'But . . .' Harry looked at the grandfather clock, which stood beside the door to the drawing room; it was just chiming the single note denoting a quarter past twelve. 'What about luncheon, milady?'

'Tell them to go ahead without me. Lucia can put something aside and I'll have it when I come in.'

'Yes, milady,' Harry said doubtfully, but Kristin was already halfway up the stairs to her suite; she had evacuated the rest of the huge house for her daughter-in-law, of whom she was very fond.

She went into her sitting room, closed the door, and surveyed herself in the mirror. Kristin Ojeda de Santos Lopez Morant, Dowager Lady Eversham, had never suffered from false modesty; all through her somewhat turbulent life she had been accustomed to heads turning whenever she entered a room. And at forty-four nothing had fundamentally changed. The auburn shoulder-length hair was as strokeable as ever, the wide lips as kissable, the deep green eyes as seductive. And her body remained, from voluptuous breasts to slender hips to long legs perhaps more compelling than ever.

But after having known so many men, she had determined to settle for just one . . . the one she could never have, on the scale she truly wanted. Kristin was not a woman who ever wasted her time on idle, guilt-inducing, and therefore ultimately depressing, introspection. She had encountered Jamie Goring, then just eighteen, it could be said, fully, in August 1939, at the close of the Cowes–Dinard Race, when she had joined her son's boat for the voyage back to England, only a fortnight before war had been declared.

She had of course known Jamie virtually all his life, as the Eversham cars had always been serviced by Goring's Garage, and Jamie had filled her petrol tank often enough. She had watched him growing into a most attractive young man, without ever giving him more than a passing thought; the gulf in their relative social standings had been too vast ever to be bridged. Until that August day three years ago when she had volunteered to do the cooking – she had sailed all of her life – and Duncan had deputed his youngest crew member to assist her. There had been a gale, and the pair of them had achieved in a few hours a considerable mental intimacy.

Even that need not, and certainly should not, have progressed, but over the next few months their meetings had become more frequent, with all the time a tremendous desire growing within her. She knew he had been shocked when she had revealed what she wanted. She knew he had reflected that she was no more than a randy old woman – from his perspective – looking for a one-night stand, but he had been unable to resist the extreme sexuality, not to mention the allure, being thrust at him.

Of course it should have been a one-night stand; the affair should have ended there and then. Instead it had grown and grown, no matter that they both knew that they were following a street that had to come to a dead end. But with a war on, a possible dead end covered just about every aspect of life.

Then, after two blissful if traumatic years – she could not imagine Duncan's reaction to discovering what was going on – of tumultuously passionate and secret trysts, they had quarrelled. Well, she supposed it was she who had done the quarrelling, in a fit of petulance when she had learned that the flotilla commanded by Duncan was being sent to the Mediterranean for a tour of duty which might last more than a year, supposing they ever came back at all. And in fact only one boat out of the six, and a total of thirty-five men out of a hundred and two, had come back. Her instincts had been correct. But when she had suggested to Jamie that he should desert rather than go, and run away with her – one of her wilder and more irrational flights of fancy, as she well knew – offering to look after him for the rest of his life, he had refused.

Even while recognizing that he had done the correct, and indeed, honourable thing, she had stormed off in a rage, and at Christmas had compounded folly with stupidity by accepting Jimmy Lonsdale's proposal of marriage. That had been the ultimate absurdity. Even if she had been in love with Jimmy, her wayward personality, fuelled by her extreme wealth, made her entirely unsuitable to be the wife of an admiral who believed in discipline and correct behaviour at all times.

So that had become history in short order, culminating in her determination to visit Malta, against Jimmy's virtual command, ostensibly to see Duncan but in reality to be reconciled with Jamie. That had been another act most people would consider irresponsible stupidity – certainly Jimmy had thought so – which had ended in her ship being bombed and her floating around the Mediterranean for two days in a life raft. But it had been worth it.

And then . . . she could remember as if it were yesterday the shock of almost physical pain she had felt when the news had been received that Duncan's boat had been lost with all hands. Her son and the most satisfying man she had ever met, gone together in a moment. She had been unable to think for a week, had hardly slept or eaten. But for the continuing comfort and support of Alison, who had had to stand up to the loss of her husband, and who was one of the only two persons in the world – apart from Jamie and herself – who knew of her mother-in-law's affair, she thought she would have gone mad.

Just as she had almost gone mad, with joy and relief, when they had turned up after all; even if Duncan had had a shattered leg, he was alive, and Jamie, unhurt, had been a hero for saving his life. That had been the happiest moment of her life, and the fact that Jamie had been unhurt, had allowed her to convince herself that he was invulnerable. But whatever had now happened, he was still alive. She had to know how much alive, how he would be when he was back on his feet.

# RELATIONSHIPS

As usual when around the house she was wearing slacks and a blouse, but she felt something more might be needed, as she had no authority to see him and she was not a relative. She changed into a flowered green silk dress bought in Paris just before the war, put on high heels, made up her face, and added three of her most expensive rings, as well as a string of pearls and a gold bracelet studded with diamonds.

Harry was waiting in the hall when she went downstairs, looking more apprehensive than ever as he took in her appearance. 'Am I allowed to tell his lordship where you have gone, milady? He may be concerned.'

'Certainly you may tell him, Harry. I have gone to the hospital. Come along, Lucifer.'

The huge white dog, who had been sitting by the front door, panting – he could tell that something was going on – got up and shook himself, and then advanced, meaningfully; his greatest pleasure was getting on his hind legs to hug his victims. As he weighed a hundred and fifty pounds and stood nearly six feet tall when fully erect, this could be either an exhilarating or a traumatic experience according to how much one liked dogs and how much one valued the clothes one was wearing at the time. But it was always both exhausting and untidy, so Kristin said, 'No, no. We're going in the car.'

Lucifer wagged his tail. He adored riding in the car. Kristin pulled on her kid gloves, and closed the door behind her before Harry could get around to asking which hospital, opened the door for Lucifer to get into the back seat of the Bentley – normally she used her other car, the Sunbeam, for local driving as it was far less petrol-hungry, but she was continuing her plan of overwhelming any opposition, and besides Lucifer preferred the bigger car – and drove the few miles from Lymington to Southampton, ignoring the No Stopping signs to park at the hospital door. 'I won't be long,' she told Lucifer, rolling down her window so that he could have lots of fresh air – there was no risk of anyone tampering with a car containing Lucifer. 'Have a nap.'

She knew the hospital well. Duncan had spent several weeks there before being allowed home, and in the summer of 1940 Alison had also been an inmate after stopping a bullet while mixed-up in the Dunkirk evacuation. Alison and Duncan had, in fact, got married there, with the girl still in bed, which Kristin happily remembered as a gloriously romantic occasion. And then, just before last Christmas, she had been here again for the birth of Baby Duncan.

Thus she was also well known here. Unfortunately, the nurse on duty at reception today was someone she had never seen before. 'Excuse me, madam,' the young woman said, as Kristin strode past the desk. 'May I ask where you are going?'

Kristin paused to give her a withering look. 'Is that any concern of yours?'

'Yes, it is. I am required to keep a note of all visitors and whom they are wishing to see. Especially, as you may not be aware, that it is not visiting hours.'

'Another beastly wartime regulation, I suppose,' Kristin remarked, surveying her more closely. She was an extremely pretty young woman, with splendidly chiselled features exposed because her hair was concealed beneath her cap. 'Well, if it will make you happy, I am on my way to the intensive care ward.'

'But . . . you can't just go there.'

'Why not?'

'Because it's the intensive care ward. The people in there are very unwell. You can only visit them with special permission.'

'Now,' Kristin said, 'You listen to me very carefully, because if you do not you may regret it. I am Kristin, Dowager Lady Eversham. You have a young man in that ward named Petty Officer James Goring. He is an old friend of my son, who as you may know, is Lord Eversham, and is at this moment incapacitated. Petty Officer Goring is, or was, a member of my son's crew, and is under the command of Rear-Admiral Lonsdale. I am visiting him at the request of both the admiral and Lord Eversham, so kindly refrain from interfering further.'

She turned away and the nurse, who had been regarding her with increasing hostility throughout her speech, now called, briskly 'Mr Walden! Mr Walden!'

The doorman hurried over. 'Trouble, Sister Broughton?'

'This lady . . .' Sister Broughton said.

'Why, Mr Walden,' Kristin said. 'How nice to see you.'

'Your ladyship. I thought that had to be your car outside. Is it going to be there long?'

'That entirely depends or how much obstruction I encounter in here.'

'May I be of assistance?'

'This young lady,' Kristin said disdainfully, 'who no doubt is doing her duty, is attempting to prevent me from carrying out a mission of mercy.'

'She wants to go to the ICU,' Sister Broughton said, still short of breath. 'Just like that.'

'Ah! You should be accompanied, milady. Let's see . . . oh, Sister Denton. A moment please.'

Another sister appeared beside them, this one a much older woman. 'Why, Lady Eversham. How good to see you.' Then she frowned. 'There's nothing wrong, I hope?'

'With me, no. I merely wish to see Petty Officer Goring.'

'Ah. Well . . . he really should not be agitated.'

'Do I look as if I am about to agitate anybody?'

Sister looked at her colleague, no doubt remembering previous visits Kristin had paid to the hospital. 'Of course not, milady. It's just that there is someone with Mr Goring, already.'

Kristin raised her eyebrows. 'This young lady informed me that he was not allowed visitors.'

'I didn't,' Sister Broughton contradicted. 'I just said she'd have to have permission.'

'Which you are about to give me, Sister,' Kristin pointed out. 'Who is this visitor anyway?'

'Mr Goring's commanding officer, milady. He's just gone up.'

'Ah! Just the man I wish to see. Shall we go?'

Sister Denton looked at Sister Broughton again, and gave

a helpless heave of her shoulders. 'You'd better come with me, milady.'

'And tell me,' Kristin said as they left the desk behind them, 'who that beastly girl is. You addressed her as Sister. How can anyone that young be a sister?'

'Well . . . she's very good, actually. And very keen. I mean, she shouldn't be on the desk at all, and today is her morning off. But she's standing in for a sick colleague. Her father is Sir Kenelm Broughton.'

'Who is Sir Kenelm Broughton, when he is not fathering monsters?'

'Well, I suppose one could say that fathering, or at least. delivering, monsters is his profession.' Sister was unmarried. 'You must have heard of him. He's the most famous gynaecological specialist in the country.'

'It is nearly thirty years,' Kristin said, 'since last I had anything to do with a gynaecologist. I didn't like that one, and I have never liked the breed since. Where is this intensive care ward of yours?'


'Of course it wasn't your fault, sir,' Jamie protested. 'You took the necessary action to save the ship.'

'I should have shouted a warning,' Richard said.

'There was no time for that, sir. You acted entirely correctly. And if I may say so, sir, you handled the entire action with skill and panache. I hope our superiors appreciate that.'

'Well . . .' Richard flushed. 'Both Lieutenant Linton and Commander Webster seemed pleased.'

'And I'm pretty sure the crew are.'

'I hope so. They were more concerned about you. So, do you think, well . . .'

Jamie grinned. 'Let's say, sir, that Lord Eversham could have done it no better.'

'Thank you, Petty Officer. Now what about you. Is the pain very bad?'

'Comes and goes, sir. They feed me painkillers every couple of hours. And they say I'm on the mend. I'm going into a general ward in a couple of days.'

'Well, that is splendid news, Petty Officer. The crew will be delighted. As am I. So when can we expect you back?'

'Now, that's not so good, sir. They're talking about at least a couple of months.'

'Hm. Well, we'll have to manage without you, for that time.'

'I hope I'm not going to be replaced?'

'Not if I can help it. Wellard can do the job on a temporary basis, can't he?'

'Oh, indeed, sir. But you'll still be a man short.'

Richard nodded. 'Leave it with me. We have to have a replacement for poor Bloom. I'll put in for a temporary additional member until you're fit again. Just remember that your berth is there, whenever you feel up to it.' He turned his head and then stood up as the door opened. 'I know, Sister. My time is up.'

But Jamie was looking past the nurse at the woman behind her, his expression a mixture of consternation and delight. 'Milady!'

Kristin advanced to the bedside. 'Jamie! What on earth have you been doing?'

'Well . . . falling down, I suppose.'

'Oh, you silly boy.'

'Excuse me,' Richard ventured, having taken in the situation. 'Would you . . . ?'

'This is the Dowager Lady Eversham,' Sister Denton explained.

'Milady.'

'And you, I take it, are Jamie's . . . Mr Goring's, commanding officer.'

'Yes, milady.'

'Name?'

'Sub-Lieutenant Richard Calman, milady.'

'And where exactly are you from? You're not English.'

'I am English, ma'am. But I was born in British Guiana.'

'British what?'

'It's a colony, milady,' Jamie explained. 'In South America.'

'Good heavens! And what were you doing to be born in such a place?'

'My father manages a sugar plantation there, milady.'

'And he took your mother with him? I thought white women were not allowed to go to places like that?'

'You're thinking of West Africa, milady. Tsetse flies. We only have the anopheles mosquito. That is actually quite as dangerous, but it can be coped with.'

'It sounds frightfully unpleasant. But frightfully romantic as well.'

'Milady . . .' Sister Denton ventured cautiously. Kristin had a penetrating voice, and although the occupants in the other five beds were fairly comatose, there was some movement.

'Of course,' Kristin acknowledged. 'I am being a nuisance. The story of my life. If you would care to wait for me downstairs, Mr . . . Calman, was it? I would love to continue this intriguing discussion. Now, Sister, I wish to be alone with Mr Goring. I won't be long.'

'Well . . . ah . . .'

'What I would like you to do,' Kristin explained, 'is draw the curtain around the bed so that Mr Goring and I may have a private discussion.'

'Well . . .'

'Or shall I do it myself?'

'No, no.' Sister drew the curtains.

'Thank you. I'll be down in a few minutes.'

Sister Denton looked at the bewildered Richard, and then ushered him through the door.

Kristin parted the curtains and sat in the chair beside the bed.

'Milady,' Jamie said – for all of their years of intimacy he had never been able to bring himself to call her Kristin – 'they're going to be relaying this all over the hospital.'

'After all these years, I would hate to cease being a source of scandal.'

'But—'

She leaned forward. 'I'm here on behalf of Duncan. That's all anyone needs to know. You're his oldest ship-mate, and when he heard you were in hospital, he worried about you. And everyone knows he can't get around very easily.'

'Then his lordship knows you're here?'

'No, he doesn't, yet. He wasn't in when I got the message, and I came straight over. I'll tell him when I get home.

But I really did not come here to talk about Duncan, you know. I want to know that you are all right.'

He grinned. 'A little bashed up, that's all. I'm going to be all right. I'm sorry about not showing on Tuesday. Were you very upset?'

'Yes, I was. But now that I know it was the call of duty I entirely forgive you. I only hope it, this, was worthwhile.'

'We sank an S-boat.'

'You did?'

'Well, the skipper did, actually.'

'That boy?' She squeezed his right hand, and then kissed it 'When Jimmy told me you'd been hurt I damn near had a heart attack.'

'Jimmy? You mean Admiral Lonsdale told you about me?'

'He thought Duncan might be interested. Don't worry. He knows nothing about us.'

'Um,' Jamie said, remembering the close call he had had from encountering the admiral in her hotel in Valetta earlier that year. 'I thought you and he had fallen out.'

'We did. But I've an idea he'd like to be friends again.'

'So that he can ask you to marry him again. Will you say yes, again?'

'Why, Jamie! You're jealous.'

'Milady, you are a woman to be jealous of.'

She got up, leaned over the bed, and kissed him, then lifted his hand to press it against her breast. 'How many times have I told you that you are all I want, now and always. Listen, when are you getting out of here?'

'This ward? I think tomorrow or the next day. But they want me in hospital for the next few weeks, and then apparently there's to be a period of convalescence.'

'You'd be just as well off at Eversham House. Better off, in fact, because I'd nurse you myself. I'll arrange it.'

'Milady!' His hand moved from her breast to clutch her arm. 'You can't do that. Please!'

'Don't you want to convalesce at Eversham?'

'I can't think of anything I'd like more. But it's quite impossible. It would be impossible anyway, but with his lordship home . . . you must see that.'

Kristin considered him for few moments, then kissed him

again. 'I must go. I'll be back in a couple of days.' She stood up. 'Jamie . . . without you I'd simply have no reason to go on living.'

Kristin went downstairs in a pleasant glow, and also on a distinct high. She had anticipated catastrophe, and now . . . she wanted to embrace the whole world. She smiled at Sister Broughton, who regarded her as she might have done a recently delivered parcel that was giving off a loud tick, and then turned her attention to Richard, seated in a straight chair on the far side of the lobby. Life, that had been becoming increasingly frustrating following the unexplained non-appearance of Jamie at their rendezvous, had suddenly become not only clear again but filled with delicious possibilities. Not least of which was the prospect of amusing herself with this handsome young man.

Not that she had any concrete plans in mind. Although she had meant every word she had said to Jamie, and had no desire or intention to change or even alter their relationship, she did like to be entertained, and as he, even if she did manage to get him to Eversham, was clearly hors de combat for the next few weeks, a flirtation with this so-attractive young officer at least promised to be amusing. She remembered having been quite fond of Duncan's immediate junior, Arnold Cooper, her interest in whom had upset Jimmy Lonsdale – Jimmy, being the most orthodox, hidebound of men, had been just able to accept that she might flirt with a junior officer, however jealous it made him, where it could never possibly cross his mind that she might have an affair with someone from the lower deck. The fact that Cooper had been killed in the Adriatic incident had not had the impact it might have as the news had arrived together with that of the apparent deaths of Duncan and Jamie.

Richard was looking somewhat anxious. 'My bus leaves in ten minutes, Lady Eversham,' he said.

'You have a bus?' Kristin was intrigued.

'I mean, the bus I have to catch to get back to Portsmouth.'

'Why do you have to get back to Portsmouth?'

'Milady, that's where I'm based. That's where my boat is.'

'I'm sure it's not going anywhere today.'

'Well . . . I have been given leave of absence until tomorrow morning. But—'

'Tomorrow happens to be Sunday.'

'Yes, milady. But as the Germans don't stop fighting on Sundays, neither can we.'

'I suppose that is a valid point. But in any event, you don't have to be back until then.'

'Yes. But—'

'Have you lunched?'

'Well, no.'

'And it is a quarter past one. You must be starving. I know I am. So I tell you what we'll do. You will come home with me, and have lunch with me, and then, whenever you're ready, I will drive you to Portsmouth myself.'

'You have a car?'

'Of course I have a car. Don't you?'

'Milady, midshipmen can't afford cars.'

'You said you were a sub-lieutenant.' She looked at the single stripe on the sleeve of his tunic.

'I was promoted just over a month ago.'

'How exciting. We must celebrate. Come along.'

She led him outside, and he goggled at the Bentley. 'This is yours?'

'I know it's a huge, cumbersome beast. But it is comfortable. And Lucifer loves it so. Now,' she said opening the door, 'kindly behave.'

Richard turned his head sharply and then realized that she was not talking to him. Instead he goggled again, at the mountain of white fur rising in the back seat, where it had apparently been asleep. 'My God!'

'Please don't be rude,' Kristin protested. 'He's very sensitive.'

The mountain gurgled and licked Kristin's hand, as she had removed her glove to greet him.

'But what is it?' Richard asked, cautiously sitting beside her.

'*He* is a Pyrenean Mountain Dog,' Kristin explained, severely.

'Ah! Oh, my God! What . . . ?

A large tongue was massaging the back of his neck while a cold nose breathed into his ear.

'He is also very affectionate. Actually, you are better off receiving him sitting down than standing up. He weighs a hundred and fifty pounds. Lucifer, please stop doing that.'

Lucifer subsided into the back seat, still breathing heavily.

'Is that his name – Lucifer?'

'What else would you call him?'

'Well . . . he's an impressive beast. But I'm sure he doesn't do this expensive upholstery any good.'

'He doesn't. But upholstery, and indeed, cars, can be replaced. Lucifer cannot.' She started her engine and drove out of the yard. 'How long have you served with MTBs?'

'Seventy-two hours.'

Kristin turned her head. 'Are you trying to be funny?'

'I wouldn't dream of it, milady. Ah, would you . . . um . . .'

Kristin turned her head back to the road, and just avoided the oncoming car; the two vehicles passed each other with a mutual blaring of horns. 'Cretin,' Kristin growled. 'Couldn't he see me?'

Richard had been using his handkerchief to wipe the back of his neck; now he wiped the front as well. 'I joined the MTB squadron just over three days ago, from *Warspite*. *Warspite*—'

'Is a battleship. I know.'

'You're very up on the Navy, milady.'

'Shouldn't I be? My son is in the Navy, as well as my . . . well, you mean you transferred to the squadron three days ago and have already been in a battle? And sunk an S-boat?'

'How do you know that?'

'Jamie told me'

'Jamie?'

'Petty Officer Goring.'

'I didn't know you knew him.'

'What did you say your name was?'

'Calman, milady.'

'I know that. I meant, your Christian name.'

'Richard.'

'Richard! I like that better. I call Jamie Jamie, Richard, because I have known him all his life. His father owns a garage outside Lymington, and he, and Jamie, have serviced my cars ever since I can remember. He also used to crew my son's yacht.'

'Yes. He told me that.'

'That was before he started crewing my son's MTBs, of course.'

'Remarkable that they managed to wind up serving together.'

'Remarkable? I organized it.'

'You? But . . .'

'I am a friend of Admiral Lonsdale,' Kristin explained, increasing speed to hurtle through the fringes of the New Forest.

Richard tried to dissociate himself from the accident he suspected could happen at any minute. 'I've never actually met the admiral.'

'Haven't you? He's coming to lunch tomorrow. You must come.'

'But . . . aren't I lunching with you today?'

'Of course you are. That doesn't mean you can't lunch with me tomorrow as well. Or are you on patrol or something stupid like that? But you said you had the day off.'

'Yes. My boat is having a few bullet holes patched up.'

'Well, then . . . and I know Jimmy would love to meet you, after you've sunk an S-boat.' He will be absolutely furious, she thought, happily.

They raced onto the gravel forecourt of Eversham House and scattered small stones as Kristin braked violently. 'Ooof,' Lucifer commented, only just stopping himself from sliding off the back seat by digging his claws into the leather upholstery.

Richard felt like doing the same, then got out and stared at the open garage at the side of the house, where there was a Sunbeam-Talbot, and . . . 'My God! Isn't that a Bugatti?'

Kristin had also emerged and was allowing Lucifer to descend and shake himself. 'Yes. Great noisy thing. It belongs to Duncan.'

'Wow! And he has a yacht as well.'

'That's in Lymington. I'll show it to you if you like. What sort of boat do you have?'

'I don't have a boat, milady.'

'Good heavens! Why not?'

'It's a little out of my financial range.'

'Hm. How old are you?'

'Nineteen.'

'How delicious. To be nineteen. I was nineteen, once. And I was already married and a mother. Then I gave up that sort of thing. I mean, being a mother, not fucking. Don't get me wrong. I adore Duncan. And I believe that one should experience everything in life, at least once. But when it comes to childbearing, once is more than enough. It consumes so much time which could be put to experiencing other things. Duncan!'

The front door had opened. 'Mother? Where on earth have you been?'

'To the hospital. This is Richard Calman. He's the latest addition to the MTB fleet.'

Richard, still recovering from both the drive and Kristin's devastating frankness, not to mention her choice of words, stood to attention. It was not that the man confronting him was actually in uniform – he was wearing bags and an open-neck shirt – but that his entire presence was commanding. He knew that the Third Lord Eversham was not yet thirty years old, and according to Linton had cut a swathe, both socially and professionally through life wherever he found it. But he had been unprepared for the sheer size of the man. Duncan was well over six feet tall, with massive shoulders and long, clearly powerful legs, even if one of them was still obviously hardly usable; he was standing on two crutches. His features were rugged, although there were traces of his mother's beauty, and his eyes were the same shade of green. His hair was black and lank, and his smile welcoming, as he held out his hand. 'Calman! Where on earth did you manage to accumulate my mother?' He braced himself against the door as Lucifer got on his hind legs for a hug and a kiss.

'Well, sir . . .'

'He didn't accumulate me,' Kristin pointed out. 'I accumulated him.'

'Actually, sir, I remember you from Scapa, in 1940.'

'Good heavens! Were you there then?' It had clearly crossed

his mind to add, can you possibly be old enough, but he thought better of it.

'Well, sir, we never actually met. I was only a snotty.'

'Richard was on *Warspite*,' Kristin explained. 'And has seen action all over the place. And we are both starving and dying for a drink. Lucifer, do behave. Come inside, Richard. Ah! Alison. Meet Sub-Lieutenant Richard Calman.'

'Milady!' Richard hesitated, unsure whether he was required to kiss the small white hand that was being extended towards him.

In the strongest possible contrast to both her husband and her mother-in-law, Alison Eversham was a little woman, in her late twenties, he estimated, not much over five feet tall, but with a full figure, attractively piquant features, and obviously long dark hair which was currently confined in a bun. Like her husband, she was casually dressed, in her case in a tweed skirt and a cashmere jumper. The only indication of her rank as at least 'county' was the string of pearls round her neck. Now she gave his hand a gentle squeeze.

'I hope I'm not intruding, milady.'

'No friend of Kristin can ever intrude at Eversham House, Mr Calman.'

'Calman was at Scapa in 1940,' Duncan said.

'Were you? I'm afraid—'

'No reason why you should, milady. I was a snotty. And you were a second officer.'

'Well . . .'

'Have you eaten?' Kristin inquired.

'We were about to.'

'Oh. good. But we'll have a drink first. Harry!' she called. 'We'll have a bottle of Bollinger. And will you please ask Lucia to set another place for lunch.'

She led the way into the drawing room. Richard took off his cap to hang it on the stand beside the door.

'Now,' Duncan said, limping behind her. 'Perhaps you'll tell us where you went dashing off to in such a hurry.'

'Come and sit on the sofa, Richard,' Kristin said, seating herself, crossing her legs, and patting the space beside her. 'If we stick together we can't be bullied.'

Richard cast an anxious glance at Alison, the only one of

his three hosts, he felt, who was remotely close to his class, and received a reassuring wink, and a quick nod. He sat beside Kristin, who waited while Harry brought in the champagne and poured, then sipped appreciatively.

'I,' she announced, 'have been at Southampton General visiting Jamie Goring. That's where I met Richard; he is at this moment Jamie's CO.'

'Jamie?' Duncan shouted. 'In hospital? What with?'

'A broken arm, a dislocated shoulder, and a couple of broken ribs.'

'Oh, my God!' Alison said.

'They tell me he's going to be all right,' Kristin assured her. 'Given a little time.'

'How the hell did he break his arm?' Duncan demanded. 'And break his ribs?'

'You explain it, Richard. He was there, you see.'

Richard related the events of Tuesday night and Wednesday morning.

'Good lord!' Duncan commented. 'And you say this was just a raid?'

'Apparently, sir. There was some talk that it might have been a trial invasion, but there were just not sufficient men and ships employed.'

'It was a raid,' Kristin said. 'And it turned out very badly. Jimmy Lonsdale told me that more than half the five thousand men involved were either killed or captured, and we lost several ships and God knows how many aircraft.'

'You've spoken to Lonsdale?'

'He telephoned this morning. He actually wanted to speak to you, to let you know about Jamie, but as you weren't here he spoke to me instead. So I felt the least I could do was go and visit the poor boy, on your behalf.'

'That was very good of you, Mother.'

Alison drank some champagne.

'And what Richard has not told you is that he got an S-boat. In his very first engagement.'

'Oh, well done,' Alison said.

'It was actually almost entirely due to Goring,' Richard admitted modestly. 'He was telling me what to do throughout. I'd never been on an MTB before, you see.'

'What did you say?' Duncan asked.

'I'd only just joined, when this came up and we were all ordered to sea.'

'And you say you'd never even had a trial run?'

'Richard went straight to MTBs from *Warspite*,' Kristin said, proudly.

'Well, all I can say is, again, well done. I hope you're going to get a gong.'

'I don't know about that, sir. As I said, Goring did all the hard work.'

'Jamie has one already, not to mention the VC,' Kristin pointed out. 'I'll speak with the admiral.'

Alison was frowning. She knew her mother-in-law far better than Duncan knew his mother. Now she gave a bright smile. 'I think it's time for lunch.'

'How were you thinking of getting back to Portsmouth?' Alison asked after the meal.

'Oh, I—' He glanced at Kristin.

'I'm taking him,' Kristin said.

'I can do that,' Alison suggested.

'Of course not. You'll be wanting to take Baby for his walk.'

'He had a walk this morning.'

'But I know how busy you are,' Kristin insisted. 'And it'll do me good to get out of the house.'

'You were out of the house this morning.'

'Are you trying to tell me when I can go and come?'

'I wouldn't dream of it,' Alison protested.

'I don't want to put anyone out,' Richard said. 'I saw a bus stop just along the road. I can catch a bus.'

'My dear boy, that would take hours. And I think we should leave now. We don't want you to be AWOL.'

Richard opened his mouth to remind her that he had the rest of the day, and tomorrow, off, then thought better of it; she was definitely not a woman he wanted to upset. 'Well,' he said, 'that was a magnificent meal, milady. And the wine was superb, sir. I've never actually tasted Chateau Margaux before.'

'Very drinkable,' Duncan agreed, getting up with the aid

of his crutches. 'I look forward to meeting you again, whenever I'm allowed back into uniform.'

'But you'll be seeing him again tomorrow,' Kristin said. 'He's coming to lunch.'

'But . . . Lucia tells me that Admiral Lonsdale is coming to lunch to tomorrow,' Alison reminded her. 'She says you invited him.'

'Yes, I did,' Kristin acknowledged. 'That was before I had met Richard. Anyway, I think it's a good idea for admirals to meet their junior officers. It's democratic.' She got up. 'Now, I shall just go upstairs for five minutes and then we'll be off. Richard, there's a washroom just down the hall.'

She left the room.

'I'm afraid,' Duncan said, 'that my mother can be a trifle overwhelming.'

'I think she's absolutely charming, sir.' Richard also got up. 'May I?'

'I think you should,' Alison said. 'The way Kristin drives, you don't want to be sitting beside her with a full bladder.'

They stood together to watch the Sunbeam drive off, Alison attempting to hang on to Lucifer's collar – he weighed considerably more than she did – as Kristin, much to his displeasure, had elected not to take him with her this time.

'I hope she doesn't scare that poor lad stiff,' Duncan said. 'Or do you think she has already done that?'

'I think he's surviving fairly well,' Alison said. And *scaring* him stiff is not what she has in mind, she thought.

It was a continuing source of concern to her that while she had determined, from the moment this gorgeous hunk of a man had asked her to marry him, that she would never have a secret from him, almost the moment she had moved in with Kristin she had been confronted with a secret that simply had to be kept.

She had already been aware that Kristin was, and apparently always had been, if not exactly sexually voracious, totally amoral and unable to resist either any handsome man or her own impulses. When at the age of fifteen she had been given permission by her parents to spend the summer holidays of 1913 sailing as crew on Douglas Morant's yacht – he had not yet inherited the title – it had been discovered, when she returned to her Madrid convent in the autumn, that she was pregnant.

Douglas, a man Alison had never met although she had watched him die as she had been on board Duncan's MTB when his father's motor yacht had been blown up off the Dunkirk Beach – immediately before she had herself been hit by a Messerschmitt bullet – had been universally reviled for seducing a young girl placed in his care by an old friend. But Alison had no doubt, nor had Kristin ever denied, that it was she who had done the seducing.

In any event, being both an aristocrat and a gentlemen he had married the girl, no doubt helped in his determination to do the right thing by the fact that her father was one of Spain's wealthiest men, and Kristin had been his only heir. But it had not taken the poor fellow more than a couple of years to discover that she was absolutely uncontrollable, and although, for the sake of convention and their son – and because her family was Roman Catholic – the marriage had been kept in being for just over twenty years, the moment Duncan had become an adult, and both Kristin's parents had died, his father had brought divorce proceedings.

Duncan knew all about Kristin's past, and although the most moral of men himself, he had always preferred to live with his mother, a decision again almost certainly influenced by the fact that when her father had died she had become one of the wealthiest women in Europe. He had long known that his father was all but penniless, and that he would there-fore not be inheriting anything in that direction, save the title, while even if Kristin clearly had no intention of dying for a long time yet, she could refuse her only son nothing.

For all this, Alison knew he loved her dearly. As did she, now. When they had first met she had been terrified, less of the woman herself than of the total uncertainty as to what she might do or say next, without the slightest warning. That had worn off very rapidly as she had realized that Kristin, for all her faults and the quickness with which she could take offence, did not have a vicious bone in her body, and like her dog, wanted only to love everybody, even if some more than others.

She had also been reassured by Duncan's certainty that his mother had turned over a new leaf, and had not had an affair for several years. But this misapprehension had been because Kristin's past amours had always been within her own social class, and there had been absolutely no evidence or even suggestion of that, save her on and off romance with Jimmy Lonsdale, and as Jimmy had been his commanding officer he had raised no objections to that, although Alison knew that he had been very relieved when they had got engaged, and equally upset when the engagement had been abruptly terminated.

What had never crossed his mind was the possibility that Kristin could fall in love – or as much in love as she was capable of falling, certainly by Alison's standards – with his own mechanic. Living in the same house, where Duncan was absent for so much of the time, Alison had very quickly realized the situation. If Jamie had never actually come to the house, at least to her knowledge – save on a few occasions over the past couple of months to visit his crippled commanding officer – there had been guarded phone calls arranging secret trysts, and then the day, two years ago now, when she had answered the phone. Kristin had come in almost immediately and taken over, but Alison, having sailed with Jamie on Duncan's boat, had recognized the voice, as Kristin had understood. She had neither apologized nor asked for secrecy, merely pointed out that it would be an impossible situation on board the boat were Duncan to know about it.

In fact, the incident had brought the two women ever closer together, and at the same time subtly altered their relationship. Kristin had become dependent on Alison's understanding and goodwill, and although she continued to bluster her way through life, at least in public, had slowly drifted into the position of junior partner in the household. And although Alison did not know where it was going to end – and neither, she was sure, did Kristin – she had thoroughly enjoyed watching the two men also growing closer together, culminating in Jamie saving Duncan's life. But in fact Jamie was such a likeable boy she almost felt that he was a member of the family, and dreaded the thought of an ultimate catastrophe.

But now . . . was it merely that he was going to be out of action, perhaps for several weeks? Or was Kristin simply growing tired of him? Alison had never had an affair, save with her husband, and she had no desire ever to have one. But she knew that where they did not involve marriage, or at least the prospect of marriage, for one to last more than two years was exceptional. But while she felt it her duty to keep a watching brief over her mother-in-law and try to make sure that she did not commit an irretrievable mistake, there was nothing she could do about this situation until she could get Kristin alone, and over the past few months, with Duncan home all of the time, those opportunities had been rare.

'Well,' she said, 'if she scares him off, he won't come to lunch, tomorrow.'

# LOVERS

'Where are we going?' Richard asked, as the Sunbeam turned off the Southampton Road.

'Lymington,' Kristin said. 'I promised to show you Duncan's boat, remember?'

He wasn't sure how to reply to that, and before he could think of something they were in the narrow streets of the little town, somnolent on a Saturday afternoon, and descending the steep hill to the harbour. 'You mean she's in the water all the time? Does his lordship ever get to take her out?'

'That's not practical, without a crew. Anyway, she's on the hard. Has been since October 1939.' She braked before a pair of wrought-iron gates set in a high fence, got out, and unlocked the padlock, then returned to the car, drove through, and got out again to lock the gates behind her. 'We don't really want the hoi polloi to know we're here.'

Another unanswerable remark. Richard looked around himself as they drove slowly across the beaten earth, through a myriad of yachts of all sizes and shapes, perched on their legs, mast-less, shrouded in their canvas cocoons. 'I've never seen so many yachts in one place. Where is all the staff?'

'Serving, somewhere. There's nothing for them to do here; none of these boats are going back into the water until hostilities end.' She stopped the car before an open shed and indicated the large yacht sheltering beneath the roof. 'Voila!'

'Wow! That's a big one.'

'Forty-five feet, overall length.' Kristin got out, walked beneath the shelter, feeling a wave of nostalgia sweeping over her. How often had she come here and looked for the reassuring sight of Jamie's bicycle leaning against the wall. They should have been here together four afternoons ago, but instead he had been required to rush off and see if he could get himself killed!

Then what was she doing here, in this most secret and

sacred of trysts, with another man? Sheer impulse. But she had found Richard the most attractive man she had met since Jamie himself, and she was still on a high.

Richard joined her to look up at the hull, rising above them on its legs. Somehow it seemed much larger viewed from underneath than from a distance. Of course she was still twenty-five feet shorter than *433*, but she gave an impression of solidity that the plywood MTB lacked. 'What's she made off?'

'The hull is Burma teak.'

'Wow! Have you ever sailed in her?'

'Of course.' Kristin walked the length of the hull. 'I sailed on her last voyage, just three years ago. That was returning from the Cowes–Dinard race, after Duncan had won his class. During the race he nicked a rock, off Guernsey. Here.'

Richard joined her and looked at the gash in the lead keel. 'That must have been scary.'

'I wasn't there. But it didn't seem to bother them too much. And it can't be repaired until after the war, when we can get hold of some lead. As I said, I wasn't in the race; I joined them in St Malo for the trip home. That was such fun. We had a gale.'

'And Goring was with you?'

'He was part of Duncan's crew. It was thanks to his local knowledge that we won the race.' She went back to where a ladder led up to the deck, some twelve feet above them. 'Come on up. I have a key to the cabin.'

Richard waited, uncertain as to the correct drill, watched her take off her shoes. 'I need your shoulder,' she said.

He stood next to her, and she rested a hand on his shoulder while she stood on one leg to raise her skirt and release her stockings. Having never been this intimate with a woman before he had no idea where to look.

'The rungs are sometimes slippery,' she explained, changing legs for the second stocking. And what legs, long, slender and yet strong. And if she did not actually raise her skirt far enough to reveal the suspender belt and anything else that might be under there, the suggestion of intimacy was growing every second.

'There,' she said, dropping the stockings on to her shoes. 'Come on up.'

He watched her climbing above him. her skirt swaying; from beneath the legs were exposed above the knee, and even more when she reached the top and swung them over the rail to gain the deck. Hastily he climbed behind her, as she opened her shoulder bag and took out another key, with which she unlocked the padlock securing the hatch. This she slid back, descending the ladder into the cabin.

'She's a bit bare at the moment,' she explained. 'All her gear is stored ashore. But there is a sleeping cabin aft –' she indicated the companionway – 'and two more forward, and of course these two settee berths can also be used if necessary. The engine is under the cockpit deck, just here.' She tapped the bulkhead behind the ladder. 'The galley is just forward, there. And there are two heads. So . . . there you are.'

'It's fabulous,' Richard said. 'To own a boat like this . . .'

'Well,' Kristin said, sitting on the starboard bunk. 'You never know how things will turn out.'

'And you know, even if she's laid up, she almost looks lived in. That mattress, and those blankets . . .'

'I put them here. And they have to be changed every so often, at least in winter, because they get damp.'

'Should they be here at all? As she's laid up?'

'I put them here,' Kristin repeated, 'so that I can come here whenever I feel like it, and be alone, and think anything I like, without the risk of interruption. You know, some people have a secret garden, or a secret glade in the woods . . . this is my secret hideaway.'

'I think you are a romantic, milady.'

'I would have thought that was fairly obvious. Anyway, everyone should be a romantic, in some way or other.'

'Absolutely.'

'Are you a romantic, Richard?'

'I like to think I am, milady.'

'I think we should put it to the test. First, take off your cap and place it on the table.'

Richard obeyed.

Kristin patted the bunk. 'Now come and sit beside me.'

Again he obeyed, this time somewhat hesitantly.

'Now,' she said. 'I have a quite overwhelming urge to kiss you.'

'Sub-Lieutenant Calman is here, sir,' said Second Officer Grace.

'Thank you, Nancy. Send him in.'

The Wren officer stepped aside, and Richard entered the office and stood to attention. 'Good morning, sir.'

After the previous two days he did not know what to expect. What he dared expect. He had actually been in close proximity to an admiral before; *Warspite* had been a fleet flagship. But while the two admirals who had served on her had been introduced to every officer, including the midshipmen, it had been a case of standing in line and having his hand perfunctorily shaken, and then keeping as much out of the great man's way as possible.

Actually lunching with so exalted a figure had been beyond the limits of his imagination. But then, so much that had happened over the past two days had been beyond his imagination. Had he really held the Dowager Lady Eversham in his arms, kissed her open mouth, touched her breast with trembling fingers? He had absolutely no knowledge of women, having gone straight from school to Dartmouth in what had been not merely a new experience but a new country, with quite different manners and mores to anything he had known in the carefree West Indies.

Although born in British Guiana, and only having left the Caribbean twice, when his parents had returned to England on leave, he had been brought up to regard the British Isles as 'home'. It was the ideal of every Englishman, Scotsman, Welshman or Irishman working in the 'colonies' to complete his career and enter a hopefully long retirement, supported by a sizeable pension, at 'home'. And he had accepted this, for all that he could remember nothing of his first visit – he had only been four years old – and his second had seemed to be very cold and very wet; it could be very wet in British Guiana on the mainland of South America, but it had never been other than hot.

Thus although Dartmouth had been a dream come true – he had been a late entry at the age of sixteen – his time there, and indeed since, had been a fairly steep learning curve. But two years in the Navy had made him feel like an Englishman, and even more, an English officer and a gentleman. But now, without warning, he had been propelled into the ranks of the aristocracy, and in a manner that involved an introduction to a way of life he had not supposed to exist.

It had not been merely the careless wealth with which he had found himself surrounded, or the unconscious arrogance, it had been the sheer amorality, at least of Kritisn; he could not bring himself to believe that Duncan, and certainly never Alison, indulged in absent-minded bed-swapping. Not that he had shared a bed with Kristin. That was the most titillating and frustrating, as well as puzzling, thing of all. She had seduced him, allowed him to kiss her and touch her wherever he chose, even to slide his hand under her dress and up her bare thighs, giving every evidence of extreme pleasure, and then, again quite without warning, had suddenly said, 'I think we should be getting you back to Portsmouth.'

Clearly, in some way he had not measured up. Or she was the biggest prick-tease in history. And yet she had insisted he go to lunch the next day, and while she had been aristocratically correct throughout the meal, she had looked into his eyes as she had said goodbye, and added, 'I have enjoyed meeting you, Richard. I would hope to do so again.' So where did that leave him? Hanging by a thread. Her thread.

'Good morning,' Lonsdale agreed. He was a stocky man, some inches shorter than Richard, with pugnacious features and crisp iron-grey hair. 'At ease. Sit.'

Richard took off his cap and cautiously lowered himself into the chair before the desk. But this hardly sounded like the beginning of a reprimand.

'I didn't know you were a friend of the Evershams?'

'I'm not, actually, sir. When I visited Petty Officer Goring three days ago, I encountered Lady Eversham. That is, the Dowager Lady Eversham. She wanted to hear all about the action, and then very kindly invited me to lunch.'

'She has a very generous streak, especially when it comes to junior naval officers. How is Goring, by the way?'

'I'm afraid he is going to be out of action for a couple of months, at least.'

'Can you manage without him?'

'I think so, sir. He is very anxious that his position should be kept open for him.'

'I wish the entire Navy could be composed of men as enthusiastic as he is. And what about your boat? I understand there was some structural damage.'

'Only some bullet holes, sir. They have been patched up and we are again ready for sea.'

The admiral regarded him for some seconds, then tapped one of the various sheets of paper on his desk. 'Is it true that this was your first action?'

'My first action in MTBs. I saw action with *Warspite*.'

'I'm sure you did. But it also says here you had no experience in MTBs.'

'That was the first time I had taken one to sea, sir.'

'That is also what it says here. Frankly, I didn't believe it. I'm not sure that Commander Webster did the right thing, sending you straight into action like that.'

'Every boat was needed, sir.'

'It was still a great risk. However, bagging an S-boat on your very first outing . . . that could well be some kind of record.'

'For the most part I was doing what Goring told me to, sir.'

'I don't think modesty is really required, Lieutenant. The reports, from both Lieutenant Linton and Commander Webster, are glowing. I'm recommending you for the Distinguished Service Cross.'

'Sir?'

'Don't sound quite so surprised.'

'I am most appreciative, sir.'

'Just keep up the good work. Thank you, Lieutenant. Carry on.'

'Sir!' Richard stood up, replaced his cap, saluted, and left the room.

'Congratulations,' said Miss Grace.

'I'm not at all sure that I deserve it.'

'Of course you do. Look at it this way: it could easily have been posthumous. And it'll look awfully good in the newspapers: junior officer wins DSC on his first mission.'

He'd never thought of that. He should get a copy of *The Times* and send the clipping to his parents; they'd be tickled pink. And then a thought suddenly crossed his mind: Kristin! She had said that she was a good friend of the admiral, as she obviously was. He wondered if she had actually done the recommending?

The important thing was that it gave him an excuse to telephone her, when all things might be possible. Was he stark raving mad? The woman was a member of the upper class, old enough to be his mother, and at the very least was an eccentric. But she was also quite the most compelling woman he had ever met. Not that he supposed that was saying a lot, as he had not met that number of women.

So he was playing with fire. He had no doubt that if she could, and almost certainly had, lift him up with a flick of her finger, she could also, if ever offended, cast him down again with a flick of the same finger. But what the hell! If he didn't chance his arm he'd regret it for the rest of his life. He felt the same sense of exhilaration as when going into battle last Wednesday. And look how well that had turned out?

He left the Command Building and hurried across to the officers' mess, where there were several telephones available, called the exchange. 'I'd like to put a call through to Eversham House. It's just outside Lymington. I'm afraid I don't have the number.'

'One moment, sir,' the woman said. There were various clicks and thuds, and then a ringing sound. 'You're through, sir.'

'Eversham House,' said a man's voice.

'Lord Eversham?'

'No, sir.' The voice was disparaging, to inform the caller that Lord Eversham did not answer the telephone. 'This is Harry, the butler.'

'Oh, Harry. I remember you. This is Sub-Lieutenant Calman. I had lunch at the house, yesterday.'

'Indeed, sir. And you would like to speak with Lord Eversham?'

'Well, actually, I'd like to speak with Lady Eversham.'

'Which Lady Eversham, sir?'

'Good point. Lady Kristin.'

'I'm afraid that will not be possible at this time, sir. The Dowager Lady Eversham is at the hospital in Southampton. Visiting your petty officer.'

'Every time that woman comes here,' said Sister Broughton, 'I feel it necessary to have my blood pressure checked. What's the matter with her today? She looked ready to bite me.'

'She's upset,' Jamie explained.

'What has she got to be upset about? Sister Denton told me she's a multi-millionairess, or something.'

'I suppose that's part of the problem. Normally, she just has to snap her fingers or open her cheque book and what she wants is done, immediately. She simply doesn't like not getting her own way.'

Sister Broughton smoothed the pillows under his head. Since this so attractive young man had been released from intensive care and placed in her ward, she had grown very fond of him, so much so that she undertook, for him, many of the duties that should have been handled by her subordinates. She was also, as were many of the people in the hospital, intrigued by the interest being taken by the Dowager Lady Eversham in a petty officer. 'And there is something she wants from you that she can't have?'

'Not in real terms,' Jamie said, truthfully enough. For his part, he appreciated and enjoyed both the sister's interest and her attention, because he found her extraordinarily attractive, with her clipped features and her obviously full figure which not even her somewhat drab uniform and apron could conceal. Her hair was just an occasional wisp of golden-brown peeping out from beneath her cap. In addition she spoke with a very good accent. He had a growing urge to know more about her, especially without her cap. Certainly he was happy to chat with her. 'It's just that she wants me to go to Eversham House to recuperate, and I don't think it would be a good idea.'

'What, pass up the opportunity to spend a couple of weeks with the very rich?'

'It isn't really my scene.'

'And, of course, you'd be constantly exposed to her

ladyship's moods,' Sister Broughton observed. 'Well, I must get on. Can I get anything for you?'

'Actually, I'd like to go to the toilet.'

'So she affects your bladder as well as my heart. I'm not sure that would be a good idea. You're still weak and to fall over could be disastrous. I'll get the bottle.'

'Shouldn't one of the nurses do that?'

Sister Broughton smiled. 'Don't you want me to?'

'I'd love you to,' he replied without thinking. 'Oh, I beg your pardon.'

'I'll get the bottle.'

'I seem to have been wrong,' she conceded, as she handed the bottle to a waiting nurse and pulled down his hospital robe. 'You're stronger than I supposed.'

'I apologize.' He was in fact embarrassed. If the ordinary nurses had had to attend to his genitals during the past three weeks, the sister was by far the most attractive woman to have done so since his last session with Kristin, and that was almost a month ago.

'Why? Do you suppose you're the first man I've held a bottle for, and had a reaction?'

'Well, no, but—'

'It goes with the job. Now, you have a rest. I'm at my desk if you need anything.'

She turned away, and he rested his hand on her arm. 'Sister.'

Her head turned back.

'Do you think I could know your name?'

'I thought you did. It's Broughton.'

'I mean your Christian name.'

Again she smiled; he loved her smile. 'Emma.'

'Emma. That's a lovely name. But . . . bit unusual, isn't it?'

'Not really. My best friend is called Emma. Our mothers were at school together, and they were both great readers of Jane Austen. I think they had to study *Emma* for their school certificate.'

'You make it sound like an up-market school.'

'Well, I suppose it is. Cheltenham Ladies'.'

'I think I've heard of it.'

'Most people have.'

'But if you went to . . . well . . . I mean, shouldn't you, well—'

'When I left school, Mr Goring, I had four choices, and, as you have obviously noticed, the nation is at war. I could have gone to university, which seemed rather puerile, I mean, studying books, in these circumstances. I could have got married which seemed totally inappropriate, apart from the fact that I knew no one I was at all keen on marrying. Or I could do something, and as wearing brogues and a heavy khaki skirt and drawers and thick stockings as well as having to drive a truck or pound a typewriter is not my scene any more than walking behind a tractor, I opted for nursing.'

'Bed pans and blood.'

'It's real, Mr Goring. Life needs to be real. Actually, my friend Emma joined the Navy. The Wrens, you know. She's a commissioned officer. I don't suppose you know her?'

'Petty officers don't actually socialize with the brass. And it's a big navy.'

'It's just that she's stationed in Portsmouth. That's where you're based, isn't it?'

'Yes, it is. What's she called?'

'Second Officer Dunning.'

'Good Lord!'

'Don't tell me you do know her?'

'I've never actually said more than good morning to her. But she's my CO's secretary.'

'Now that is interesting. Small world and all that. I'll tell her.'

'Tell her what?'

Emma Broughton smiled. 'That we met, Mr Goring. Hospital intimacies like bedpans are strictly confidential. Now you have a rest.'

'And how are you today, Petty Officer?' asked Dr Clifton.

'Right as rain, sir. When do I get out of here?'

'Hm. When did the sling come off, Sister?'

'A week ago, sir,' Emma said.

'Hm. Let's see . . .' He held the arm and moved it, gently. 'That hurt.'

'Not at all, sir.'

'Petty Officer,' Clifton said severely. 'I could tell from your expression that there was at least a twinge.'

'A twinge, sir. I get that from sleeping awkwardly.'

'And the arm itself?'

'No problem.'

'And your ribs seem to have got back together. Well, I'm going to discharge you, mainly because we need the bed. But there is no way that you can return to duty for at least another three weeks, and I will so inform your commanding officer.'

'Yes, sir. Thank you, sir.'

'I can, of course, send you to a convalescent home. Or do you have a home of your own to go to?'

'I'll go to my parents. They live just outside Lymington.'

The doctor nodded. 'Sister, will you make up the necessary paperwork and arrange transport?'

'Yes, Doctor.'

'Now, Petty Officer, I do recommend that you do some walking to get strength back into your legs, but be sure to use a stick, and while you should exercise the arm, do not use it for any lifting or other feats of strength. You will return here in a fortnight's time, when we will assess whether you are fit for duty.'

'Yes, sir.'

The doctor continued on his rounds, followed by his entourage. It was half an hour before he finished with the ward, and Emma was able to return to Jamie. 'I never knew you lived in Lymington.'

'Just outside. My father owns a garage.'

She snapped her fingers. 'Of course. Goring's Garage.'

'You mean you know it?'

'Well, I've seen it, often enough, when going in and out of the town.'

'Don't tell me you live in Lymington?'

'No, no. My father keeps his boat there.'

Jamie stared at her in consternation. 'Your father has a yacht?'

'Well, yes. Shouldn't he?'

'May I ask what he does for a living?'

'He's a doctor. Well, a specialist, really. I suppose that's why I enjoy nursing.'

'And became a sister so young.'

She grimaced. 'I know. I'm afraid strings were pulled. But I am twenty-three, you know.'

'I'm sorry. I didn't mean . . .'

'So don't worry about it. Do you have a boat?'

'My father has a Bristol pilot cutter.'

'Ooh. Lovely, romantic things.'

'And I was part of Lord Eversham's racing crew, before the war.' Which was stretching the bow a bit; he had only crewed Duncan on one race, that famous Cowed–Dinard. But there was no way this most attractive young woman could know that.

'Gosh! Not in that tremendous schooner of his?'

'That's right. You mean you've seen her?'

'From a distance. She must be a dream to sail.'

'She is, yes. Unfortunately, she's not going anywhere right now; she's up on the hard. But . . .' He drew a deep breath. Yet she seemed interested. And perhaps even more than that. 'Would you like to see her? Go on board?'

'You have access?'

Jamie drew another long breath. 'I look after her for his lordship. When I have the time. I could show you over her. When you have the time.'

'You mean Lord Eversham wouldn't mind?'

'Good lord, no. He trusts me, absolutely.' Which was no lie. As to what Kristin might say, or do, if she found out he had taken another woman to their secret tryst, he didn't care to think. But there was no reason for her ever to find out; she never went to the yacht save to meet him, by arrangement.

'It's a lovely idea,' Emma said, thoughtfully.

'Do you go to Lymington often?'

'Not nowadays; we live at Eastleigh. It would have to be on my day off.'

'Which is when?'

'Which is when I can be spared from here. Anyway, we have to get you well, first. Then we'll see what we can fix up.'

She went about her duties, and Jamie stared at the ceiling. Of course it was pie in the sky. She was older than he, at an age when age differences mattered, and she was the daughter of a high profile doctor, not a garage owner. Equally, a girl as attractive as Emma Broughton had to have a boyfriend, perhaps even a fiancé . . . although she was not wearing a ring. And she had said she was not currently interested in any man.

But she had seemed interested in him! And Kristin had taught him that miracles could happen. And Kristin? For just on three years she had been everything to him, when he had not been on duty. But to live his entire life in a fog of guilt, relieved only by flashes of sexual ecstasy, and now increasingly outrageous demands . . . her growing determination that anything she wanted she could have was beginning to border on megalomania.

Of course, as regards herself, she was absolutely correct. She was invulnerable, something that had always fascinated him, had always suggested a shield beneath which others could shelter; she had offered him that shield more than once. But to accept it would end his life as a man, and he would become a pet, like that fabulous dog of hers. Oh, she would look after him with the same loving care as she lavished on Lucifer, he had no doubt, but entirely on her terms. And moving into her house, when her son and daughter-in-law were there all the time, would be tantamount to giving up the Navy, because she would be unable to keep out of his room, and someone had to notice that.

The personal problem, apart from the preservation of his identity, was that she had introduced him to a way of life that was irresistible. Over the past three years the pleasure he had felt at going home, even for a couple of days, had increasingly been less at the prospect of seeing his parents and sleeping in his own bed, than of seeing Kristin, with all the unbridled sex that would ensue. And yet he had been becoming increasingly aware that he at least was heading for catastrophe. So . . . oh, Kristin! But then . . . oh, Emma Broughton! If he dared.

'The telephone is for you, milady,' Harry said

'Who is it?' Kristin asked, coming in from the garden and stripping off her earth-stained rubber gloves; Lucifer as always panted at her heels, his nose also mud-stained where he had been digging.

'Southampton General Hospital. Dr Clifton.'

Kristin took the phone. 'Good morning, Doctor. May I help you?'

'Well, no, milady. You asked me to keep you up to date on the progress of the young sailor, Petty Officer Goring.'

'Did I?'

'Well . . . I have a note of it.'

'How efficient of you. Well, how is Goring?'

'I saw him this morning, and have passed him fit to return to duty.'

'To . . . hasn't he got to spend some weeks convalescing?'

'He's been doing that for the past three weeks.'

'Doing it where?'

'At home, so far as I know.'

'You are saying that Petty Officer Goring has been at home for the past three weeks? That he was discharged from hospital three weeks ago?'

'That is correct, milady.'

'Why was I not informed? I left you that message.'

'I'm sorry, milady. I was under the impression that you merely wished to know when Mr Goring would be fit for duty.'

'Well, really,' Kristin snapped. 'And you say he's fit for duty now. You mean he's rejoined his boat?'

'No, no. As today is Thursday, I've given him a last weekend off. I've informed Portsmouth that he will be reporting for duty on Monday morning.'

'I see.' The words were drips of ice. 'Thank you, Dr Clifton. You have been most helpful.'

She hung up, glared at the telephone. Three weeks, and he had not tried to get in touch. The poor boy obviously thought she was still mad at him. She snapped her fingers. 'Come on, Lucifer. We're going out.'

'There's a telephone call for you, Jamie,' Mary Goring called.

Shit! Jamie thought, rising from his chair; she's found out I'm home. But he supposed he'd have to take it. The house telephone was in the kitchen. He joined his mother, picked it up. 'Hello?'

'Mr Jamie Goring?'

Breath rushed through his nostrils. 'Emma? I do apologize. Sister Broughton! I thought you'd forgotten all about me.'

'Of course I haven't forgotten about you. And I think Emma is far more appropriate than Sister, you're no longer a patient. I'm sorry I missed you this morning. But I gather you're back on duty on Monday.'

'Yes, I am.' His heart was singing; she was interested, after all.

'So I thought . . . is that invitation to look at Lord Eversham's yacht still open?'

'Of course.'

'Well . . . I could get down to Lymington this afternoon. I'm off duty.'

'That would be tremendous.'

'Three o'clock all right?'

'Oh, yes. How will you get here?'

'I have a car.'

'What?'

'A present from Daddy for my twenty-first birthday. It's never had much use, so I've stacks of coupons saved up.'

'That's tremendous. Where will we meet?'

'I'll pick you up, if you like.'

He hesitated for a brief moment. He was so conditioned to his clandestine relations with Kristin he had to assimilate the fact that there could be nothing wrong in his parents knowing about a possible romance with a hospital nurse of roughly his own age, even if obviously of a higher class. 'That would be magnificent.'

'Three o'clock,' she repeated, and hung up.

'She sounds very nice,' Mary remarked. Small and fair, she was half the size of her son, although facially he took after her. 'Someone we know?'

'I don't think so. She's a nurse who looked after me in hospital.'

'And she wants to see some more of you? You must have scored a hit.' She squeezed his hand. 'I'm so glad, Jamie.'

'Mother, she's just an acquaintance. I can't even call her a friend, yet.'

'If she didn't want to be your friend, she wouldn't have telephoned, would she? Do you know, this is the first time you have ever been interested in a girl?'

If you only knew, Jamie thought. 'Life's been a bit hectic, these past few years.'

'Well, you know what they say: all work and no play makes Jack a dull boy.' She looked through the window; the house overlooked the garage forecourt. 'Hello, look who's here.'

Jamie stood beside her. 'Shit!' he commented.

'What did you say?'

'Sorry, Mother. It just slipped out.'

'Her bark is worse than her bite,' Mary said. 'It's just that it's been over a month since she was last here. Your father was beginning to worry that we'd lost her custom.'

'Good afternoon, Mr Probert,' Kristin said. She had known him for years. 'Fill her up, will you.' She handed him the book of coupons.

'Yes, milady.' Probert got busy with the pump.

Kristin got out of the Sunbeam. 'I'm told Mr Jamie is home.'

'Oh, yes, milady. He came home three weeks ago.'

'How nice. Is he in?'

'As far as I know, milady. Milady, the tank appears to be full.'

'That's why I'm here.'

'Yes, but it's only taken two gallons.'

'How odd. I must have filled it more recently than I thought. Put it on the account, will you, please. I'll be back in a moment, Lucifer.'

'She's coming over here,' Mary said. 'I wonder what she wants? Your father is in the office.'

'I'll find out,' Jamie said, as he knew what she wanted, just as he knew that this confrontation had to happen, and was safest on his own ground. He opened the door and stepped outside. 'Milady! How nice to see you.'

'And you, Jamie. And looking so well. I understand that you've completed your convalescence and are ready to return to duty.'

'Yes, milady. I report on Monday.'

She lowered her voice. 'And you never contacted me?'

'Well, I thought . . . I mean, after the hospital . . .'

'Silly boy. I'm free this afternoon.'

Jamie drew a deep breath. 'I'm sorry, milady. I have an appointment this afternoon.'

She frowned at him, as if unable to believe what he had said. 'Then cancel it.'

He refused to lower his gaze. 'I'm sorry, milady. I cannot do that.'

The frown deepened. 'What is this appointment about? Who is it with?'

'I'm sorry, milady. I cannot tell you that, either.'

That really would provoke a scene. And for a moment as her eyes became hard as flint, he supposed there was going to be one anyway. Then she said, 'Then keep your beastly appointment,' turned, and went back to her car.

'She looked a bit annoyed about something,' Mary observed as Jamie returned to the house.

'I have no idea what, Mother. Every time I see her ladyship, she seems to be in a fury about something or other.' Which, he reflected, was not altogether untrue.

He could hardly eat a bite of lunch, his brain a maelstrom of, what have I done, competing with, what am I going to do? If he didn't do something he knew he was going to regret it for the rest of his life. But equally, if he was hasty and lost Emma now, he would regret that for the rest of his life; he had only his instincts that she was interested in anything more than looking at Duncan's yacht.

He was in the forecourt at five to three, wearing a light jacket over civilian clothes; at the end of October the weather was distinctly autumnal. And Emma was on time, driving a small dark-blue Hillman. 'Hi! Not late, am I?'

'Spot on.'

He got in beside her, taking her in. Disappointingly, if sensibly, she was wearing slacks; he'd never seen her legs above her calves. But her woollen jumper was very well filled, and she was hatless. Her hair was everything he had wanted it to be, yellow-brown and straight, cut just below her ears, so as to neatly frame her face.

'Well,' she said, 'Do I pass muster, Petty Officer?'

He flushed. 'I'm sorry. I . . .'

She gave one of her entrancing smiles. 'Forget it. That is, as long as I do pass muster.'

'You're absolutely gorgeous. Oh, I—'

'You have to stop this apologizing. You have just paid me an enormous compliment. Where are we going?'

'You said you wanted to look at Lord Eversham's boat.'

'So I did. But I don't know where it is. You said it was out of the water.'

'Lymington. Hallam's Yard. Do you know it?'

She engaged gear and drove out of the forecourt. 'I know it. But it's closed down for the duration, isn't it?'

'Yes. But I have a key.'

'You're organized. I suppose that goes with being a petty officer. Are you a professional, or did you join when the war started?'

'When the war started.'

'And have you seen much service?'

'A bit.'

'Dr Clifton said you were in MTBs. Aren't they very dangerous?'

'They can be.'

She gave him a sideways glance as they entered the town. 'Have you ever been sunk?'

'Yes.'

Now she was looking straight ahead as they descended the hill; her ears were pink. 'I have a distinct feeling that you have an awful lot to tell me about yourself. Or is it too traumatic to remember?'

'No. But—'

'Don't tell me you're a hero in disguise. Have you got any medals?'

'I have one. But I believe I'm going to get another, whenever the king can spare the time.'

'Wow! What's the one you have?'

'The DCM.'

'That's the Distinguished Conduct Medal, right. Isn't that awarded for gallantry in action?'

'Well . . . let's say it's awarded for doing the right thing at the right time. That's usually in action.'

'So what is the other one for? I mean, you can't get

anything higher than that, can you? To get something like
the DSO you have to be an officer, don't you?'

'That's right. But apparently they award the Victoria Cross
to enlisted men as well as to officers.'

Emma stopped rather abruptly; they had in fact reached the
boatyard gates. She continued to rest both hands on the wheel.
'I really do not like people who poke fun at me.' She turned
her head, frowning. 'You aren't, are you? I mean, making
fun of me.'

'No, ma'am. You asked. I'll just unlock the gates, shall I?
You can drive in.'

He got out, and as he reached the gates the car gave a
little jerk as if she had taken her foot off the brake; in fact,
the engine stalled. He opened the gates, and she restarted
and drove through. He closed and relocked the gates behind
them, and got in beside her.

'I feel the most awful fool,' she said.

'Please don't,' he begged. 'I've been looking forward to
this afternoon for weeks. The shed is over here.'

Another quick glance, then she drove between the yachts
to park outside the shed. As she did so, it started to rain.

'Come on.' He held the door for her and urged her under
the roof. 'At least this should ensure privacy. But actually,
no one ever comes here.'

She made no comment.

'So,' he said, 'here she is. How big is your father's boat?'

'Thirty-three feet,' she said in a low voice.

'That's actually ideal. You only need two people, or in
fact, you can handle it on your own. Forty-five feet now, you
can sail her with two, but you want at least four to get the
best out of her. When racing, Lord Eversham always had
six, including himself.'

'You've raced with Lord Eversham? Of course, you told
me. Is that why he sent his mother to make sure you were
all right?'

'Ah . . . Yes, I suppose so. One reason, anyway. But I
suppose he worries about me. I'm getting the VC for saving
his life.'

'Good lord! Was it worth saving?'

'I beg your pardon.'

'I'm sorry. That was a terrible thing to say. Any life is worth saving. What I meant was, is he anything like his mother?'

'He is not in the least like his mother. He is the finest man I have ever known. Would you like to see inside?'

'You mean, I'm forgiven?'

'I think I could forgive you anything, Emma.'

She considered this, again her ears pink. Then she said, 'You mean you have a key for the cabin as well?'

'Yes. Up the ladder.'

She was wearing sensible, low-heeled shoes, and revealed her yachting background by climbing the ladder as quickly and confidently as Kristin, if less seductively. 'Wow!' she remarked, standing on the deck and looking forward. 'I've never been on a boat this size. Apart from cross-Channel or Isle of Wight ferries, I mean.'

'You should come and see my MTB.'

'How big is she?'

'Seventy-two feet, all but.'

'Gosh. And this is forty-five?'

'Forty-five.' He sidled past her and knelt to unlock the hatch, sliding it back. 'Enter.'

'My parlour, said the spider to the fly.' She gave him one of her quick glances as she went down the ladder. 'Full head room.'

He followed her. 'Well, fractionally over six feet. His lordship has to stoop a little.'

'Is he that tall? I've never met him. But I suppose there are times when it pays to be five foot four.' She looked around her. 'Comfortable, too.'

'She can sleep eight. Apart from these two, there are four forward and a master cabin with two more aft. And there are two heads. But she's most comfortable with just four. She was actually designed for cruising more than racing. I mean, she has a diesel, an eighty-horsepower Perkins. That's really too heavy for racing. But Duncan likes to try everything, and he was quite successful. As he usually is.'

Emma looked at the name plate over the forward doorway. '*Kristin*. Isn't that . . . ?'

'Yes. The Dowager. She paid for it. Actually, they're very close.'

'Must be nice to have a millionairess for a mother. How many girls have you brought here?'

'What?'

'When boats are laid up, their contents are usually removed. All of their contents, as has been done here. But things like blankets, mattresses and pillows are usually the first to go.' She was looking at the starboard settee berth.

He felt utterly helpless. 'You'll be thinking me the most utter cad.'

'Well, I don't know. Are you an utter cad?'

'I . . .' But having embarked on a deception, he had to go through with it, at least until they knew each other a whole lot better . . . or they would never get to know each other a whole lot better. 'I like to come here, and relax, and think.'

'You're a terrible liar.' She held up a finger, and sat on the bunk. 'It's not my business to pry. But I think I'm entitled to know one thing, truthfully: am I a stand-in, or a casual pick-up?'

He sat beside her, his heart pounding as he realized it might be going to happen. 'You could never be a stand-in, Emma. Or a casual pick-up. I've wanted to . . . well . . .'

'Get your hands on me,' she suggested, helpfully.

'Well . . .' He could feel his cheeks burning.

'Since when?'

'Since I was moved to your ward. And you sort of, showed an interest in me.'

One of those smiles. 'And was able to have my way with you.'

'I can't believe you found that very edifying.'

'Quite the contrary. I found you very edifying, certainly when compared with most of the inmates of my ward. Bedpans are things I usually leave to the junior nurses.'

'Is that why you're here, now?'

She made a moue. 'Just let's say, I'm here.'

They gazed at each other.

'So,' she said, 'what do you usually do with the girls you bring here?'

A last hesitation, then he took her in his arms and kissed

her. Her lips parted readily enough, and her tongue was eager. Still kissing her, he allowed his hand to slide from her shoulder on to her delightfully full breasts, and then further to her waist and her thigh. But when he got to her belt and fumbled at it, she closed her hand on his, and gently moved her head back.

'There is something you should know.' Her cheeks were pink. 'I'm a virgin.'

His hand fell away, and he also moved back.

'Is that so devastating?' she asked.

He licked his lips. 'But—'

'I'm here. With my tongue hanging out. I don't want you to think I'm a prick-tease.'

'You mean—'

'As I said, I'm here. And I had a pretty good idea what you had in mind when you invited me.'

'I thought—'

'That I was a tart?'

'Oh, good God, no, Emma! It's just that . . . well, you're twenty-three, and seemed to have been around a bit, and there's a war on, and—'

'All very cogent reasons for me to have got off the mark long ago. I suppose I have always been reluctant to take such an irrevocable step. How old were you when you lost yours?'

'Eighteen.'

'Wow! Was she a virgin?'

'No. No, she wasn't a virgin. I've never been with a virgin.'

'I can see that I'm way behind in the experience stakes. So . . . unless I've completely put you off . . .'

'You could never put me off, Emma. But you mean . . . ?'

'As we keep having to remind ourselves, I'm here. I think there comes a time in every woman's life when she needs to make a decision. You are the first man I have ever met who I have remotely felt like sharing a bed with. And since then, everything I've learned about you has increased that feeling.'

'You mean because I'm a VC? What nobody seems to appreciate is that I was saving my own life as well as those of Duncan and Wilson. I would have behaved in exactly the same manner had I been on my own. Only then nobody would have dreamed of giving me a medal.'

'So you're an accidental hero. I'm only interested, as far as that goes, in the fact that you have been in action, several times, and have apparently never shirked doing what needed to be done.'

'You should be a philosopher.'

'I like to think I am. However, I think the time for philosophy is past, so . . .' She gazed at him, eyes enormous.

He held her hands. 'There's just one thing more.'

She waited, her face expressionless.

'I want you so badly,' he said. 'But I don't want there to be recriminations. What about afterwards?'

'There can't be an afterwards, Jamie. Until there's been a before.'

'I mean, suppose there really is an afterwards. I . . . well, I wasn't sure . . .'

'So you didn't anticipate too much.' She felt in her pocket and produced a packet of condoms. 'I did.' She studied him as he did not immediately reply. 'You do know what these are for?'

How to tell her that he had never used one? He couldn't possibly do that. 'Yes.'

'Well, then . . . or do you feel that I'm being impossibly forward?' She gave a little shrug. 'I suppose I am.'

He held her shoulders, brought her against him for another kiss.

'It's just,' she said, when she got her breath back, 'when I make up my mind to do something, I do it.'

'You have got to be every man's dream.'

'You'll have to tell me what we do first.'

'I'd like to look at you. Everything.'

'Oh,' she said. 'Everything.' She kicked off her shoes, then lifted her jumper over her head, laid it on the bunk, then took off her white brassiere. Her breasts were not large, but perfectly shaped, and the nipples were hard. Cheeks now glowing, she stood up, unfastened her belt, and allowed her pants to slide down her thighs. Her legs really were perfection. Her knickers were white to match her bra, and these followed her pants; he felt that she was hurrying before she lost her nerve.

But now she looked at him, anxiously, the same thought

having apparently crossed her mind. 'I should've done that more slowly, shouldn't I?'

'You did it perfectly.' He put his arms round her buttocks and brought her against him to nuzzle her pale pubic hair, while a long tremor went the length of her body. Then raised his head. 'And I have nothing to show you that you haven't already seen.'

'You have a great deal I would like to view again,' she reminded him, and watched him undress in turn. 'I feel I'm in the presence of old friends.' She stretched out her hand to stroke the scar on his lower rib cage. 'That could have been catastrophic.'

'But as you can see, it wasn't.'

'I'm so glad about that.' She bit her lip. 'I suppose it's going to hurt like hell. I mean, you're kind of bigger than most. At least when you're like this.'

'I'll be as gentle as possible. But that's one reason why you have to be sure.'

She stood against him to kiss him and hold him. 'I'm sure. And besides, I have to experiment with these little things.' She drew the packet of condoms across his neck.

# PART TWO
# OPERATION SEVERE

Impossible? That will be done.

*Jules Michelet*

# THE PROPOSAL

'Captain Lord Eversham is here, sir,' said Miss Dunning.

Fitzsimmons rose from behind his desk, for once his face wreathed in smiles. 'Duncan! By God, it's good to have you back.'

'It's good to be back, Harry.' Duncan shook hands.

'Although why you're here, I can't imagine,' Fitzsimmons said.

'I'm told I'm replacing you.'

'You are. But why? With your record they'd surely give you a battleship. Or at least a heavy cruiser.'

Duncan went to the window and looked down at the pontoons. 'My record, Harry, was earned on MTBs. The thought of me in command of a forty-thousand tonner would turn their lordships' collective hair white. It probably already has. Anyway, I'm too young. My place is here, with what I know. So the moment I heard from Lonsdale that you were moving on—'

'You volunteered to take over. Well, horses for courses, I suppose.'

'So where are you going?'

'Whitehall. The staff.' Fitzsimmons made a face. 'They won't give me a battleship, either. I suppose because I'm too old. Well, old man, it's all yours. You have thirty-six MTBs to play with; they're in squadrons of twelve, so we can operate a rotating system, one out on patrol all the time, one on stand-by to respond to any emergency, and one being checked out while the crew have a spell ashore.'

'Sounds efficient. And there's nothing special coming up?'

Fitzsimmons grinned 'Not that anyone has told me. They're probably waiting for you to turn up.'

'What about the Second Front?'

'God knows. I have an idea they're still licking their wounds after that Dieppe disaster.'

'Harry, that was damn near a year ago.'

'They still remember it. Well, I'll leave you to it. Second Officer Dunning knows where everything is. She's a treasure.'

'Thank you. And good luck.'

They shook hands again, and Fitzsimmons left. Duncan sat behind the desk, did a bit of savouring as he remembered the many occasions on which he had stood in front of this desk, watching Fitzsimmons working himself up into a fuss. Not that he intended to make this quite such an office job as his predecessor. He looked up as there was a knock on the door. 'Come.'

Second Officer Dunning stood there. 'May I say how pleased I, and all the staff, are to have you in command, sir.'

'Thank you, Miss Dunning. That's very kind of you.'

She was looking at the crimson ribbon occupying the place of honour in front of the other ribbons on the breast of his uniform. 'I . . . we have never previously had the privilege of serving under a VC.'

He leaned back in his chair and studied her. She was a small woman, but then all women – save for his mother – seemed small to him. She was also quite young, not yet twenty-five, he was sure, and extremely attractive in a gamin fashion, with blue eyes. She wore her yellow hair in a bun, as required, but he had the impression it would be quite long when released. She also spoke with a distinctly upper-class accent; he put her down as Roedean or Benenden or perhaps Cheltenham. 'Well, I hope you will continue to find it a privilege.'

'And to have two VCs in the same command. That has to be some kind of a record.'

'You've met Goring?'

'Only socially, sir. But I feel that I know him quite well. He's my best friend's boyfriend.'

'Ah . . . I follow you. You mean she's in the service too?'

'No, sir. She's a nursing sister. Apparently when Goring was hit last year, he was in her ward at Southampton General, and, well, one thing led to another.'

'Good Lord!' Maybe I was wrong about this girl's class after all, he thought. Or her age. 'Isn't that very irregular?'

'Well . . . I don't know whether it is or not, sir. Emma is in rather a special position. Privileged.'

This grew more interesting by the moment. 'I did have the feeling that if she is your best friend she's a bit young to be a sister.'

'Thank you, sir. But as I said, Emma is in rather a special position. Her father is Sir Kenelm Broughton.'

'Not the gynaecologist?'

'That's the one, sir.'

'And his daughter is seeing Petty Officer Goring? You mean, seriously?'

'I think it's quite serious, sir. Oh, I know what you're thinking. And I'm not sure that Sir Kenelm approves. But Emma, well, he did not approve of her going into the profession, either. But she's inclined to go her own way.'

'Apparently.'

'And she's a most beautiful girl. You couldn't blame any man for going for her.'

'Then he sounds like a lucky fellow. May I ask your name, Miss Dunning?'

She raised her eyebrows, as he had just said it. 'Dunning, sir.'

'I meant your Christian name.'

'Emma, sir.'

'The same as Miss Broughton?'

'Yes, sir. Our mothers were, are, close friends. And we went to the same school.'

'Which was?'

'Cheltenham Ladies' College, sir.'

So I was right after all, he thought. Even if . . . 'I see. Emma. I like that. Is there anything urgent pending, Emma?'

'Not urgent, sir.'

'Well, will you let me have the complete list of crew members for the squadron.'

'Yes, sir.'

She hurried off and returned a few moments later with the thick file.

'Thank you. Carry on.' He riffled through the various sheets, found the one he wanted. He would have gone down there anyway. As they had attended different investitures – Jamie had

been back in uniform long before himself – they had only seen
each other once or twice since their return from the Adriatic,
on the few occasions Jamie had been able to spare the time to
visit him at Eversham House, and over the past year he hadn't
seemed able to make it at all. So he would have wanted to
contact him anyway, now that he was again his CO. But now
also he was curious; the boy seemed to be growing up very
fast. Of course, he was now nearly twenty-two years old . . .
but to have accumulated a girlfriend from several classes above
himself . . .

He got up, put on his cap, went into the outer office. 'I'm
going to take a walk down to the pontoons.'

'Yes, sir.'

He went down the stairs, returning the salutes of those of
his staff he encountered who happened to be wearing hats
– the others merely stood to attention as he passed – and
out into the bright spring sunshine. More memories.

He stood at the top of the gangway and looked down at
the pontoons, again evoking moments from the past. Then
he went down the sloping ramp and along the slatted wooden
platforms. He had ascertained from the duty roster that
Commander Roberts' Number Two Squadron – Webster had
been moved on – was on stand-by today, and turned towards
the waiting boats.

His visit had to be conducted in its proper order, so he
stopped beside *444*. 'Good morning,' he said, courteously,
to the rating mopping the deck.

The sailor looked up, gulped, and stood to attention. 'Sir!'

'Would Commander Roberts be on board?'

'Yes, sir.' He turned his head. 'Petty Officer! The
Commanding Officer is here, to see Commander Roberts.'

Men appeared from all over the place, to stand to attention.

'Carry on,' Duncan said. 'Good morning, Petty Officer.
Permission to come on board?'

'Please, sir.'

Duncan stepped on board at the same time as Roberts
emerged from the hatch. 'Captain Eversham! Welcome
aboard, sir. It's a privilege to have you in command.'

Duncan went up to the bridge, shook hands. 'It's a
privilege to be here, Mr Roberts.'

'Shall I assemble the crew for inspection, sir?'

'No, no, Commander. This is an informal visit. I'm just renewing memories. I will wish to see all the officers and men, in the near future, as I gather that they're nearly all new men, at least as far as I am concerned.'

'I'm afraid so, sir. We have a fairly high turnover, as we take casualties almost every time we go out. But every man is thrilled at the idea of serving under you.'

'Even if, in my time, I have been responsible for most of the casualties?'

'That was a legendary raid, sir. Everyone here now would have given a year's pay to be on it.'

'Even if only twenty of us came back? Believe me, Commander, I don't really have any desire to lead so many men to death again. And even less, as my new position requires, to send them. But it's good to know they're as enthusiastic as ever. Very good, Mr Roberts, I'll leave you to it. I would like you to assemble all your officers in the mess this evening for a chat.'

'Aye-aye, sir.'

'I take it you're out tomorrow.'

'Yes, sir.'

'And the day after that you're on R & R.'

'Yes, sir.'

'I wouldn't want to interfere with that. I'll address your crews on their next stand-by day.'

'Aye-aye. sir.'

'Thank you, Commander Roberts. Carry on.'

He returned to the pontoon, went to *432*. This crew had of course observed his visit to the flagship, and were already assembled at attention, as were those on *433* outside her.

'Welcome back, sir,' Linton said.

Duncan shook hands. 'It's good to be back. All well?'

'With me, sir. Yes. And . . .' He glanced down at Duncan's leg.

Duncan grinned. 'Only when it rains, eh? And this is . . . ?'

'Sub-Lieutenant Todd, sir. My exec.'

'Todd.'

The young man saluted.

'At ease.' Duncan shook hands.

'May I say what a privilege it is to serve with you, sir.'

'I think you should have a talk with Mr Linton before you form that opinion. Now, Bob, I'm going to have a chat with you all this evening. Right now, with your permission, I'd like to visit *433*.'

'Of course, sir.'

Both officers stood to attention as Duncan crossed their deck. Richard was waiting for him. They had seen quite a lot of each other over the last year, as Richard had lunched at Eversham House often enough, and he had known that Duncan was going to take command of the MTB fleet before anyone else, although he had been requested to keep it to himself.

Duncan was well aware that the boy was his mother's current protégé. As Kristin had clearly turned over a new leaf during the past few years, and abandoned the wild flights of fancy that had earned her so much notoriety in the past, and was indeed, rather obviously, toying with the idea of again taking up with Jimmy Lonsdale, he had no objection to her mothering young officers, providing they were socially acceptable, and Richard was certainly that, more so, he felt, than her previous toy boy, Arnold Cooper. And in fact he liked the young man himself.

Richard saluted as he boarded. 'Good morning, sir. It is good to see you in uniform.'

'It is very good to be in uniform again, Mr Calman.' There were crew members within earshot. 'Petty Officer.'

'Sir!' Jamie stood to attention.

'All well?'

'Indeed, sir. Thank you.'

'No ill effects?'

'Oh, good Lord, no, sir. I'm as fit as a fiddle.'

'And I gather that episode, even if painful at the time, has brought romance in its wake.'

'Sir?'

'Second Officer Dunning is my secretary.'

'Of course, sir.' Jamie was unable to control a flush.

'So, are we going to hear wedding bells?'

'Early days, sir.'

'Indeed? But you left hospital six months ago.'

'Yes, sir.'

'Well, it's none of my business. But congratulations, if it happens. I understand that she's a lovely girl.'

'Yes, sir. She is.'

'Well done. Carry on. I'll see you later, Mr Calman.'

Richard saluted, watched him visiting the next boat. 'Romance in the air, Petty Officer?'

'With luck, sir.'

'Well done. I look forward to hearing more.'


Emma Dunning was waiting for him. 'Admiral Lonsdale would like a word, sir. ASAP.'

Duncan nodded. As Lonsdale had known for some time that he was taking over today, and had already congratulated him, this could hardly be an official welcome.

'Pleased to have you with us, Captain Eversham,' Miss Grace said. 'You're to go right in.'

Duncan nodded, gave a tap on the door, and entered the admiral's office, checking as he discovered there were two other men already present, neither of whom he knew. One wore the uniform and insignia of a captain, the other was in plain clothes.

'Come in, Duncan,' Lonsdale said. 'All settled in?'

'Getting there, sir.'

'Excellent. I'd like you to meet Captain Collins, from the Admiralty.'

'Collins.' Duncan shook hands.

'I've read your file,' Collins said. 'It's a pleasure to meet you.'

'Thank you.'

'And this is Mr Lawton. Mr Lawton, Lord Eversham is our commanding officer, MTBs.'

Lawton was on his feet, also to shake hands. 'A pleasure, Captain. You have a considerable reputation.'

As he was both rather nondescript in appearance, and wore a nondescript business suit, and was yet in the admiral's office as, apparently, an equal and accompanied by a staff officer, Duncan did not need to be a genius to deduce that what he should have been wearing was a slouch hat, a cloak and carrying a dagger. 'My pleasure, Mr Lawton,' he said, keeping an open mind for the time being, even if the man's presence had to mean either that there was something nasty going on in the Navy, or that there was an unpleasant assignment for his people in the offing.

'Sit down, Captain,' Lonsdale invited.

Duncan took off his cap and sat beside Lawton.

'Mr Lawton is from MI6,' the admiral explained.

Duncan gave a faint sigh of relief; the fact that the visitor was from the external rather than the internal branch of the Secret Service at least meant that no traitors had been found in his command.

'He has a project to put to us, of vital importance to the war,' Lonsdale went on. 'And thus everything we say is classified.'

When is it not? Duncan wondered, somewhat cynically.

'And this is a preliminary exploration of ways and means, which we would merely like you to consider. Should you conclude that the plan is practical, then you, and I, will be required to attend a full planning conference in London. Should you conclude that it is not practical, then we will have to turn elsewhere. The decision will be yours.'

Thanks a bunch, Duncan thought, and wondered if the project had been saved for his assumption of command, on the grounds that he would be more likely to go for a difficult assignment than Fitzsimmons. But he said, 'It sounds interesting, sir.'

'It is. Mr Lawton?'

The agent cleared his throat. 'I believe I am correct in saying that you, and thus various members of your command, know the island of Oleron, in the lower half of the Bay of Biscay?'

'You would not be correct, sir.'

Lawton gazed at him in consternation. 'Did you not lead the famous raid up the Gironde in 1941?'

'I did, sir.'

'Well, surely some of those people are still serving.'

'Some of them are. But that raid did not go near the Isle d'Oleron. That is situated within a couple of miles of the French coast. Our objective in 1941 was to gain the mouth of the Gironde without being detected by the enemy. Thus we laid a course far out into the bay and only approached the shore at night. We came back the same way.'

'Hm. But . . . you're a famous yachtsman. Did you never sail along the coast of Biscay in pre-war days?'

'No, sir, I did not.'

Lawton sighed. 'Then I seem to have had a wasted journey. Thank you for your time, Admiral Lonsdale.'

Lonsdale did not reply, but continued to watch Duncan, whom he had known all his life; he could tell that his protégé was not finished.

'I have not said, sir,' Duncan said, 'that I would be unable to help you. If you would tell me what help you are looking for.'

Lawton gave him a frosty stare. 'We wish to know, Captain Eversham, if it would be practical to make a landing on the island of Oleron.'

'Is this to be a raid, or a reconnaissance?'

'It is to be a mission, Captain. To be conducted in the utmost secrecy.'

'In other words, you wish to rendezvous with someone on the island. I think that may be practical, and obviously the entry would have to be made in complete secrecy. That also is practical. Getting back out again, while it may just be practical, will be impossible in secrecy.'

'The question is, in any event, academic. We understand that the approaches to the island are so very difficult that they can only be undertaken with local knowledge. Lacking that . . .' He shrugged. 'We have no desire to send your men to their deaths.'

Duncan gave him an old-fashioned look: as far as he could see this would be very close to a suicide mission in any event. However, he said, quietly, 'I may be able to provide the local knowledge you require.'

Lawton raised his eyebrows. 'From amongst your crews?'

Lonsdale snapped his fingers. 'Goring!'

'Who?'

'Petty Officer Goring,' the admiral explained. 'Tell him, Duncan.'

'It is simply that I have in my crews a man named Goring,

who has sailed the French coast ever since he was a lad. I do not know if he has ever visited Isle d'Oleron, but if anyone in the British Isles has done so, it will be him.'

'But that is splendid. And he would undertake such a mission?'

'He will tell you whether or not it is practical, sir. As to whether he will undertake it, well, you will have to ask him. I am sure you appreciate that such a mission, into enemy controlled coastal waters, must be a voluntary one. And that goes for the entire crew of the MTB involved.'

'Hm. Yes, of course. But first we need to know if the plan is practical. When can I meet this chap . . . ah . . . ?'

'Goring,' Duncan said. 'You can meet him now, Mr Lawton. If I may use your telephone, Admiral.'

'Help yourself.'

Duncan called his office. 'Miss Dunning, would you please get hold of Petty Officer Goring, *433*, and tell him to report to Admiral Lonsdale's office, immediately. I know he's on board, because I spoke to him not half an hour ago.'

'Aye-aye, sir.'

Duncan replaced the phone. 'I think, sir, that it would be helpful if, when Goring gets here, we have a large-scale chart of the French Biscay coast available, as well as the Admiralty Biscay Pilot.'

'Good lord!' Richard said. 'What the devil do you suppose is up?'

'It looks as if I am, sir,' Jamie said, hastily making sure that his tie was straight and putting on his cap before joining Emma Dunning, waiting somewhat uncertainly; she did not often come down to the pontoons, and his weight was causing it to sway.

'What's happening?' he asked, as they walked back to the ramp. If she was superior to him in rank, she was Emma's best friend, and although he would never have dreamed of allowing their friendship to impose on naval protocol, they were well away from any risk of being overheard.

'I haven't a clue,' she admitted.

'But, I mean . . . you're still Duncan's secretary, aren't you?'

'Yes. He's up there now. With the admiral.'

'And they've sent for me?'

She allowed her hand to brush against his. 'You'll be all right. I don't think they've ever actually cashiered a VC.'

They entered the Command Building. 'You're on your own,' Emma said. 'Good luck.'

Jamie swallowed and climbed the stairs, knocked tentatively on the door of the admiral's outer office.

'Come.'

He turned the handle and stepped inside. Second Officer Grace gave him a bright smile. 'You'll be Petty Officer Goring.'

'Yes, ma'am.'

'Just a moment.' She got up, knocked on the inner door, opened it. 'Petty Officer Goring is here, sir.'

'Thank you, Miss Grace. Have him come in.'

She gave Jamie a quick nod, and he stepped past her; the door closed behind him. He stood to attention. 'Sir!'

'At ease,' Lonsdale said. 'Captain Eversham tells us that you have some experience of sailing on the French coast.'

Although standing at ease, Jamie continued to stare straight in front of himself. 'Yes, sir, I do.'

'This gentleman would like to put some questions to you.'

Jamie turned his head, his gaze first of all encountering Duncan, who also gave him an encouraging smile, then Collins, stony-faced, and then Lawton, who was studying him with a frown, which deepened as he took in the medal ribbons on Jamie's left breast. Then he looked at Duncan. 'Good Lord!' he commented.

'Oh, indeed,' Lonsdale agreed. 'You have in front of you the pride of the Command.'

'But . . . he's very young.'

As if I wasn't actually here, Jamie thought.

'There is no age requirement involved in winning the Victoria Cross,' Lonsdale pointed out, mildly. 'At Jutland in 1916, Boy Cornwall won the award, posthumously, at the age of sixteen. As for Petty Officer Goring's rank . . . how old are you, Goring?'

'Twenty-one, sir.'

'Now that is young, to have reached warrant officer rank. But he has earned every step of it.'

'I was merely thinking,' Lawton protested, realizing that he had rubbed all four of the Navy men up the wrong way, 'that he is very young to have accumulated the sort of detailed knowledge we require. I mean, the war has been on now for more than three years. He can't have been cruising Biscay in that time.'

'Actually,' Duncan said, 'he has cruised Biscay during that time, on operation. However, pre-war . . . how old were you when you first went to sea, Mr Goring?'

'Six, sir.'

'This was in your father's boat?'

'Yes, sir.'

'And in the dozen years that elapsed between your first voyage and the outbreak of war, how much sailing, cruising, did you do?'

'We cruised every year for three months, sir.'

'By cruising you mean . . . ?'

'The west coast of Europe, sir.'

'From . . . ?'

'The Netherlands to the north coast of Spain, sir. We never went further afield than that because my father's boat is not very fast.'

'I'm impressed,' Lawton admitted. 'So would you ever have sailed by the island of Oleron?'

'Isle d'Oleron, sir? Oh, yes, several times.'

'Have you ever landed there?'

'Yes, sir.'

'I see. Would you be prepared to pilot a boat there?'

'Are we talking of from the Bay, sir? It is an exposed coast. I could take a boat to within a few hundred yards of the beach, but to go closer could involve getting caught up in rollers and stranded.'

'That agrees with my information, certainly. What about the other side?'

'That is quite practical, sir. That is, in normal circumstances. Right now . . . well, it is very close to the mainland.'

'And we are at war. Our information is that because of

the difficulties of navigating the passage, it is not very heavily guarded.'

'One gun covering the Pertuis d'Antioch, which as you say, is narrow, would be all that is needed.'

'There is actually a battery,' Collins put in. 'But could it not be done at night, without lights?'

Jamie considered. 'It's possible. Much would depend on how thoroughly it is covered by radar.'

'Our information is that the enemy has only a few, widely spaced, stations down there.'

'Then sir, it could be possible to get in.'

'And out again?' Duncan asked. 'I assume the island is garrisoned, Mr Lawton?'

'Yes, it is. Or at least a post. We don't believe it is heavily manned. Well, Mr Goring?'

'Everything would depend on what we're going in for, sir. If it's a raid, and we stir the whole place up, well . . .'

'It would not be a raid,' Lawton said. 'But it could well stir the whole place up. Would you be prepared to take that risk? If the reason were vital enough?'

Another consideration.

'Couldn't you,' Collins suggested winningly, 'use the entrance called the Pertuis de Maumusson? Certainly for getting out. Our information is that this is not guarded at all.'

'I would like to be shown all of this,' Lonsdale said, indicating the chart on his desk.

'Yes, sir. With your permission.' Jamie went round the desk to stand beside him. Me, he thought, Jamie Goring, literally rubbing shoulders with an admiral! And what an admiral! Even if Lonsdale might be blissfully unaware of it, they had been rivals in love for three years! But he was actually totally absorbed in what was being suggested to him.

Duncan, Collins and Lawton leaned over the desk from the other side.

'Here is La Rochelle,' Jamie explained, 'sheltered by Isle de Re. South of Isle de Re there is the inshore passage, entered from the Bay by the Pertuis d'Antioch, which leads to Rochefort. This used to be an important French naval base.'

'It still is,' Collins commented. 'Although it's a German base now.'

'Yes, sir. This water, as you see, is known as the Coureau d'Oleron, and is sheltered from Biscay by Isle d'Oleron. This is a big island, stretching twenty-odd miles. And as you also see, only a few miles south of Isle d'Oleron is the entrance to the Gironde River.'

'Up which Lord Eversham led three boats in 1941. Were you with him on that raid?'

'Mr Goring was our pilot,' Duncan said, 'He knew the river. And I should remind you that only two of my boats got back out.'

'And as you said, you entered from seaward. But this Pertuis de Maumusson looks straightforward enough to me,' Collins commented.

'It is, sir, on the chart,' Jamie agreed. 'And it is, probably, unguarded. But there is a reason for that.'

Duncan had been thumbing the Admiralty Biscay Pilot. 'It says here that this entrance is listed by the French as SEVERE. Doesn't that mean . . .' He looked at Jamie.

'Yes, sir. It is a warning that the passage is extremely dangerous, and is only to be attempted at your own risk. In other words, if you take it, and get into trouble, there is no point in calling for assistance, because there won't be any offered. We are, of course, talking about yachts or other small craft in time of peace. It is not navigable at all to ships of any size.'

'So you don't actually know it.'

'Oh, I know it, sir.'

'You mean you've been through it?'

'Yes, sir.'

'Then . . .' Lawton looked from face to face. 'What is the risk?'

'The risk, sir, is that the bottom end of the Coureau d'Oleron is encumbered with shallows and sandbanks and the Pertuis is merely a channel through these hazards. It carries only about four feet at low water springs, and therefore can only be attempted at half-tide up with a boat of any size. The tidal flow through the passage is strong, and as the passage has to be taken slowly, it is only really practical on the ebb, which flows south. But any wind across tide situation – and the prevailing wind is of course south-westerly – sets up surf right across the entrance.'

'But you have been through it,' Collins said. 'In what?'

'My father's pilot cutter.'

'With what sort of draft?'

'Five foot with the centreboard down, two feet with it up.'

'And an MTB?' Lawton looked at Duncan.

'Four foot six. We don't have a centreboard to take up.'

'But it would be practical?'

Duncan looked at Jamie.

'Quite practical, sir, in the right conditions. That is given absolute choice of time and weather.'

'Well, then,' Lawton said. 'There we have our code name for the mission. Operation Severe. I like the sound of that.'

'But suppose a choice of wind and weather were not available?' Duncan asked.

'In those circumstances,' Lonsdale said, 'we cannot undertake this mission. I cannot send seventeen of my people to certain death or imprisonment, and as that would include any passengers they may have with them after leaving the island, the entire exercise would be totally pointless. I'm sorry, Lawton, but while I am proud of the reputation my boats have achieved for carrying out the most daring of ventures into enemy waters, there has always been at least a fifty-fifty chance of survival. Here there is none at all.'

Lawton looked at Collins. Who cleared his throat. 'I must inform you, sir, that their lordships regard this operation as absolutely vital to our chances of carrying out a successful invasion of the continent, and have commanded me to instruct you that it is to be attempted if there is even one chance in ten of it being carried out successfully.'

It was Lonsdale's turn to clear his throat, while he went very red in the face.

'I will now ask Mr Lawton to put you in the picture,' Collins went on.

Throughout the exchange Lawton had continued to gaze at Jamie; now he addressed the young man more than his superiors. 'What I am going to say must never be repeated to a soul outside this room. As I am sure you know, and as

Captain Collins has just indicated, we are preparing for a return to the continent, that means, to France, in the near future. The Second Front, eh? The plans are being drawn up now, by General Morgan. They are a long way from being finalized, but they will involve the landing and maintenance of several million men on the French coastline. Unfortunately, they cannot all be landed at the same time, therefore the first few days are going to be hazardous in the extreme for every man in the expeditionary force that is put ashore. If the Germans are able to bring all their resources to bear on the bridgehead, we could well be dislodged and driven back into the sea. That would mean not only a massive loss of life in the ranks of our best soldiers, but the prolongation of the war for at least another year, that is, three hundred and sixty-five days, and the death rate, worldwide, is currently running at better than three thousand a day.'

He paused to look around their tensed faces. 'So the landings cannot fail. But it is agreed, both in London and Washington, that they can only succeed if there is sufficient disruption behind the German lines to prevent him from concentrating all his forces. The RAF and the USAAF will do what they can, of course, but it is not considered that this will be sufficient. The real disruption has to be on the ground, that is, it has to be provided by the French Resistance. The Resistance claims to be able to put into the field a hundred thousand men and women, armed and determined. But there is a caveat. These men, and these women, all belong to different groups, separated not only by distance but by ideology, by different backgrounds, different beliefs and different aims. To be of any use to us, they have to be united, and that means, they have to follow, and obey, a common directive from a common leader. And the leader has to be on the ground, not in London as is the case with General de Gaulle.

'Now, our agents in France have informed us that there is such a man. His name is irrelevant, and it would mean nothing to you anyway. His code name, and the name by which he is known in the movement, is Colonel Morte, which is sufficiently descriptive of both his methods and of his achievements over the past three years in killing the enemy and disrupting their arrangements. We have been in contact with him for some time. Unfortunately, as I suppose was inevitable, a month ago his headquarters were betrayed. He escaped, but has had to go into hiding.'

'And you think he is on Oleron?' Duncan asked.

'We know he is there, Captain. He has been in contact with us since his betrayal. But he also knows that he is on borrowed time. The Gestapo will find him, sooner or later. We have got to get him out of there before that happens. Once he is here, he can safely contact his various people by radio, and when the invasion is ready to go, he can be put back in by parachute. Unfortunately, we cannot get him out by plane; owing to the uneven surface and the considerable wooded areas there is nowhere to land even a Lysander in Oleron. It has to be by boat.'

'And if coming out by boat involves his death?' Lonsdale had recovered.

'He is prepared to risk that. The point is that to remain where he is involves almost certain capture, which will mean death, which will of course only follow sufficient torture to force him to reveal not only a great deal of classified information, but also lead to the arrest and execution of a large number of other leaders, who are all known to him. Worst of all, while he lives, he is the embodiment of the Resistance. Were the Germans able to claim his death, and prove it by exhibiting his body, the effect on morale would be inconceivable.'

Lonsdale sighed. 'You realize this is emotional blackmail?'

'It is a fact of life, Admiral,' Collins said, 'and is recognized as such by their lordships. Now, there is one other detail. You say, Petty Officer Goring, that you can navigate your boat through the Pertuis d'Antioch, and hopefully, out the other side. However, there is the matter of the pick-up. Mr Lawton?'

'Ah. Yes. Would you know the harbour of Le Chateau, Mr Goring?'

'I do, sir.'

'We understand that it's a fishing port.'

'Yes, sir. Just about the oldest fishing port in France, and dates back to the seventeenth century. It is where the first

Maritime Laws, later accepted by the entire rest of Europe, were drawn up.'

The officers exchanged glances, and Duncan felt it necessary to explain. 'The study of history is a hobby of Mr Goring's.'

'Excellent,' Lawton said. 'But have you been there, Mr Goring?'

'Yes, sir, I have.'

'Tell us about it.'

Jamie understood that the blighter had obviously read it up in some guidebook, and was waiting for a mistake.

'It is a small town, sir, which is entirely enclosed within the walls of the citadel, hence it's name, Le Chateau. The harbour is small, and largely dries, but the bottom is soft mud. When we were there we lay alongside the quay and took the ground quite comfortably, but I don't think that would suit an MTB. But if we are to pick somebody up and be off again, it would have to be done on one tide, anyway.'

'Excellent,' Collins said in turn. 'Now, we intend to give you all the assistance possible. We obviously cannot help with the actual operation, as that necessarily has to be carried out with a single shallow draft vessel. But once you are out again, you will rendezvous with a submarine, which will relieve you of your passenger.'

'If I may say so,' Jamie said. 'In an MTB we can get the passenger back to England far quicker than a sub.'

Collins looked disapproving, at having his dispositions questioned by a petty officer. 'That may be so, Mr Goring. But I doubt as safely. Work out your times and co-ordinates, and we will arrange a preliminary rendezvous on the way in. As I assume this operation will take place at night, the sub will then remain on station until you return the following morning. Do you wish to say anything else, Mr Lawton?'

'Simply that I shall, of course, be accompanying the mission,' Lawton said. 'I assume there will be room for me on your boat?'

The sailors exchanged glances; that was really putting the boot in as regards courage and determination. And necessity. Lonsdale looked at Jamie. 'This has to be your call, Goring.'

Jamie had been considering as he listened to Lawton's speech. Now he drew a deep breath. 'Who knows, sir. We might get lucky.'

Lawton and Collins left the sailors to it, their sole require- ment being that the plan should be worked out as rapidly as possible, and taken to London by Lonsdale and Duncan for final approval, when the Resistance in Gascony would be informed and the submarine rendezvous set up. Lawton would then join the mission, on the day it was sailing.

'You must say that he has guts,' Lonsdale commented. 'Although I don't like the idea of revealing our plans to the Frogs. I don't like that at all. We're told that this has to be absolutely top secret, and then that our arrangements are going to be blabbed over the radio.'

'Well, sir,' Duncan argued. 'If they don't know when we're coming, they can't have their man ready to join us. Now, Jamie, which boat?'

'With permission, sir, I'd like to take my own. *433*.'

'That is . . . ?' Lonsdale inquired.

'Lieutenant Calman, sir,' Duncan said.

'Ah. A bit of a tearaway, isn't he?'

'With respect, sir,' Jamie protested, and glanced nervously at Duncan, 'Lieutenant Calman's aim in life, from his first day, has always been to act as he supposes Lord Eversham would.'

The admiral gazed at him for several moments, then suddenly smiled. 'I see you have more inside that brain of yours, Petty Officer, than just guts and knowledge. You'll have *433*, but your commanding officer will have to volunteer to accompany you, as will every other member of the crew. The danger involved will have to be made perfectly plain, Duncan, without of course revealing what those dangers actually are.'

'Yes, sir,' Duncan said, thoughtfully, and Jamie shot him another quick glance. He had sailed with his hero for more than three years, and had heard that tone and seen that expression on more than one occasion.

Lonsdale apparently had not. 'Well,' he said, 'I will leave you to it. Work out your tides, select your crews, and report back to me, obviously ASAP. But the planning must be meticulous.'

'Aye-aye, sir,' Duncan acknowledged.

'Mr Goring, it has been a pleasure meeting you. I would very much like to do so again. Thank you, gentlemen.'

# THE PLAN

D uncan and Jamie went down to his office, where Emma Dunning regarded them somewhat quizzically. The idea of a petty officer being closeted with an admiral for more than an hour was unique in her experience. But Duncan merely said, 'No calls, Miss Dunning,' and closed the door.

He indicated the chair, and Jamie removed his cap and sat down. Duncan sat behind the desk. 'Is it possible?'

'Given the right conditions, sir, yes.'

'And those are?'

'A moonless night.'

'But that'll mean a neap tide.'

'Yes, sir. But there'll be enough water a couple of hours either side of High, and if it's wind across tide when we want to get out conditions will be better for us with the slower movement.'

'It will still be extremely dicey. And what about getting in?'

'We'll have to use the same tactics as we did for the Gironde raid, sir, stay out in the Bay and then make for the Pertuis d'Antioch, aiming to arrive there an hour before high water. The tide will still be running north, and we will have to take it slowly, but the full flood will have ended; on a neap it shouldn't hold us up too much.'

'There are several caveats. One is that it's May, not February, as it was when we went up the Gironde. Even if your plan is approved and you can be ready in a week from today, you're still running out of darkness. Another is that the Pertuis d'Antioch is about half the width of the Gironde at Royan, and instead of a couple of guns there is a complete battery, and again, unlike 1941, whatever Lawton says, they'll almost certainly have radar covering it.'

'I never supposed it would be easy, sir. Like I said, maybe we'll get lucky.'

'There is a third caveat, which didn't exist when we went in in 1941. The submarine pens in L'Orient have been repaired and are again fully operational. Biscay is now a regular channel in and out for U-boats. They are usually on the surface for speed.'

Jamie grinned. 'Maybe we'll bag one, sir.'

'And if there are several together?'

'Then we'll have to miss them. Even on the surface, we can go twice as fast as any U-boat.'

Duncan considered him for several seconds. 'You don't have to go through with this, if you feel the risk is unacceptable, Jamie.'

'Sir?'

'I mean if, when we analyse what is involved and the conditions we require, you realize that it simply cannot be done, no one will hold it against you if you say so. And I will back your decision. As will the admiral.'

'We've exposed ourselves more dangerously in the past, sir, and got away with it. And we do have the opportunity to choose our time.'

'I'm afraid the word 'we' does not apply in this case. You have no idea how much that bothers me.'

'I understand that, sir. You have a greater responsibility than just one mission. But I think Sub-Lieutenant Calman has what it takes.'

'You understand that he must volunteer.'

'He'll volunteer, sir.'

Duncan gave a brief smile. 'Because you've convinced him that he must ape me in all things.'

'He didn't need much convincing, sir.'

'Well . . . have you any idea how he is situated domestically? You understand that no married men can be accepted for this project.'

'Yes, sir. Mr Calman is not married. I believe his people live in the Caribbean.'

Duncan snapped his fingers. 'Yes, of course. British Guiana. That's actually on the mainland of South America. And he has no one over here? No girl or anything like that?'

'Not so far as I know, sir.'

'And what about you? You're an only son. You shouldn't be included.'

'With respect, sir, I have to be included, as I'm the only person with the knowledge necessary to get us in and then out.' He spoke with not a suggestion of false pride or arrogance. But Duncan had long realized that Jamie Goring was totally lacking in either of those two vices; their absence in one so talented and so courageous was his most enduring quality. 'As for my parents, well, they accepted from the day I joined the MTB squadron that I was in a high risk occupation. They're used to it, now.'

'Because you've always come back.' He gave one of his quick grins. 'Even when reported dead. But now you do have a girl. You are planning to marry her?'

'I would like to do that, sir.'

'But there's a but. You mean she isn't that keen?'

'Oh, no, sir. She's keen. It's her parents who aren't.'

'Have you met them?'

'Yes, sir. It was not a great success.'

'Were you in uniform?'

'No, sir.'

'Mistake. There is no parent in his right mind could resist those medals you're wearing.'

'Unfortunately, sir, I don't think even a chest-full of medals would make any difference. Emma's father, well, he's a knight of the realm, comes from a very posh background . . .' He paused in embarrassment.

'I get the message,' Duncan said, equably. 'And you're a petty officer, son of a garage owner. I suppose snobbery is endemic in our society.'

It was Jamie's turn to reflect that perhaps Duncan's most endearing quality was that, for all his wealth and background, he was totally lacking in that vice; he well remembered the shock waves that had gone through British society when Lord Eversham had ditched his upper-crust fiancée to marry a simple Wren second officer, with no pretensions to class or background.

'But you say that Emma wants to marry you.'

'That's what she tells me, sir.'

'Hm. I'd like to meet this girl.'

'Well, sir, I'm sure that can be arranged, when this business is over.'

'And if you come back.'

'There wouldn't be much point if I don't, sir.'

Another long consideration. Then Duncan said, 'Very good, Jamie. Work out your dates and tides and I'll put the plan before the admiral. And I'm going to do something else: when you come back, you will be recommended for a commission.'

Alison woke up with a start, instinctively felt the space beside her. It was empty, but the sheet was still warm. She sat up, blinked in the gloom, and saw her husband standing in the window, silhouetted against the night sky; he had drawn the curtains. 'Duncan?'

He turned. 'Damn! I didn't mean to wake you up.'

'Isn't that what wives are for, to be wakened when their husbands have too much on their minds to sleep?'

He returned to the bed, sat beside her, and took her into his arms. 'I'm not sure that is a universally held opinion. But then, you are a unique wife.'

Alison blew a raspberry into his neck. 'I shouldn't think that's a universally held opinion either.'

'It's a fact. No one else could have survived three years of me, and Mother. Not to mention Lucifer.'

'If I've survived, it's because I've become part of you. All of you.'

As much to her own surprise as anyone else's. She could still remember the mixture of excitement and apprehension she had experienced when this entirely lovable man, so many light years above plain Alison Brunel, Second Officer, daughter of a country doctor with no family background, had asked her to marry him. She had put it down to post-traumatic shock after his boat had been the only one to survive that encounter with the German navy; it had taken her a little while to appreciate that Duncan Morant did not suffer from things like post-traumatic shock, not because he lacked depths or imagination, but because in his code of conduct officers and gentlemen did not allow such weaknesses to exist, at least in themselves.

Other moments of equally confused emotions had followed thick and fast. Her first meeting with his incredible mother! Her first encounter with the no less incredible Lucifer, when she had found herself lying flat on her back with a monstrous dog standing over her, licking her face.

And then, the fabulous lifestyle, all without the slightest apparent awareness that it was fabulous, because Kristin and Duncan had never known anything else. But then she had realized that she had been invited to join them in this never-never world. Even if she hadn't been madly in love with Duncan, she would have found it irresistible. And now she was in a position of equality, able to treat her husband as a man, rather than a demi-god.

'So tell me what's on you mind,' she said. 'It's something to do with the visit to London yesterday, isn't it?'

'Something.'

'They're not moving you on, already, are they? You've only been there a week.'

'They're not moving me on.'

'Well, then . . . don't tell me you've gone off the job itself? I thought that commanding an MTB squadron was always your ambition. And now you have three.'

'And no captain could ask for a better crew. Every one of them is worth his weight in gold.'

'But you don't enjoy having to send them out, day after day, to risk their lives, when you're not actually doing it yourself, leading them into battle.'

He pulled his head back to look at her face, a sliver of white in the darkness. 'Who's a deep thinker, then?'

'Doesn't require thought, just observation. It's been pretty obvious this past week. Ever since you took command. But you knew what went with the job.'

'Yes,' he said, thoughtfully. 'You mean Mother has noticed it too?'

'With the deepest possible respect, darling, and you know that I love your mother more than anyone else in the world, saving only you and Baby Duncan, Kristin is not given to observing other people very closely, save as projections of her own plans and attitudes.'

And since her love life has gone sour, she thought,

she has not even been able to make any plans. Kristin had not confided in her what had actually happened, but as she watched her mother-in-law very carefully, if only in the hopes of preventing her from embarking on any irrevocable catastrophe, she was quite sure that she was no longer seeing Jamie.

And she had not yet, apparently, found an adequate replacement. The boy Calman had obviously been in line. He had been invited to lunch on several occasions since the first, last year, and Alison personally enjoyed his company. She also knew how good Kristin was at concealing her feelings, when in company, principally beneath an abrasive exterior. But she couldn't bring herself to believe they were sleeping together, because Kristin had entirely ceased to *glow*, as she had so often glowed during the past three years, almost always after returning from one of her mysterious afternoon jaunts. So maybe she had tried him and he didn't measure up, or more likely, he was not as subservient as Jamie had obviously always been . . . although clearly he had ceased being sufficiently subservient since his spell in hospital.

As for the admiral . . . Jimmy had been re-admitted to the fold, and was also again a regular visitor, but Kristin obviously remembered too well her disastrous experiment of the previous year, and was in no hurry to repeat it.

But in any event, Kristin's emotional problems had to be subordinate to Duncan's, simply because he had never had any emotional problems before, at least as far as she had been able to observe. 'It's never kept you awake before.'

Duncan sighed, and hugged her so tightly that she ran out of breath. 'I'm awake because I have come to a decision. I'm going to have to ask you to forgive me. I'm not sure anyone else is going to.'

Oh, my God! She thought. It's not the job: he's having an affair!

'I am being required to send one of my crews to almost certain death, or at least imprisonment.'

Breath rushed through her nostrils; but what a terrible thing to be relieved about! 'Tell me.'

'I can't, Alison. You know that. I can tell you that it will make that raid up the Gironde seem like a Sunday school picnic.'

'And the Adriatic?'

'I would say this is more dangerous even than that.'

'You lost three boats, including your own.'

'I think that was bad luck. Our chances of survival were higher. And the raid was basically a success; if we hadn't crippled *Napoli* she'd still be afloat. This time . . . if the boat doesn't get back, the mission is a complete failure, and we'll have squandered seventeen lives.' Actually, it will be twenty, he thought.

Alison reached past him to switch on the bedside lamp, so that she could study his face. 'And one of them is Jamie Goring, isn't it?'

'Well . . .'

'Is he that important to you?'

'He's my oldest living shipmate, apart from Harry. And he's a friend. And he did save my life. And more than that; he's hoping to get married in the near future.'

'Jamie? My God!'

'What's so surprising about that?'

'Ah . . . I just never put him down as the marrying kind.'

'That's because we all still think of him as a boy. But in a couple of months he's going to be twenty-two.'

'Um. Do you have any idea who the young lady is?'

'I don't know her personally. But he seems to be stepping up a class. Her father is Kenelm Broughton. The gynaecologist.'

'Good lord! How on earth did Jamie Goring meet someone like that?'

'It's rather a romantic story, really. She's serving as a hospital sister, and he was in her ward when he was wounded last year, and, well, I suppose one thing led to another.'

'But, if she's a sister, isn't she old enough to be his mother?' And reflected, isn't Kristin?

'Apparently not. She's only a couple of years older than he is. When she went into nursing, her father seems to have pulled strings.'

Again, just like Kristin, Alison thought.

'And you know what really is a hoot,' Duncan said.

'My secretary is her best friend. Seems they both went to Cheltenham Ladies' College. One thing you have to say for wars, they do break down the barriers. But it would seem that they are very much in love.'

'And Papa Broughton isn't happy with the situation?'

'No, he is not. But that's because Jamie is an enlisted man. But I intend to put that right. When we return from this mission, I'm recommending him for a commission. Mother will be tickled pink.'

Mother, Alison thought, is going to blow a gasket, the consideration causing her to overlook his slip of the tongue. 'And is that why he has to go on this one?'

'He's the only one who can possibly pull it off.'

'I can see it's a horrid decision to have to make. But . . . wait a mo. If Jamie's going, then—'

'It's to be *433*, yes.'

'Calman?'

'I'm afraid so. He and his entire crew have volunteered.'

'Shoot. Does Kristin know?'

'She does not, and she cannot. It's top secret. I shouldn't be telling you.'

'But you are. Because –' suddenly she realized what he was trying to say – 'oh, my God! Duncan, you can't. You're the captain of the squadron. They'd throw a fit.'

'If by they, you mean Lansdowne and the brass, they are not going to know until after we get back.'

'And if you don't get back?'

'Well, then it won't matter, will it?'

'It'll matter to me.' Her voice was low.

'That's why I'm telling you. I couldn't just disappear without saying goodbye.'

'Duncan . . .' Her fingers were like claws, eating into his flesh.

'But I'm not going to disappear. If anyone can bring this off, it's Jamie and me.'

'You're not immortal. No one is.'

'We are more experienced than any other men in the Navy. Certainly when it comes to handling MTBs.'

'That still doesn't mean you can do the impossible. You said it was impossible.'

'I said it was extremely risky.'

'The most risky thing you have ever been required to undertake. That's what you said.'

'Maybe it is. That doesn't mean it can't be done.'

'But why? Tell me why, Duncan.'

He sighed. 'I can't put it into words, my dearest girl, I only know . . . these people are my friends. The best friends I have in the Navy. Jamie has to go. As I said, he's the only one who can navigate us in, and then navigate us out again. I can't just stand by and say goodbye and good luck. He saved my life.'

'And so it's something you feel you have to do.' Her turn to sigh. 'So . . . When?'

'Wednesday night. We'll be back by Saturday.'

He could see her brain working. 'Then it's on the French coast.'

'That's right. Please don't ask me more than that. Alison, I'm telling you this because I know you're strong enough to handle it. Don't let me down.'

'I will never let you down, Duncan. Even if . . . well, it doesn't matter.'

'And you won't say a word to a soul. Especially Mother.'

'Especially Mother,' she agreed, and kissed him. 'Not before Wednesday night, anyway.'


'Guess what?' Jamie asked. 'I'm to get a commission.'

'What?' Emma sat up, a splendidly tousled, naked sight, all erected pink nipples and with her normally immaculate hair scattered. 'And you never told me!'

'I just have. I didn't want it to get in the way, while we were both on the boil.'

She turned on her knees and straddled him. 'That's marvellous. But . . . do you have sufficient seniority?'

'It's going to be an award for meritorious service.'

'Then you deserve it.' She frowned. 'Or haven't you done the service yet?'

'In a couple of days.'

'You mean you're going to get shot at again.'

'Well, there's a risk of being shot at every time we leave harbour.'

'And they don't always miss.'

'Angel, I have been in the Navy, being shot at, for more than three years, and I've only been hit once. That's a pretty poor percentage.'

'But if the brass seem to think this one is worth a leg up, it must be pretty important.'

'Well, it is. Or they think it is. They say it will be a vital step towards winning the war.'

'In the hands of a petty officer?'

'Well, yes, in a manner of speaking. It involves a whole crew, with a lieutenant in command. But it's a tricky navigational job, and it seems I'm the only one who has sufficient local knowledge to get us in and get us back out.'

'Must be nice to be unique.' She lay down again, but left one leg draped across his thighs, and rested her head on his shoulder. 'Jamie . . . you *are* coming back?'

'Don't tell me you'd miss me? Ow!' She had sunk her teeth into his shoulder.

'You have taught me what life is all about,' she said. 'I think I'd be a little lost without you to look forward to.'

'My idea is that you should always have that. Emma, when I come back, and get my commission, do you think your dad will agree to us getting married?'

'Jamie, when you come back, I'm going to marry you, with or without a commission, and with or without Daddy's permission. I'm twenty-four years old, for God's sake.'

'Duncan!' Admiral Lonsdale was looking ebullient. 'Come in and sit down.' He tapped the paper on his desk. 'Young Goring seems to have gone into this pretty thoroughly.'

'He does everything thoroughly. He is quite meticulous. In my opinion, he is born officer material, and when we, I mean, he gets back from this mission, I intend to recommend him for a commission.'

'Hm.' Lonsdale stroked his chin. 'He's very young.'

'Sir, if he had been able to attend Dartmouth, he'd be at least a full lieutenant by now.'

'Good point.' He remembered that he had always felt that if his parents had allowed him to go to Dartmouth at thirteen instead of taking a late entry after completing his public school education, he might have been a vice-admiral by now. 'I will certainly endorse your recommendation. But first we have to get him back, eh? In that regard, I have had the most brilliant idea.'

'Sir?' Duncan could not keep a trace of scepticism out of his tone.

'What we need is some kind of distraction, to keep Jerry occupied while *433* sneaks in. Goring seems to feel that coming back out by that 'Severe' passage will be the easier option.'

'Providing the weather doesn't act up.'

'Oh, quite. But we can't do anything about that; what we can do is assist with getting in. I've been on to London, pointing out that if this operation is as vital as they say it is, we are entitled to all the help we can get. The submarine is a splendid idea, but it's only of any value after the oper-ation has been successfully carried out. They saw the point. Therefore on –' he glanced at the paper – 'Thursday night the RAF will deliver a heavy raid on Rochefort, commencing at –' another look at the paper – '2300, which is fifteen minutes before Goring estimates he will attempt to enter the Pertuis d'Antioch. The raid will be maintained until 2330, by which time he should be well inside the Coureau d'Oleron, and, of course, we estimate that the disruption and distrac-tion caused by the bombing will last for several hours, by which time they should be out the other side. What do you think of that, eh?' he demanded proudly.

'That would be excellent, sir. Providing the bombers remember that Rochefort is only a couple of miles up the Charente River, and that the Coureau is only about a mile wide, so that we don't want any bombs dropped short.'

'I will certainly remind them of that.'

'And this fellow Colonel Death has been alerted?'

'That is happening now. Lawton guarantees that he will be on the Le Chateau dockside at 2400 on Thursday night.'

'I suppose we can't ask anything more than that, providing he is there.' He stood up. 'Well, I had better get on with it.'

'When are you going to tell Calman exactly what is involved?'

'Tomorrow afternoon, sir. Just before he leaves.'

'Does he know that he will be carrying an MI6 agent?'

'Yes, sir. I suspect that he supposes he is delivering Lawton to some secret destination. Which, in effect, he is. I will give him his sealed orders at that time.'

'He's liable to have a bit of a shock when he opens them.'

'The envelope will be marked that it is only to be opened in the presence of both Lawton and Goring, who will be able to put him completely in the picture.'

'Hm. You're not afraid that could brew some resentment? That one of his crew knows more than he does?'

'I don't think so, sir, if I have judged Calman's character correctly. In any event, in the orders I will explain in detail Goring's importance, both in the planning and execution of the mission, and I may say that ever since Calman took command, and this is very nearly a year now, he has relied extensively on Goring's know-how and experience.'

'Well, I hope you're right. It would be tragic if this went wrong because of personal feelings in the command.'

'There is no other way to handle it, sir.'

'No doubt. You will, of course, let me have a copy of the orders.'

'Of course, sir. You will get a copy tomorrow afternoon, as soon as it is drafted.'

'Very good. Carry on, Captain Eversham.'


'Good afternoon, Emma,' Duncan said brightly. 'I hope you had a good lunch?'

'Yes, sir, I did.' Emma Dunning tried to control her surprise. Her commanding officer had never asked after her lunch before.

'Excellent. Now will you bring your book in? And make sure that we are not interrupted for the next hour.'

'Aye-aye, sir.' She was back in a moment, settled in the chair before his desk, pad on her knee, pencil poised. Duncan dictated with hardly a pause for fifteen minutes, and her pencil flew over the paper, even if she had increasing difficulty with her breathing. When he had finished, she stared at him.

'I wish two copies of that, now,' he said.

'Yes, sir.' She stood up. 'Sir . . . is it . . . well . . .'

'If all goes well, it will not be as dangerous as it sounds. If it doesn't, well, that is a hazard of all naval operations. I also wish you to telephone the Met Office and get me the weather forecast for Biscay over the next three days.'

'Aye-aye, sir.' She left the office, and Duncan looked at his watch. 1600. Tension would be mounting. All the squadron knew was that *433* had been told off for a special mission under sealed orders, and that every man of her crew had had individually to volunteer. Feelings, he suspected, would be running the gamut from envy, in a few, to relief in the majority, that they hadn't been selected.

He leaned back and half closed his eyes as he waited. As always, once a decision was made, he felt perfectly calm. There was no point in feeling anything else, if he was going to carry out his plan successfully. He had to feel, as he had made himself feel through all his major engagements, from the inadvertent attack on the German fleet in 1940, through the Dunkirk evacuation, through the raid on Guernsey, the mission up the Gironde, the hazardous voyage up to the North Cape looking for Rebecca Strong and her father, and of course the chase after *Napoli*, that he would survive. And he always had done, although the last one had been entirely thanks to Jamie Goring. But Jamie would be at his side on this mission also. That was the most comforting thought in the world.

Emma returned, laid the two sheets of paper on his desk. He scanned them, then raised his head. 'And the forecast?'

She read from her pad. 'Pressure is dropping over Biscay as a front moves in from the Atlantic. On Thursday afternoon the wind is expected to freshen from the south-west, reaching Force Five to Six. This may increase to Force Eight for a while overnight, but will decrease by Friday morning as the front moves through. Sea state moderate to rather rough for a time on Thursday night, decreasing thereafter.'

'Thank you, Emma. May I have that, please.'

She tore out the sheet and handed it to him.

'Now,' he handed back one of the typewritten sheets. 'I wish you to place this in a sealed envelope, and personally deliver it to Admiral Lonsdale. Personally, remember. Don't let that dragon of his try to take it off you.'

'Aye-aye, sir,' she acknowledged, doubtfully.

'I will deliver the other one to Sub-Lieutenant Calman. When you have done that, I wish you to go home.'

'Sir? It's only five o'clock.'

'So take an hour off. And Emma, you do realize that what you have heard here this afternoon is absolutely confidential.'

'Yes, sir. I do.'

'Very good. Carry on.'

Duncan waited for the door to close, then took a sheet of his own notepaper, and wrote a note:

> *Emma, I shall be out of the office for the next few days. Don't broadcast it, but if you are asked a direct question, say that I have reported sick. Should the matter be pressed, refer them to my wife. But I know you will handle everything. Yours. Duncan.*

He had no real idea how she would cope, but she was a sensible girl, and appeared to be devoted to him. If he did not return, of course, that would be a different matter, but in that case, he had no doubt that Alison would prove a tower of strength. But he had every intention of returning.

And the forecast? That would have to be up to Jamie. But knowing Jamie as well as he did, he did not suppose he would be too disturbed.

He got up, surveyed the office. There was no way he could take any change of clothing or even any toiletries with him without giving away his intention, but it would only be two days before he was home again. He folded the two sheets of paper and placed them in his pocket, then tucked the cylindrical chart case under his arm, put on his cap and left the office, acknowledging the salutes of his staff as he went down the stairs and then the ramp to the pontoon.

Roberts was waiting for him beside *444*. 'Sir!'

'Commander.'

'I don't suppose . . . ?'

'I'm afraid not, Mr Roberts. Believe me, I don't like

sending one of your boats off into the blue any more than you do. But they'll be back within seventy-two hours.'

'Aye-aye, sir. I see they are taking a passenger.'

'That's why they're going. I will see you later.' Duncan went along to *432*. 'Permission to cross your deck, Mr Linton.'

'Yes, sir.' Linton, and his crew, stood to attention; like Roberts, they were all tense 'I wish this was my assignment, sir.'

Duncan grinned at him. 'With your experience? You'd be bored stiff.'

He stepped on to *433*, and was again greeted by the paraded crew. 'At ease, gentlemen. All set, Mr Calman.'

'All set, sir. But—'

'And Mr Lawton is on board?'

'Below, sir. Taking pills.'

'I'd better see how he looks. Will you come with me, please? I am about to give you your orders, and it should be in his presence, so there can be no misunderstanding.'

'Of course, sir.'

'And I would like Mr Goring also to be present.'

Richard raised his eyebrows, but said, 'Petty Officer.'

'Aye-aye, sir.'

Jamie followed the two officers down the after companionway to the captain's cabin, where Lawton was sitting on the bunk; he certainly looked far from tranquil, but managed a nod. 'Captain Eversham.'

'Mr Lawton. Ready to go?'

'As ready as I can be. I'm afraid my stomach has never been partial to the sea.'

'You'll be fine once we're out on it.' Duncan sat at the desk. 'Come in Jamie.'

'I'm afraid it's a bit tight, for four, sir,' Richard said. 'But I suppose you know that.'

'Yes, I do. Close the door, will you, please, Jamie.'

Jamie obeyed, remained standing against the bulkhead, as did Richard.

'First things first,' Duncan said, and took the forecast from his pocket. 'Study that, Jamie.'

Jamie took the sheet. Richard continued to look both apprehensive and confused. Lawton obviously had no idea what was going on. 'Jamie,' Duncan explained, 'has been involved, at the request of Admiral Lonsdale, from the beginning of this concept, because, thanks to his yachting experience, he know the waters in which you are going to operate better than anyone else.'

'I see,' Richard said. He revealed no sign of being upset, but Duncan knew he had to be thinking, as his superior officer, surely I should have been involved as well.

'Well?' Duncan asked.

'Not ideal, sir,' Jamie said. 'But beggars can't be choosers.'

'The point is, once this front passes through, the weather will improve, at least for a while. We could postpone the operation.'

'Isn't the gentleman waiting for us, sir?'

'Well, yes. But I believe he can be contacted.'

'Going by what Mr Lawton said, sir –' Jamie glanced at the agent, who for once was taking no part in the conversation – 'every day is vital, and a delay of even one could be fatal. From our point of view, every day means the moon will be filling, and puts the tides more and more out of timing, for us, as well as getting bigger, which means less margin for error. Tomorrow is ideal. The next ideal day may not come along for another month, and there's no guarantee that the weather will be better, while the nights will be shortening all the time. I think we should go now.'

'Very good, Jamie. You're the expert.' He took the second sheet from his pocket, handed it to the patiently waiting Richard. 'Here are your orders. They are supposed to be in a sealed envelope, not to be opened until you are at sea. But I am giving them to you now, because . . . well, read them.'

Richard studied the words. 'Understood, sir.'

'You appreciate that this is a highly risky operation, both as regards navigational dangers and enemy action.'

'Yes, sir. But you say that Goring, Jamie, is familiar with the waters.'

'He is. And all things being equal, he will take you in and bring you back out. However –' he opened the chart case and took out the large scale chart of the French Biscay coast from La Rochelle to the mouth of the Gironde – 'I have just been informed by Admiral Lonsdale, that we are to have

additional assistance. The RAF will commence a raid upon
Rochefort at 2300 tomorrow night. According to your
calculations, Jamie, that is fifteen minutes before you will
enter the Pertuis d' Antioch.'

'Yes, sir. But—'

'I know. I have pointed out to Admiral Lonsdale, who is
relaying it to the Bomber command, that the Coureau is an
extremely narrow stretch of water, and so we cannot have
any shortfalls or jettisoned explosives. The raid will last for
half an hour, by which time you will be at Le Chateau. The
idea is that the whole area will be too stirred up to be
worrying about one small boat.'

'But enemy action on the ground will be my responsibility?'
Richard asked, wishing to be sure of his position.

'Not entirely,' Duncan said, 'I'm coming with you.'

'Sir?' The two men spoke together in equal consternation.
Lawton opened his mouth and then shut it again.

'I do not intend to muscle in on your command,
Lieutenant,' Duncan said. 'But I have done this sort of thing
before. I therefore think that my experience may be of
assistance, in an advisory capacity.'

Richard gulped. 'Very good, sir.'

'However,' Duncan said, 'no one save for you three
gentleman, and my wife, knows of this decision, and no
one can know until we are out at sea and cannot be recalled.'
He looked at his watch. '1730. Therefore I shall remain in
this cabin until after we are at sea. However, both Mr Linton
and Commander Roberts know that I have come down
here, and I suspect that Admiral Lonsdale will also be here
in a few minutes to wish you God's speed. Commander
Roberts knows nothing more than that I came further down
the pontoon, presumably to bid you goodbye, and I do not
wish to involve him. Mr Linton saw me come on board,
and will know that I have not yet crossed his deck to return
to the pontoon. So will you ask him kindly to join me here
for a few minutes.'

'Aye-aye, sir.' Richard left the cabin.

'With respect, sir,' Jamie said, 'did you say that Lady
Eversham knows what you are about?'

'Yes, she does. I felt obliged to tell her. And in answer to your next question, Jamie, no, she is not happy about it. But she is my wife, and she is Lady Eversham, and she can be trusted.'

'Of course, sir. And . . . ah . . .'

'My mother does not know about it, Jamie, and cannot know about it, until, as I said, we are beyond recall.'

'Yes, sir,' Jamie said, somewhat doubtfully. 'May I ask a question?'

'I thought you just had. But you're welcome.'

'Are you coming with us because you don't think we're going to come back?'

'I am coming with you, Jamie, because I feel that you and I, working in harness, provide the best chance *of* us coming back. But that is between you and me.'

'Yes, sir!' Jamie said enthusiastically.

'Very good. Carry on. We leave in half an hour.'

'Aye-aye, sir.'

Jamie left.

'I'm sorry about this contretemps, Mr Lawton,' Duncan said. 'There is no need for you to be involved.'

'I would not dream of it, sir. My sole aim is to get there and get back, hopefully with Colonel Morte. If having you along increases our chances of that, I'm all for it.'

'Good man. We'll have a drink together when this is over.'

A few moments later a bewildered Linton arrived.

'Mr Linton,' Duncan said. 'We have served together for a very long time.'

'Yes, sir.'

'So I am going ask you to do me a favour.'

'Of course, sir. Name it.'

'You saw me come on board this boat.'

'Yes, sir.'

'Now, you did not see me leave again, but that is because, having spoken with me, you retired to your cabin to do some paperwork. Although you did not see me leave, you have no doubt that I did leave. I mean, I must have done. Am I right?'

'Ah . . . yes, sir.'

'Thank you, Mr Linton. I shall not forget your co-operation.'

'May I wish you God's speed, sir. And I say again, I wish I could be going with you.'

'So do I, Mr Linton. But we only need, and can only spare, one boat. Carry on.'

He held out his hand, and Linton squeezed the fingers, saluted, and then left.

A few minutes later Duncan heard Lonsdale's voice on the upper deck. 'You've received your orders, Mr Calman?'

'Yes, sir.'

'You understand that they are not to be opened until you are at sea?'

'Yes, sir, I do.'

'Very good. I assume Captain Eversham has been down to say farewell?'

'Yes, sir. A few minutes ago.'

'You wouldn't happen to know where he is now?'

'No, sir, I do not.'

'Hm. Well, it's 1800. I'll wish you God's speed, Mr Calman, and look forward to your safe return.'

'Aye-aye, sir. And thank you.'

'Carry on.'

Duncan waited, and a few minutes later Richard entered wiping his neck with his handkerchief. 'Do I get cashiered when we return, sir?'

'You get commended and another gong. All you have done is obey orders given to you by your superior officer. Now, Mr Calman, I'd like you to take this boat to sea.'

'Six o'clock,' Alison remarked. 'Feel like a drink?'

'I always feel like a drink,' Kristin announced. 'Duncan's late.'

Alison poured two scotches. 'Duncan isn't coming in tonight.'

'What? Why not?'

'He's gone away for a few days.'

'What? Without telling us? Oh, he seems to have told you.'

'Well,' Alison said. 'I am his wife.'

'And I'm his mother. Where's he gone?'

Alison handed her a glass, and sat beside her, her own

glass held in both hands. 'He's gone to France, to pick somebody up.'

Kristin had been sipping. Now she slowly lowered her glass. 'Would you like to say that again? Oh, don't bother. Have you gone completely mad?'

'This character,' Alison said, not looking at her. 'Is apparently terribly important to the invasion plans, and is needed here.'

'So how is Duncan involved? They normally fly people like that out.'

'Well, yes. If they can put a light aircraft down. But this chap is holed up on a small island just off the coast, and the Gestapo are closing in, so he has to be brought out. And it can only be done by boat. By a small, fast boat. So they've sent an MTB.'

Kristin stared at her. 'I still do not see,' she said in an icy tone, 'how Duncan is personally involved. He no longer commands an MTB. He commands the entire south coast fleet.'

'Well, yes. But he felt he had to go. It's apparently quite risky. Oh,' she hastily added, 'he's quite sure he's coming back. But . . . well, he has this sense of responsibility towards . . . well . . .'

Kristin continued to stare at her, but her gaze had slightly softened. 'It's *433*.'

'Yes.'

'With Jamie. And Richard.'

'Yes.'

Kristin put down her glass and stood up. 'That is the most absolute rubbish. I'm calling Jimmy.'

'Jimmy has nothing to do with it.'

'Don't be naïve. An operation of this importance can only be ordered by an admiral.'

'Well, yes, apparently the orders did come from Jimmy. On instructions from the Admiralty.'

'The Admiralty couldn't possibly have chosen *433*. They probably don't know she exists.'

'Probably not. But she is the only boat that numbers Jamie in her crew.'

Kristin had already lifted the phone. Now she replaced it on the table.

'Jamie,' Alison explained, 'is the only man they have who knows the island where they are going, and the coast, and the hazards.'

Kristin went to the sideboard and poured herself another drink.

'Anyway,' Alison said. 'I didn't know you and he were still . . . seeing each other.'

'He seems to have taken umbrage because I suggested he come here to convalesce, last year. And I am certainly not going crawling after him. That Malta business was a once in a lifetime madness. But I don't want him killed. He'll come back to me, given time. He's very young.'

Alison drew a deep breath. 'Kristin, he's not going to do that.'

'What do you know about it? About Jamie?'

'Not a lot. But I do know that he's planning to get married.'

'What? Jamie, married? That's nonsense. Who's he supposed to be marrying?'

'A sister he met in hospital. Girl named Emma Broughton. One thing you have to say for Jamie: he always aims at the top drawer. This girl's father is Sir Kenelm Broughton, the famous gynaecologist.'

Kristin sat in the chair opposite. 'That ghastly little prig?'

'You mean you know her?'

'I have encountered her, on more than one occasion, doing her little Hitler act at the hospital. If Jamie marries her he needs his head examined. In fact, he deserves to have it blown off. But there is absolutely no reason for Duncan to go with him.' She reached for the phone again.

'Who were you planning to call?' Alison inquired.

'Why, Jimmy, of course. I told you. To put a stop to this madness.'

'Kristin, you cannot do that.'

'Are you telling me what I can or cannot do in my own house?'

'Yes,' Alison said, still speaking quietly. 'Because it happens to be my house as well. Just as Duncan is my husband, and he is doing what he wants to do, and in that he has my full support.'

Kristin stared at her, then her shoulders sagged. Alison

had always known that she had the stronger personality, despite her mother-in-law's exterior persona of invulnerable dominance. She got up, and rested her hand on Kristin's shoulder. 'They'll come back. Together. They always have.'

Kristin's hand closed over hers.

# THE OPERATION

'We're through the Needles Channel, sir,' Richard said.

'Thank God for that.' Duncan got up. 'Do you know, Richard, I have spent four years in a cabin exactly like this, on and off, and this is the first time I have realized how small it is.' He glanced at Lawton, who was stretched on the bunk, his eyes closed. 'We'd better leave him be.'

'Do you think he's going to wake up, sir?'

'I would say so. As to whether he's going to get up, that's another matter. Severe sea-sickness usually takes about two days to wear off. If all goes well, we'll be back here in two days. Do you have an oilskin for me?'

'Right here, sir.'

Duncan put it on and left the cabin, climbing to the bridge to the amazement of those members of the crew he passed on the way, who to this moment had had no idea their commanding officer was on board. Jamie was on the helm, and Duncan stood beside him to take deep breaths of fresh air and look around him at the moonless but clear and therefore starlit night, and experienced the reassuring feeling of the boat skating up and down the gentle Channel swell. 'Course?'

'Two six zero to south of the Scillies, sir. Maintaining thirty knots, we will be there at midnight. Then we alter course two four zero to give Ushant a wide berth. Our rendezvous is forty-six north, ten west. We should be there at 1300 tomorrow. Then it's zero nine five. That's the long haul into the Bay, but ETA off the Pertuis d'Antioch should be at 2315, as arranged. It should not take us more than an hour to collect our passenger and be out. In fact, if it takes more than that we won't be coming out. Return rendezvous, 1415 Friday, home on Saturday morning.'

'Is that satisfactory, sir?' Richard asked.

'Two questions. You are maintaining thirty knots throughout?'

'We have to, in view of the time parameters.'

'We're talking about better than sixty hours.'

'Yes, sir,' Jamie agreed. 'At thirty knots, say forty gallons an hour, that will be two thousand four hundred gallons.'

'And we have?'

'Two thousand seven hundred and forty.'

'So we'll be cutting it fine.'

'Yes, sir. But once we deliver the passenger to the sub, we no longer have a schedule to keep, and we can reduce speed and save fuel that way, if necessary.'

'Very good. Now my second question. You understand that you will be crossing the Bay, or a large part of it, in daylight. Both going and coming.'

'It's a risk we have to take.' Richard said. 'There would be a greater chance of being spotted if we closed the French coast earlier.'

'Very good. Lastly, you understand that you will be on German radar screens from about forty miles out.'

'Yes, sir. Mr Lawton did say there weren't too many radar stations operating on that part of the coast.'

'I'm quite sure there'll be one or two. As we discussed earlier, I think we need to assume the Pertuis d'Antioch will be covered.'

'Well, sir,' Richard said, 'forty miles means we'll be within an hour of the coast, and by the time they decide to do something about us, the RAF should have arrived.'

'Good thinking, Richard. Well, gentlemen, tally ho.'

Wilson served dinner, and they settled down to a normal sea-going routine. Duncan paid a visit to the cabin and found that Lawton was awake, with a basin clutched in his hands. 'Do I gather that your pills haven't worked?'

'I'd probably be worse off without them,' the agent groaned. 'Does this banging go on throughout the voyage?'

'I'm afraid it does,' Duncan said. 'We have to maintain this speed to keep to our schedule.' He decided against warning him that if the weather did deteriorate the movement would be far more severe. 'Look, old man, I think you really should have some nourishment.'

'I couldn't eat a thing. And it'd be straight back up. Waste of food.'

'I'm going to send you down some salt biscuits. Try nibbling one. And a bottle of water. It's essential that you keep sipping it, or you'll become dehydrated and fit for nothing.'

'Tell me, Captain, if I understand the situation, you are not supposed to be here at all.'

'I think I should be here, Mr Lawton.'

'Believe me, sir, I am very glad you are. But again, I've gained the impression that Rear-Admiral Lonsdale would not agree with either of us. When he discovers the situation, won't he call you back?'

'No, he will not, for two reasons. One is that the mission is too important to be aborted, and the second is that he can call until he's blue in the face, but we shall be maintaining radio silence until your passenger is delivered to the submarine. And he knows that. Wilson will bring you down the food.'

'What do you reckon?' Richard asked. 'Will he survive?'

'He'll survive,' Duncan assured him. 'They always do. Tell me your watch rota.'

Now that they were well out in the Channel, Jamie had handed over the helm to Wellard to take a watch below.

'I'm on until midnight, sir,' Richard said.

'Very good. I'll relieve you then.'

'You mean you're going to take the Middle Watch? There's no need for that, sir. We've a full crew.'

'It's over a year since I was at sea, Richard. I need the feel of it. I'll see you at midnight. You've no objection if I use the spare cabin?'

'Of course not, sir.'

'And your razor tomorrow morning?'

'Please do. And ah . . . ?'

'Oh, I'll just gargle till we get home. Wilson doesn't generally use garlic, and I'm not planning on kissing anybody till then. I will see you at midnight.'

When Duncan went up again, Jamie was back on the helm, and the course had just been altered to south-west. Although there was no moon, it was a brilliantly bright starlit night, and the sea remained calm. With binoculars, it was even possible to make out the humps of the Scillies gradually disappearing behind them. 'Can't complain about this, sir,' Jamie said.

'It would be nice to have some cloud cover tomorrow. What's the glass doing?'

'It is dropping, sir. But slowly. So we should get something. May I say what a pleasure it is to have you on board, sir? Quite like old times.'

'I'm delighted to be here, Jamie.'

'Will there be repercussions, sir?

'Nothing that will matter. If we don't come back, it won't matter at all. And if we do, we'll have been successful. And I intend to enjoy every moment of it, because you know, the way they keep kicking me upstairs, this may well be the last time I shall ever have the opportunity to be at sea. At least, in an MTB.'

'We'll miss you, sir.'

'This time next year, Jamie, you'll have your own boat. You will regard interfering captains as nuisances.'

My own boat, Jamie thought. He had never expected to achieve that. Why, it might be worthwhile staying in the Navy after the war, and making a career of it. And all because of this so remarkable friendship. Suddenly he had the wildest desire to use this opportunity to confess his relationship with Kristin. But that would be not only disastrous but criminal. The only person who could ever tell Duncan the truth was Kristin herself. He had in fact half expected her to do that, when they had parted, last year. But obviously she hadn't. And in any event, to do so now, when they both needed all their concentration, and indeed all their comradeship, would be to risk the entire mission.

So he asked, 'Would you like to take her for a spell, sir?'

'I would like that more than anything else in the world. I thought you'd never offer.'

By dawn the weather was definitely on the change. Duncan, having come off watch at 0400, was up for breakfast at seven, regarded with some awe by the crew, none of whom had ever sailed with a captain on board before, or with so famous a man as Lord Eversham, save of course for Wilson, who greeted him like a long-lost brother.

He then went below, and discovered that Lawton was sleeping peacefully. The basin, which had been used at some time during the night, was still clutched in his arms, but the mere fact that he was deeply asleep was promising, and in fact he surprised everybody by appearing on the bridge at twelve thirty, looking distinctly haggard and untidy, but at least on his feet.

'Good afternoon, sir,' Richard said, enthusiastically. 'Isn't it a lovely day?'

'Is it?' Lawton instinctively ducked as a rattle of spray flew aft and scattered across the windshield, then peered about him in utter bewilderment. 'There's no land.' He sounded quite offended.

'We are some couple of hundred miles from land.' Duncan had shaved courtesy of Richard's razor. 'That is the object of the exercise.'

'But do you know where we are?'

'Yes.' Duncan had in fact just taken a sight. 'We should make the rendezvous in about fifteen minutes.'

Lawton peered forward. 'I don't see anything.'

'Well, he won't be hanging about on the surface in broad daylight. But he'll be able to see us. Have you had lunch?'

'Ugh!'

'I do think you need to bear in mind,' Duncan said mildly. 'That if you collapse from malnutrition you are going to be no use to us or Colonel Morte.'

'Well . . .'

'I have him,' Richard said. He had been using his binoculars.

Duncan levelled his.

'I don't see anything,' Lawton complained.

Duncan gave him the glasses. 'Just breaking the surface.'

Lawton studied the disturbed water. 'How do you know he's ours? He could be a U-boat. What will you do then?'

'If he's a U-boat, Mr Lawton, we'll attack him and hopefully sink him.'

Lawton gulped.

Richard was ringing the action stations bell, and the crew

were emerging on deck, wearing life jackets and steel helmets, and manning the guns. Jamie as always taking the six-pounder.

'He's ours,' Richard commented. 'Stand down,' he said into the tannoy, at the same time reducing speed. *433* came off the plane and eased to a halt a hundred yards away from the submarine, which was now fully surfaced. 'Lamp, Mr Goring.'

Jamie returned to the bridge and picked up the Morse lamp.

'Make,' Richard said, '1400 tomorrow.'

The light flashed, and there was an immediate response. Jamie interpreted. 'Acknowledged. Good luck.'

'Very good. Course 095, and it will be two thousand re-volutions. And I think we can swap flags. Did you bring along that German ensign I suggested?'

'I have it,' Richard said. 'But aren't we a bit small to be mistaken for an S-boat?'

'There are times, Richard, when even a thirty-second delay while the other chap is working things out can be crucial.'

The MTB raced away from the soon to be setting sun, her black, red and gold ensign, with its swastika centrepiece, streaming in the wind, while the submarine submerged.

'Think we'll meet any of these U-boats?' Lawton asked.

'I think the odds are in our favour,' Duncan said. 'The U-boats generally leave port just before dusk, so that they can cross the Bay in darkness. On the surface they are just as vulnerable to air attack as are we. So it's actually aircraft we need to look out for.'

Richard kept two men on watch on the pom-poms throughout the afternoon, but although vapour trails were visible high in the sky, no one came down for a closer look, This was partly because throughout the afternoon the cloud increased, as the wind freshened; the resulting whitecaps made the MTB's wake difficult to separate from the breaking water, certainly when viewed from any height.

Duncan insisted that Lawton go below and have some-thing to eat, and then sent him back to his bunk. 'We're going to need you tonight,' he pointed out. 'Get some sleep.'

He rejoined Jamie and Richard on the bridge.

'Will he be all right?' Richard asked.

'It's up to us to make sure that he is. I'd hate to pick up the wrong man. Now, Richard, you also get below and have some sleep. We need you to be fresh later as well.'

'Jamie's the man we need fresh,' the lieutenant objected.

'He'll be turning in as well. Down you go, Jamie.'

'But, sir . . .'

'I can handle her for a couple of hours.' He grinned at them. 'I have done it before, you know.'

'Aye-aye, sir.' They went off together, and Duncan checked the compass and then settled down to doing what he liked best. The seas, coming in on the starboard quarter, were inclined to throw the boat about, but that merely brought back memories.

Leading Seaman Wellard joined him. 'Any time you feel like a spell, sir.'

'I'm enjoying it. It's been too long.'

'It's a privilege to serve under you, sir. I wish I could have done so in the old days.'

'Why, thank you, Wellard. You do need to remember that of the men who started out this war under my command, only three are left, including me.'

'That may be, sir. But Cook Wilson says there has never been a commander to equal you. In any event, serving under you now will be something to tell my grandchildren.'

'Then keep your fingers crossed that you'll be around to tell them. I think it's time to take a sweep before it gets dark.'

'Aye-aye, sir.' Wellard wedged himself against the mast and levelled the binoculars. Then focussed more carefully, looking to the south-east. 'There's something over there, sir. Low in the water.'

'Take the helm.' Duncan levelled the glasses. 'That's a sub.'

'Ours, do you think, sir?'

'Not here. It's a U-boat.'

'Think she's spotted us?'

'I doubt it; she's at least ten miles off, and she's more interested in looking out for aircraft than in anything on the surface, this close to the coast. But even if she has, she won't do anything about it. Her business is to get out into the Atlantic to attack our shipping, and to maintain radio silence until she's on station. Pity we have a prior engagement, or we could get over there and sort her out.'

Wellard did not comment; he was still digesting the utterly calm way in which the captain had, firstly, evaluated the situation, and secondly, had considered attacking an enemy more powerfully armed than himself.

At eight o'clock Duncan turned in for a couple of hours, then had dinner and went up to the somewhat crowded bridge; in addition to Jamie, on the helm, both Richard and Lawton were also present, peering into the darkness. All three were now wearing oilskins, as was Duncan himself.

'How on earth can you tell where we're going?' Lawton asked; he seemed to have made a full recovery.

'We know it's there,' Richard pointed out.

'Do you think they'll have us on their radar yet?'

'I thought you said there was no radar coverage down here,' Duncan said, wickedly.

'I said there was no blanket coverage,' Lawton protested.

Duncan looked at his watch. '2210. Even if they can spot us at all, they won't have identified us yet; we're still forty miles out.'

'But we'll get there on time.'

'Of course we will, Mr Lawton.'

Lawton wiped his forehead, but that might have been because the occasional volley of spray was still flying over the bridge screen; even if they were going away from the wind, the seas were definitely increasing, and the occasional trough was deeper than average. 'And you say there will be sufficient water to get in and out of this place Le Chateau? You said it dries.'

'There will be enough water.'

'How can you be sure?'

'Explain it to him, Jamie.'

'Yes, sir. Well, Mr Lawton, you see, tides never change their habits. They obey certain fixed rules, and have done for billions of years. These rules are made by the moon, by how full it is. Full moon means a big tide, no moon means a small tide.'

'And tonight there is no moon.'

'Yes, sir. But there will still be a tide, sufficient for our purpose. You see, because of the constancy of the tides, it is possible to work out not only the times of high and low water in every part of the globe, but also the range in feet of every tide, again in every part of the globe. In peace time, one can buy tide tables covering every coast or port in Europe. These may not be available in war, but they can still be worked out. So tonight we know there will be a ten-foot tide in the Coureau d'Oleron and its approaches. That is the range, which is to say, at the top of the tide, which is 2355, there will be twelve feet over the bar in the Pertuis Maumusson.'

'You have lost me, Petty Officer. At the conference in Admiral Lonsdale's office, you said there was always four feet of water over the bar. Surely, if you add ten to four you get fourteen.'

'Yes, sir. But tidal height has to be related to Chart Datum. That is to the height of water shown on the chart, which is always the lowest possible, or ever recorded, tide. The depths shown over the Maumusson bar is two feet which means that on a high tide of ten feet there will be twelve feet of water.'

'I see. But that will be at high water, which you say is just before midnight. We will not be there until perhaps an hour after that. Will there still be sufficient water?'

'Oh, yes, sir. If we get there at 0100, there will be –' he made a hasty calculation – 'eleven point one seven feet of water over the bar.'

'How in the name of God can you possibly know that?'

'Because again, sir, it is the tidal law. Every tide rises and falls for fractionally under six hours to an unchanging rhythm. This is called the rule of twelve. In the first hour after dead low, a tide will rise one-twelfth of the range for that day. In the second hour it will rise a further two-twelfths, or be a quarter of the range. In the third hour it will rise a further three-twelfths, to take us to half-tide. That is obviously when the tide is running at its hardest. This will continue for the fourth hour, that is, a further three-twelfths. In the fifth hour, it slackens to two-twelfths again, that is, a total of eleven-twelfths. And in the last hour, as we approach slack water, it is down to one-twelfth again, either full tide or, when it's falling, full ebb. Then after a very brief period of completely slack water, it repeats the cycle as it falls. We shall enter the Pertuis d'Antioch in the last hour, just before the tide turns. Now, supposing we do not reach the Maumusson until an hour after high water, we know the tide will have fallen one-twelfth of ten feet. That is, point eight-three of a foot. Therefore, there will be eleven point one seven feet over the bar. But I would actually hope to get there sooner than that.'

'My God!' Lawton commented, 'You mean you carry all that in your head?'

'Every seaman does, sir.'

Lawton scratched his own head.

'I'll take her for half an hour, Jamie,' Duncan said. 'I'd like you back at 2245.'

'Aye-aye, sir.' Jamie relinquished the wheel, while Wilson brought up steaming mugs of coffee. 'I think I'll just nip down and check out the engine room.'

'Still your first love, eh?' Duncan asked.

'Well, sir, if it wasn't, I wouldn't be here now. We wouldn't be here now.'

'Good point. Carry on.'

Lawton was blowing into his coffee. 'That is a singularly self-possessed young man.'

'He is that.'

'You wouldn't say he's overconfident?'

'There are two types of confidence, Mr Lawton. One is of the emotional variety, and can be influenced by several factors, even what you had for dinner, as to whether you are feeling indigested or not. It can certainly be influenced by alcohol, but also by comradeship, incitement, or, for that matter, excitement. Because all of those factors are either emotional or physical, they are essentially unreliable. The other sort, true confidence, is based upon knowledge and experience. If you know what has to be done, exactly, and you know that you can do it, either because you have done it before, or because you have studied the subject in depth and fully understand whatever hazards or possible assets may crop up, then you possess a confidence which is unshake-able. And rightly so.'

'That is a profound psychological analysis, Lord Eversham.'

'If you omit the word psychological, I'd say I was flattered. Psychology has nothing to do with it. I'm a seaman, and have been, on and off, all of my life. At sea you have to be always aware that you are trespassing upon a realm over which you have absolutely no control. No human being can fight the sea, with any hope of winning. You can enjoy its moments of tranquillity, but you must always be aware that it is not going to last. And when the weather changes, all you can do is what you have learned from experience are the right things. You have no option of saying, I've had enough of this, and opening the car door to step out and walk away because the road has become too rough or too dangerous, or simply because you're too tired. You don't even have the option of just sitting tight and hoping things will improve. You have to keep on doing the right things, the things you have learned from experience, regardless of how tired you are, until things do improve. On the other hand the more experienced you are, the more you can be certain that things will improve; no storm lasts forever. Just as again, by experience in watching the sky and the sea and the use of your instruments, you know when the weather is coming, and how severe it is likely to be, and how long it is likely to last. Although there again, you don't have the option of saying, I simply don't feel like a storm today. I think I'll stay in bed.'

'You are saying that a sailor is an entirely different breed of human being from a landsman.'

'Yes, I am. The reason is that a landsman, most landsmen, and most of the time, have room for optimism. A sailor has only room for realism. And if you can accept that, it makes you more confident in yourself and your ability to cope.'

'As I said,' Lawton commented. 'Profound. So tell me this, is the weather going to hold for us to get in and get out?'

'I'm afraid not, Mr Lawton. It is extremely likely to be blowing at least half a gale by midnight.'

'I think it's time for another pill,' Lawton said, and went below.

\*   \*   \*

It was 2255 when Richard, on the helm, said, 'I have land, dead ahead.'

Although there was no moon, and considerable cloud cover, it was still a bright night, and now Duncan could also make out the low-lying blacker darkness in front of them. 'We're ten miles off,' he said. 'Reduce speed. Jamie, we need a positive identification.'

'Aye-aye. sir.' Jamie levelled the binoculars.

'So where's the RAF?' Lawton had reappeared.

'They'll be here,' Duncan assured him.

'Like now,' Richard said.

*433* had come off the plane, and while they were immediately made aware of the following wind, which had hitherto been travelling only a few miles an hour faster than the boat, but which now was howling, and the increased motion of the sea as the waves caught up with them; the roar of the engine had been reduced to a growl, and they could hear the drone from above them.

'I don't see anything,' Lawton complained.

'Well, they won't be showing lights,' Duncan pointed out.

'There they go,' Richard said.

They could see the first flash from in front of them, and also the smaller flashes lower down as the anti-aircraft batteries opened up, while searchlight beams criss-crossed the sky.

'That should keep their minds, and their lights, off the sea,' Richard remarked, with some satisfaction.

'It's starting to rain,' Lawton observed.

'Better for us,' Duncan said, 'You'll con us in, Jamie. Richard, your men should take action stations.'

'Aye-aye, sir.' Richard used the tannoy. 'Action stations. Life jackets and steel helmets. You stay on the helm, Jamie; I'll take the gun.'

Wilson appeared up the hatch with an armful of gear, and Lawton squeezed himself into a jacket over his oilskin top and fitted a helmet on his head. The crew emerged to take their battle stations, while Duncan stood beside Jamie. 'OK?'

'I have the Pertuis d'Antioch, sir.'

Duncan peered into the gloom, which seemed greater down here on the sea because of the spread of the clouds which were now blotting out the stars, while the rain diffused the brightness of the backdrop, as bombs exploded, and lights flashed across the sky. It did not appear as if any of the raiders had been hit, but now it was necessary to concentrate on the water. The mainland loomed to port, where there was a light tower, although this was in darkness, and now the bulk of Oleron was visible to starboard. The channel was unmarked – he presumed that the buoys had been removed by the Germans – but Jamie seemed certain of where he was going.

'There is a light flashing over on the left,' Lawton said.

'They've spotted us and are seeking identification,' Duncan explained.

'What do we do?'

'Ignore them. We're through. Richard, we'll have side arms if you please, and issue rifles to the crew, just in case there's trouble when we enter the port.'

'Aye-aye, sir.' Richard went down the hatch, summoning Wilson to accompany him.

Jamie was altering course to starboard, and now they were entirely surrounded by land. And within the Coureau there were even buoys, mostly leading away to the left, to the mouth of the Charente, beyond which Rochefort was a glow of flame, only partially shrouded in smoke. They were still in the deep water channel, but a few moments later, their passage was marked with withies sticking up out of the mud.

Jamie had now throttled right back to dead slow, and the last of the tide was still running north, further retarding their progress. But slack water was only a few minutes away, and then the tide would carry them south. On the other hand, now that they had turned south, they were also going into the wind, which seemed to be stronger than ever, although Duncan did not reckon it had reached gale force as yet, but it was driving the now quite heavy rain into their faces. He himself struck the ensign, but did not replace it with the white ensign yet, as it was dark.

Richard returned, and Duncan strapped on the revolver holster. 'I assume it's loaded?'

'Yes, sir.'

Wilson was passing out rifles and cartridge belts to the sailors.

The fires of Rochefort dropped astern, and the land to their left also virtually disappeared, receding as it did behind several hundred yards of shallows and oyster beds, but Oleron continued to glide by on their right, the channel still marked by withies. But they had not yet reached Le Chateau when the drone of the planes suddenly ceased, and almost immediately the repeated explosions of the anti-aircraft guns also stopped; across the night there wailed the all-clear siren, while the searchlight ceased their constant exploration of the sky.

'What happens now?' Lawton asked.

'I imagine everyone starts to come out from shelter to see how much damage has been done,' Duncan said. 'But I should think it will take them a few minutes to get organized.'

'But we're not yet at Le Chateau.'

'I have the buoy,' Jamie said quietly.

The red and white can loomed out of the wet darkness, and Jamie altered course to starboard to round it.

'How much water, do you reckon?' Duncan asked.

'It's the top of the tide, sir. Even on a neap there should be, oh, twelve feet.'

'That doesn't sound very much,' Lawton grumbled.

'More than enough for us, sir. But it shallows inside the harbour. Right there.'

The pier heads emerged from the gloom. Beyond Duncan could make out a considerable number of fishing boats, moored together against the main quay, behind which the castellated walls of the town rose romantically.

'Shit!' Jamie muttered.

'Say again?' Duncan asked.

'The fishing fleet is still in. It should have left on the flood, a couple of hours ago.'

Duncan peered into the wet darkness. There were certainly a considerable number of men, and a good deal of activity around the boats, 'Will they resist us?'

'I shouldn't think so, but it means I can't go alongside that dock. To get mixed up with that lot would risk being held up if we need to leave in a hurry.'

'And the other side?'

'It dries. There should be enough water, right now. But will our man know to go there?'

The pier heads were now very close.

'That looks pretty narrow,' Lawton said.

'There's room, sir.'

But as they passed between them a voice cried out. 'What ship is that? Identify yourself.'

The man was speaking French, and as far as Duncan could make out, he was in uniform, although beneath his greatcoat whether he was a gendarme or a harbour official could not be certain in the gloom. He replied, 'Schnell-boot Vier Drei Drei. Guten Morgen.'

'I didn't know you could speak German,' Lawton said.

'I can't. That's schoolboy stuff.'

Jamie had now altered course to bring the boat alongside the vacant quay opposite the fishing boats. 'This is where Dad and I moored last time we were here,' he remarked, as quietly as ever.

'You said you had grounded,' Lawton reminded him.

'Yes, sir. But that was because we spent the night here.'

Duncan watched the stone wall slowly approach as Jamie slipped into neutral. 'Fenders,' he said, not daring to use the tannoy. Wellard and the three men on the torpedo tubes went to the rail; the tubes were not viable weapons in these circumstances.

By now there was a considerable racket from the other side of the little harbour as the fishermen took in the size and shape of the dark monster – considerably larger than any of their boats – easing alongside.

'Where's your friend?' Duncan asked.

'It's not midnight yet. He'll be here. I know he'll be here,' Lawton said.

The official had followed them along the piers, and now reached the dock, speaking German at great speed, while Jamie brought the boat neatly alongside, and two men stepped ashore with the mooring warps. They did not make them fast, but waited, merely preventing the boat from drifting away.

Duncan unclipped the flap of his holster, left the bridge and stepped ashore. The man came up to him, and he could ascertain that he was indeed the port captain. 'You'll excuse me,' he said in French. 'I do not speak German.'

'But—'

'I'm afraid that was the extent of my vocabulary.'

'You are English! Here?!'

'Actually, we have come to collect somebody.'

'My God! You are for . . .' The man swallowed.

'You'd better finish that,' Duncan suggested.

'There was a rumour . . .'

'Oh, shit!'

'Captain?'

Lawton had also come ashore. 'What's happened?' Apparently he spoke French.

'It seems that your secret has been leaked.'

'Oh, my God! You mean he's under arrest?'

'No, no, monsieur,' the port captain said. 'But the Germans are suspicious.'

'Then where is he?'

'I know he was in town. But . . .'

'What do we do?' Lawton asked.

'How much time do we have, Jamie?' Duncan asked.

Jamie had already been leaning over the side with a boathook. Now he pulled it up and studied it by the light of a torch held by Richard. 'We have four feet under the hull, sir. That gives us over an hour.'

'Here. What about the Pertuis?'

'It's the top of the tide, sir. About twelve feet right now. But the tide is now falling.'

'Oh, my God, my God!' Lawton moaned. 'And you draw five feet? Can't we go back the way we came?'

'With the whole country around Rochefort on high alert, I think we stand a better chance in the Maumusson. There'll be enough water for the next couple of hours. But we may not be able to wait that long. Monsieur, are you for France or the Nazis?'

'Vive la France?'

'Absolutely. How many men are in the German garrison?'

'It is only a post. Twenty men and a lieutenant.'

'It'd still be a gun battle, and I don't want to risk your civilians. Are you prepared to help?'

'Of course, Captain.'

Duncan looked at his watch; 2355. 'He's due out in five minutes. When does your fleet leave?'

'They should have gone by now. But they waited for the bombing to stop.'

'Well, will you get round there and tell them to delay their departure for another ten minutes; we may have to leave at speed and we can't afford to get mixed up with a bunch of slow-moving trawlers.'

'Of course I will do that.'

'And will you also tell them to keep away from the town gate. There may be some shooting.'

The port captain nodded. 'I will do this.'

'Like now?'

'Of course. Monsieur, may I shake your hand?'

Duncan squeezed the offered fingers, and the Frenchman hurried round the dock.

'I'm glad you've done this sort of thing before,' Lawton commented.

'Actually,' Duncan said. 'There is a first time for everything. Just let's say I've been under pressure before. Keep your eyes skinned on that gate, Jamie.'

'Aye-aye, sir.'

In fact, the entire crew were staring at the town; even Wilson and Brewster were in the hatch. The port captain had now reached the other side and was speaking with the fishermen, most of whom were still staring at the MTB.

'I hope to God,' Duncan said, 'that none of them gets the idea of being heroic Frenchmen and tries to help us get away.'

'I have movement,' Richard said. He had swung the six-pounder to cover the gate, and now Duncan also saw the three shadowy figures emerging. But as they did so there came the wail of a siren and some shouting from beyond the wall.

'Is this them, do you think?' Lawton asked.

'It had better be. But you said he'd be coming alone.'

'Well—'

'Trouble!' Richard said. 'Shall I—'

'Let them get clear.'

The three figures were running along the waterfront, but

now the men who had appeared in the gateway opened fire, while shouting, presumably calling on the fugitives to stop; they did not as yet seem aware of the presence of the MTB. One of the running men threw up his arms and fell. The other two checked and turned back.

'Blow that gate,' Duncan snapped.

Richard pulled the lanyard, and the gun exploded. The shell smashed into the wall some yards to the right of the opening.

'Left ten and fire again,' Duncan commanded.

This time the shell burst exactly in the gateway, scattering both men and masonry, and halting the fire. The fugitives had now abandoned the man on the ground, who presumably was dead, and were on the dock.

'Stand by,' Duncan said.

'Aye-aye, sir.' Jamie had left the engine murmuring in neutral.

The fugitives came up to them. 'Mon Dieu!' one said. 'That was close.'

'It still is,' Duncan assured him.

'Colonel Morte?' Lawton inquired.

'I am he, monsieur.'

'Will you board, please. And this is . . .' He peered at the colonel's companion, and gulped.

'My woman,' the colonel explained. 'Severine.'

'We were not told of her.'

'You expect me to abandon my woman?'

'Of course we do not,' Duncan said. 'If you would come on board, madame. Wilson, show the lady to Mr Calman's cabin, and –' he peered at the bedraggled figure – 'see if you can find some dry clothes for her to wear. And madame, I would like you to stay there until we are away from this place. There may be some shooting.'

As he spoke, a shot rang out, followed by several others; the Germans had recovered, but their shooting was wild, as the MTB remained an indistinct blur in the darkness. Morte helped Severine over the rail, and followed. Lawton was behind him, and Duncan came last. 'Let's get the hell out of here, Jamie,' he said. 'Richard, cover.'

Wellard's men had already cast off, and Jamie put the

engine astern to clear the dock. The six-pounder exploded, and again, and the firing from the shore slackened, the noise being submerged in the immense hubbub rising from the town, added to by the shouts of the fishermen gathered on the other dock.

'Turning, sir,' Jamie said.

'Can you?'

'Just about.'

They were clear of the dock, but had backed close to the fishing boats. Jamie put the engine ahead while spinning the wheel. The MTB surged ahead and there were shouts of alarm from the fishermen. But he had already gone astern again, and although there was an agonising wait – it was no more than a couple of seconds although it felt like an eternity – as the bow seemed certain to crash into the first of the fishing boats, before the propellers gripped astern and she checked and moved backwards.

While this was going on, Richard continued to pump shells at the gate, but the Germans were now organized and several men had got outside and were spraying the harbour with bullets.

'Clear the foredeck,' Duncan commanded, using the tannoy as concealment was no longer necessary. Except for the gun crew, who were partly protected by the shield, the men hurried aft and into the cabin. Duncan glanced at Jamie, who was ignoring the flying shot as he continued to manoeuvre, and now got the boat straight and between the pier heads. The fishermen cheered as the MTB slipped through and into the channel.

Duncan looked at his watch. 2420. 'Are we all right?'

'Tidewise, sir, yes.'

Within the harbour, and under the lee of the town walls, they had been less aware of the wind, but once they emerged from the marked channel it seemed to leap at them.

Richard joined them on the bridge. 'What do you reckon this is?'

'Six going on seven,' Duncan replied.

'Can we do it?'

'Well, sir,' Jamie said, 'we can't go back.'

Richard looked astern, and gulped. The night back there

was as bright as day, with huge fires blazing at Rochefort, and now searchlights playing across the Coureau.

'Yes,' Duncan agreed. 'Someone in Le Chateau has been on the blower.'

'But they seem to think we're going back out the way we came in.'

'That's because they don't feel the Maumusson is practical in these conditions.'

Richard gulped.

As there seemed to be no immediate interest in what they were doing – although no doubt soon enough someone would realize that a boat that had left Le Chateau at just after midnight and had not appeared in the Coureau or at the Pertuis d'Antioch half an hour later had to have gone the other way, no matter what the risk – Jamie took the increasingly narrow channel slowly, checking left and right for landmarks; the channel itself was still marked with withies, although these were difficult to see in the dark, and more than once the boat actually brushed against the thin branches. In here, sheltered by Oleron on their right and enclosed by the mainland on their left, the sea was nothing more than a series of wavelets, over which the seventy-two-foot boat coasted easily enough.

Lawton joined them on the bridge. 'Well, gentlemen, I must congratulate you on a masterful feat.'

'It's not done yet,' Duncan pointed out. 'How are the passengers?'

'I think they're finding it difficult to grasp that they're out of the wood.'

'They aren't.'

'Because of the tide? Isn't it still high?'

'It's falling, but it has a way to go, yet. We should make it, but it may be a little boisterous. I think you should go below and warn your passengers of this. Bring them up to the cabin, and equip them with a life jacket each. Then tell them to sit tight. Richard, I think the crew should also retain their life jackets, but I don't want to use the tannoy.'

'Aye-aye, sir.' Richard disappeared down the hatch.

Duncan stood beside Jamie, peering into the darkness.

He could still see nothing, but he could hear, brought towards them by the wind, a rumble. 'Sounds like surf.'

'It is, sir.'

'Hm. And we will have perhaps six feet under the hull. Maybe less.'

'I know what's on your mind, sir. We're carrying four extra hands, say seven hundred pounds in weight. Could well be an extra six inches of draft. But . . .' He thumbed the intercom switch. 'How's it going down there, Billy?'

'Not too badly, Petty Officer.'

'Fuel?'

'Just on half. That's a bit less than I had hoped, but it should get us back.'

'Thank you, Billy. There's going to be a bit of a bobble in the next few minutes. If you're happy, I think you should come up to the saloon and put on a life jacket.'

'Aye-aye.'

'So you reckon we've shed a lot more than seven hundred pounds in weight,' Duncan suggested.

'Yes, sir.'

'But if I remember rightly, your original calculations were based on losing that weight anyway.'

'Yes, sir. But the only weight additional to my calculations is the lady, and she can't be more than one twenty. I think our only problem is wave height.' He pointed. 'There it is.'

Duncan stared into the rain, and swallowed. In front of the boat, at a distance of perhaps a hundred yards, there was a line of white, rising and falling. He could see no markers, but as the line was at least a hundred yards wide, that was obviously the width of the Pertuis. Of course it would carry the greatest depths in the centre, and it was towards this that Jamie was steering. 'Will you, sir?' he asked.

Duncan thumbed the intercom. 'We're at the passage,' he said. 'All hands stand by.'

He heard a sound behind him and half turned his head; Richard had returned to the bridge.

'Hold on, please, sir,' Jamie suggested. He never turned his head, and his hands were tight on the spokes. Now the boat, even if still within the Coureau, was starting to rise and fall to the swell coming through the gap, and a few moments later they struck the first of the surf. *433* went up, and came down again with a thump, and was entirely lost beneath a sheet of water breaking right over her, landing squarely on the three men. Duncan, holding on to a grab rail on the port side of the bridge, all but lost his grip, while Richard had both arms round the mast.

Jamie never released the helm, and *433* soared through the water and out into the air again, only to come down with another thump in the following wave. Again water flew everywhere and there was a shattering sound from below. Once again she went up, Jamie slightly increasing speed, and again she came down, this time with even greater force than before. Now there was a jar which went the whole length of the boat.

'Christ!' Richard shouted. 'What's that?'

'We've struck, sir.' Jamie also had to shout above the howl of the wind and the roar of the sea, but his voice remained calm.

'But . . .'

'She's manageable. I think we're over the bar.'

And indeed the next wave, if breaking over the bow and flooding the deck, did not fly over the bridge.

'Damage report,' Duncan snapped. 'On the double, Richard.'

'Aye-aye, sir.' Richard slid down the hatch.

'Sorry about that, sir,' Jamie said. 'I'd like to alter course, now.'

The wind was on the starboard bow, and starting to throw the boat off course.

'You do that,' Duncan said. 'And you got us through. What do you reckon we hit?'

'The bottom, sir. Those first two waves were eight-footers.'

He had now altered course to turn up into the wind, and although the waves were big they were no longer dangerous. They had done it! Providing . . .

Richard emerged.

'Report.'

'I'm afraid we're making water, sir.'

'From where?'

'Just aft of the engine room, sir. We've had the boards up in the lobby, and Brewster estimates we've cracked a seam.'

'Can we cope?'

'We've started the pump.'

'Very good. I want an up-date in the next fifteen minutes.'

'Aye-aye, sir.' He disappeared again.

'Engine and helm all right?' Duncan asked.

'Yes, sir. I reckon we may just have got lucky, and touched a slight inequality in the bottom. If the pump can cope . . .'

'What about having to head these seas? Will it open the broken seam?'

'It may do that, sir. But if we touched in the aft lobby, well, that's forty feet away from the bow, which is where the pounding is.'

'You understand that we cannot reduce speed if we're to make the rendezvous?'

'Yes, sir. But . . . do we have an alternative to carrying on?'

'Good point. On the other hand . . . in the old sailing days, when they had a problem like this, didn't they use to spread tar over a spare sail, and then pass the canvas under the hull, over the damaged timbers, drag it tight and secure it, to keep the water out? Or at least, lessen the intake.'

'Yes, sir, they did. But things were a little different. As you say, they used a spare sail coated with tar. We do not have a spare sail, or any sail at all.'

'We have bedclothes that could be tied together.'

'Yes, sir, we do. But that would not keep the water out, once it became soaked, unless it was tarred. We do not have any tar. And then, those old sailing ships made about eight knots. To make our rendezvous, we have to maintain thirty. There is nothing that could be passed under our hull that would not be swept away in minutes at this speed.'

'Jamie, you are the ultimate realist. Do you think we'll make it?'

'Depends on the pump, sir.'

'I think I'll go down and have a look.'

\* \* \*

There was a thin layer of water on the lobby floor, and considerably more in the engine room bilge. However, Richard had taken charge down there, and was rigging up the hand pump connected to a hose which was fed up the companion and through the cabin to flow over the side; this meant that the cabin door had to be opened sufficiently for the hose to have an exit, and with the largely head seas the occasional wave sloshed across the deck and water came in. But this, although uncomfortable for everyone, especially as some inevitably found its way down the forward companion and into the galley and forward cabin, was bearable.

It was also extremely hard work, pumping the long handle up and down. Two men were required, and they had to be regularly relieved. 'We'll manage, sir,' Wellard said, confidently.

They went to the engine room, where there was water over the floorboards. But the noise was reassuringly normal.

'Will she make it, Billy?' Duncan asked.

'As long as we can keep the water below the plugs, sir.'

'We'll do that,' Duncan promised.

'You couldn't ask for a better bunch,' Richard confided, as he and Duncan left them to it.

'I know it. Where are our passengers?'

'I sent them back to my cabin, sir. They'd only be in the way out here.'

'Are they all right?'

'I don't know, sir. I don't speak French,'

Duncan grimaced. 'I suppose I'd better have a look.'

The door of the captain's cabin was closed. He knocked and went in, blinked at the scene, which reminded him, on a very small scale, of prints he had seen of aristocrats awaiting the summons to the guillotine. Lawton sat at the desk, his head in his hands. The redoubtable Colonel Death sat on the bunk, his shoulders hunched, looking very much like one of his victims. The woman Severine, strong-featured and attractive, wearing a seaman's jumper and not a lot else that he could see, sat beside him, holding his hand.

Duncan surmised that their dejection, apart from the constant pounding, was caused by the water sliding to and fro across their feet. But at least no one had been sea-sick, so far as he could tell.

He gave them a bright smile. 'Only a few hours to go.'

Severine raised her head. 'Are we sinking, sir?'

'It is not our intention to do so, madame. The Royal Navy dislikes having its ships sunk.'

'But this storm—'

'Will soon be over.' Provided the weather forecast is correct, he thought. 'Would you like something to eat?'

'Well . . .'

Lawton groaned.

'I'll have the cook bring something.'

He went forward, to where Wilson was sloshing about the galley, looking morose. But he brightened up when Duncan appeared. 'Reminds me of that day in the Adriatic, sir.'

'I'm afraid I do not remember too much about that day, Mr Wilson.'

'Ah, well, sir, you were unconscious most of the time.' His tone suggested, you can't win them all.

'Exactly. Do you think you can get some food to the people aft?'

'Yes, sir. What would they like?'

'I'm not sure they know what they'd like. I think your best bet would be bowls of hot soup, and salt biscuits.'

'Aye-aye, sir.' He got busy.

Duncan went back to the bridge. 'You must feel like a spell.'

'I'm fine, sir. Dawn isn't that far. And look up there?'

The rain had stopped and the stars were visible.

'Clearing all the while. It's going to be a good day.'

His optimism was infectious, and justified. By dawn the seas were no more than moderate, and the water was no longer rising. Duncan made him turn in for a while, and took the helm himself, sharing it throughout the morning with Richard. Now the sky was absolutely clear, save for the odd puffball. The two officers took turns at studying it, both aware that it would be the height of irony were they to be sighted by an enemy plane after having all but completed their mission.

But there was nothing to be seen, and the seas steadily went down, until by noon they were skating over no more than a big swell. 'We're gaining on it, sir,' Wellard was as enthusiastic as ever.

'Well done, Mr Wellard,' Duncan said. 'I hope you're all having some lunch?'

'Yes, sir. But what about you?'

'I'll be down in a little while.'

Wellard was replaced by Lawton, unshaven and haggard, but almost cheerful.

'How are our passengers?' Duncan asked. He was again on the wheel while Richard scanned the horizon with his binoculars.

'Bearing up. I must say, Captain, you and your people have done a magnificent job.'

'We haven't finished it yet, Mr Lawton.'

But at that moment Richard said, 'I have the sub.'

'Hallelujah.'

'What are you going to do?' Lawton asked. 'Abandon ship? I'm sure they'll be able to squeeze us all in.'

'Mr Lawton, it is my intention to take this boat into Portsmouth. We'll be there tomorrow morning. Jamie, will you make, we have three passengers for you to take.'

'Aye-aye, sir.'

'Hold on a moment,' Lawton said. 'There are only two to be picked up.'

'You're going with them.'

'Captain Eversham, if you intend to take this boat home, I intend to come with you. I feel I'm a part of the crew.'

# PART THREE
# THE VORTEX

And now I see with eye serene
The very pulse of the machine;
A being breathing thoughtful breath,
A traveller between life and death.

*William Wordsworth*

# A CELEBRATION

Lucifer was barking his happy bark. Kristin looked up from her morning paper. 'That can't be Duncan, at this hour.'

Alison got up and went to the window. 'It isn't. My God! It's Rebecca Strong!'

'What?!' Kristin joined her.

As it was the third week of December, it had snowed during the night, and the entire drive was carpeted; the taxi had left tracks up to the front door. Outside the door, they watched a woman apparently waltzing to and fro, almost totally enveloped in Lucifer's paws.

'I must rescue her.' Alison ran for the stairs.

'Don't hurry,' Kristin suggested. 'She's his favourite toy.'

But she went to the stairs herself. Rebecca Strong was one of her favourite women, as well.

Alison got to the door, where Harry was also waiting, helplessly. 'Lucifer,' she commanded. 'Do please get down.'

Lucifer subsided down Rebecca's front, a journey filled with obstacles. Rebecca Strong was not a tall woman, but was very solidly built. In her mid-thirties, she had large, splendidly sculpted features, a description that could also be applied to her bust and hips, although her mink coat made her seem larger than she actually was. Hatless, she wore her yellow hair loose and longer than Alison remembered.

'Rebecca!'

Rebecca ran a hand over the front of her blouse to establish how many buttons had gone; there were three left. Then she embraced Alison in turn. 'Darling! It is so good to see you.' She spoke with a quiet Massachusetts accent. 'And looking so well. Say, do you think your man could bring my gear in? I guess this poor guy would like to get back to Southampton.'

Alison recalled that Rebecca used taxis as other people

might take a train, regardless of the distance or the cost. 'You mean you've come to stay?'

'Well, sure. I've come to spend Christmas with you. And I can tell you, getting here through all the check points and red tape took some doing. Kristin! You look great, as usual.'

'And you,' Kristin said, 'Have put on weight.'

Rebecca patted her hip. 'That's the way the cookie crumbles. Darling!'

This time the embrace was long, and slow, and intimate. Alison would have given a great deal to know what had gone on during that trip to Malta two years ago. She did remember that Rebecca had appeared in their lives, inadvertently, the year before that, when, on her way to England on a hush-hush mission for the United States Government, she had been torpedoed, actually in the Channel. She had been rescued by the MTB commanded by the then Lieutenant Eversham, which had earned her undying gratitude.

But it had also earned what had seemed likely to be Kristin's undying enmity, when it turned out that when she had been dragged from the freezing sea – it had been January – Duncan had deputed his youngest and, as he had supposed, most innocent crew member, to carry her down to his cabin and take care of her . . . which had entailed removing her sopping clothing, drying her with a towel, and then wrapping her in a blanket: she had been virtually unconscious and unable to help herself.

Kristin's jealousy – accentuated when she had discovered that Rebecca was married to an American billionaire and was thus even wealthier than herself – had only increased when a few months later Duncan's boat had been despatched – at Rebecca's request – to the north of Norway to rescue her and her atomic-scientist father from the clutches of the Gestapo, when there had been another series of mishaps involving clothes, and she had returned to England wearing Jamie's shirt and socks, and very little else.

And yet, a year later, when Kristin had discovered that Rebecca, again travelling on a diplomatic mission, and by then a widow, provided her only hope of getting to Malta in search of Jamie, she had volunteered to be her secretary. That had ended in the pair of them sharing a life raft for twenty-four hours. Kristin, unusually, had always refused to confess what had happened between them, but the adventure had ended with the pair the very best and closest of friends, and that it was on-going was revealed in the warmth of the embrace.

'I assume you're on some diplomatic job,' Kristin said, escorting Rebecca into the house, while Harry collected her bags from the taxi.

'All very hush hush,' Rebecca said, a sure sign, Alison knew, that she would soon be telling them all about it. 'To do with this invasion we're trying to get off the ground. But the mission doesn't officially start until 2 January. So . . .'

'You can stay with us till then?'

'If you'll have me.'

'You'll have to ask Alison.'

Rebecca raised her eyebrows, but turned to the younger woman.

'Of course, we'd love to have you,' Alison said. 'I'll tell Lucia to prepare a room for you.'

'And you'll be here for Christmas lunch,' Kristin said happily, leading her up the stairs to her private sitting room. 'Your old friend Jimmy is coming.'

'Is he? Oh, I'd love the see him again. Kind of make it up for the way we parted.'

'You must tell me about it,' she said, as if she didn't know that Jimmy had fallen head over heels for the glamorous American, proposed and been accepted, before Rebecca, like her, had realized that she didn't really want to be a Navy wife, with all the protocol and tradition that would involve. 'And we have a lovely young man, coming as well. A South American.'

'A what?'

'He's actually English,' Alison explained, pouring sherry. 'He just happened to be born there.'

'And Duncan, I hope.'

'Of course.'

'I read about his VC. Isn't that tremendous? You must be very proud.'

'We are.'

'And that gorgeous kid, Jamie . . . I never can remember his name.'

'Goring,' Alison said. 'He's about. He's actually in the process of getting a commission.'

'Oh, my! That's tremendous. You must be over the moon about that, Kristin.'

Because, as Alison knew, Rebecca was the only other person in the world who knew of the relationship.

'Why should I,' Kristin remarked, 'be interested in anything to do with Jamie Goring?'

The train wheezed to a halt, and the platform at Southampton General became flooded with disembarking soldiers. The station had become used to this over the past few months, as the entire south of England had been turned into one vast military encampment, but the tall figure in naval uniform stood out, not merely because of his height and bearing, but because of the strange collection of medal ribbons on his breast. He wore the insignia of a sub-lieutenant in the Navy, and yet, side by side with the crimson stripe of the Victoria Cross was that of the Distinguished Conduct Medal – awarded to enlisted men – and bar. Those close to him hurriedly saluted and then made way for him, as he slung his kitbag and went to the exit.

'Jamie!' Tim Goring embraced his son, then stood back. 'Or should I address you as sir?'

'Really, Dad!' Jamie embraced him again. 'I see things are really building round here.'

'You can't hardly turn around without falling over a soldier. And of course, it's all very hush-hush. Even if it's hard to believe that Jerry doesn't know about what's happening, and why. But for us poor civilians . . . our mail is censored, and we can't leave the area without permission, and that's only given on account of a family emergency or something like that. But I'm just an old moaner. Come along, your mother is dying to see you.' He led the way through the throng to where his old Morris was parked. 'How much time have you got?'

'I have Christmas off. I'm to report on the twenty-seventh.'

'That's absolutely tremendous.' He got behind the wheel, then shot his son a glance. 'Or will you be spending it some-where else?'

'I'm going to be spending as much of it as possible with you. If you don't mind four of us. Which is supposing she can spare the time.'

'She'll make the time,' Tim asserted, 'She's been to see us, you know.'

'I never knew that. And . . .'

Tim threaded through the traffic and headed for the New Forest. 'She is an absolutely lovely girl. No trace of side. She and your mother get on like they were related.' Another sideways glance. 'So tell me, how was it? All those public school boys?'

'I had no problems. Having had four years combat expe-rience, and wearing these –' he touched his ribbons – 'gave me a lot of clout. I think even the instructors were in awe of me.'

'Great stuff. And did you learn all about being an officer?'

'To tell you the truth, Dad, having spent a large part of those four years rubbing shoulders with officers, I didn't have all that much to learn.' He looked out of the window at the massed trees to either side. 'Gosh, it's good to be home.'

They turned off the road into the garage forecourt . . . and saw the Sunbeam at the pumps, being attended by Probert. Shit! Jamie thought; this was the last meeting he wanted, right now.

Then he realized that the smartly dressed, but distinctly small young woman in a mink coat standing beside the car was not Kristin.

Tim parked, and got out. 'Milady! Good to see you, as always.'

'Thank you, Mr Goring. But –' she looked past him as Jamie got out – 'Jamie?! Good lord!' To his consternation she crossed the court and threw both arms round his neck, having to stand on tiptoe to kiss his cheek. 'How marvel-lous to see you. And looking so, well, so splendid.'

'Thank you, milady. It's great to be home.'

'And in time for Christmas. You will be here for Christmas?'

'I will, milady.'

'That's tremendous. Listen, you must come to lunch. Christmas lunch.'

'Milady?' He could not stop himself looking at his father.

'Of course,' Alison said. 'You must come too, Mr Goring, And Mary.'

'Well, milady . . . if you're sure.'

He was clearly delighted, but Jamie said, 'With respect, milady—'

'Of course,' Alison said again. 'You'll want to spend as much time as possible with Miss Broughton. She must come too.'

'Ah . . .'

'Don't worry,' Alison said. 'I'll invite her, personally. Southampton General, is it? Leave it with me. Oh, Duncan is going to be so pleased to have you back. And I know how anxious he is to meet your fiancée. We've toyed with the idea of contacting her several times while you were away, but, well, we weren't sure it would be appropriate, without you. Now . . . all finished, Mr Probert? Thank you, so much.' She went to the car. 'Twelve o'clock, Christmas Day. All your friends will be there.' She started the engine and drove away.

Jamie stared after the receding car. All my friends, he thought. But the only friends Alison Eversham would be thinking of would be officers, and that could only mean Richard Calman. He was plunging into unknown territory, at least socially.

'Wow!' Tim said. 'When I remember the timid little girl who turned up here four years ago . . . now she's starting to remind me more and more of her mother-in-law.'

'I suppose that's inevitable,' Jamie commented, 'as for four years they've lived in each other's pockets.' But lunch, with Kristin and Emma! On the other hand, Kristin could not possibly know anything about Emma, other than that she was a rather forceful hospital sister. And Alison obviously had no idea of his own past relationship with Kristin. But

Emma! But she could not possibly ever know anything about him and Kristin. What a tangled world he had got himself into! But surely all he needed was a cool head and careful navigation.

'Jamie!' Probert, having entered the recent transaction in the book, returned from the office.

'Bill!' Jamie shook hands.

'It's good to have you back. And looking so . . . so . . .'

'Splendid,' Jamie suggested.

'That's exactly it.'

'Jamie!' Mary Goring hurried from the house. 'Oh, Jamie!' It was time for another hug and kiss. 'Oh, you look so . . . so . . .'

'Splendid,' it was her husband's turn to suggest.

'That's it. Come inside. I bought a bottle of champagne especially for today. Oh. you too, Bill. We'll see from the house if any custom turns up.'

They went towards the house.

'You'll never guess what's happened,' Tim said.

'Oh, no!' Instinctively she looked at her son.

'Oh, it's to do with him, all right,' Tim said. 'We've been invited to Christmas lunch, at Eversham House.'

'What? You're pulling my leg.'

'You saw her ladyship leaving.'

'But . . .' Mary looked at Jamie.

'It's quite true, Mother. Now that I'm an officer, I'm apparently also socially acceptable.'

'Good lord! But what about our turkey? It's ordered.'

'Well,' Tim said. 'If you can't cancel the order, we'll have it on Boxing Day. Jamie isn't reporting until the twenty-seventh.'

Mary sank into a chair in the lounge, while Tim opened the champagne. 'I've nothing to wear.'

'You wear exactly what you were going to, for lunch here,' Jamie said. 'If they don't like it, they can lump it.'

He was desperate to get on the phone to the hospital, waited, heart thumping, to the various clicks and thumps.

'Frobisher Ward!'

Breath rushed through his nostrils. 'Remember me?'

'Jamie! Oh, Jamie! Where are you calling from?'

'The garage.'

'You mean you're home? And you're—'

'I have a stripe on my sleeve, yes.'

'I can't believe it. How much time have you got?'

'A week.'

'Tremendous. I can get down tomorrow, I think.'

'I can hardly wait. And Christmas?'

There was a moment's hesitation. Then she said, 'That's off.'

'Ah.'

'Actually, there isn't going to be one. For me. They're in London.'

'And they won't come down for Christmas?' He found that hard to believe.

'It's not like that. Dad's office is in London. That's where all his work is. His normal pattern was always to come home for weekends. But since the military have virtually taken over the south of England, getting in and out has become such a hassle, passes to be presented, etc, etc. So he asked Mummy to go up and be with him, close up the house in Eastleigh and that sort of thing.'

'So you haven't had the chance to speak with them about us. In the new circumstances.'

'I did. Well, I tried. But I don't think they believed me when I told them you were going to be commissioned. But they'll have to now. And listen, if they won't go along with us, I . . . I'll lunch with you. If you'll have me. I am going to marry you, you know. No matter what.'

'No matter what. So where are you living now?'

'At the nurses' hostel. I mean, I have a key to the house, and can go there if I wish, but it's no fun being all alone in that huge pile. On the other hand, it's there. Empty. So we don't have to use Eversham's boat any more. When I collect you tomorrow, I can drive you back there. Would you like that?'

'I would love that. But about Christmas—'

'Oh, no. Don't tell me your parents—'

'Good lord, no. But the fact is that I, all of us, have been invited to lunch at Eversham House.'

There was a moment's silence. 'And you're going?'

'I said all four of us, my dearest girl. Me and mine. You're mine now, aren't you?'

Another brief silence. 'You asked them to invite me?'

'I did not ask them to do anything. Lady Eversham was here when I arrived, and she issued the invitation then. And specifically included you.'

'But . . . I can't really accept a second-hand invitation like that, Jamie.'

'You don't have to. I'm just warning you that you are going to receive an invitation, some time soon. Probably today.'

'Let me get this straight. You are saying that that dragon is going to telephone me and ask me out to lunch? I got the impression that she hates my guts.'

'As cordially as you hate hers,' Jamie agreed. 'But this wasn't the old lady, this was Alison.'

'Shoot! And she can do that sort of thing? I mean, invite people off her own bat?'

'My darling, Alison is the Lady Eversham. Kristin is only the dowager. She may make a lot of noise, and Alison gives her her head in a lot of things, but when push come to shove there is only one boss in that house.'

'I'm glad to hear that.'

'Then you will accept.'

'I wouldn't miss it for the world.'

'And you'll be down tomorrow.'

'Three o'clock. Love you.'

Alison slowed when she was out of sight of the garage, and drove the remainder of the short distance to Eversham House rather thoughtfully. What have I done? she asked herself.

She had acted on impulse, another bad habit she had picked up from Kristin. But the fact was, they were such genuinely nice people, and before she had been metamorphosed into a member of the aristocracy they could easily have been friends of her and her family, had they lived in the same town or village – her father was a GP. And Duncan, she knew, would be delighted, and he was the only one who really mattered.

So Kristin would just have to grin and bear it. On the

other hand, she had no intention of having her lunch party spoiled by anything remotely resembling a scene. So the bull would have to be taken by the horns, right now: Christmas was only four days away.

She parked and went into the house, necessarily pausing to allow Lucifer his obligatory hug and kiss, and then hung up her mink and went up the small staircase, as she did so checking to make sure she still had all her pearls and tucking her blouse back into the waistband of her skirt.

'Alison, darling!' Kristin was reading *The Times*. 'Did you get what you wanted?'

'They didn't have it. What stock they have left is all being consumed by these millions of overpaid GIs who have nothing to spend their money on but gifts for the girls back home. Oh. I do apologize, Rebecca.'

Rebecca had been reading the *Tatler*. 'I agree with you. GIs are like locusts. But then, you must remember they're here to die for you.'

'Point accepted. Anyway, they offered to order it for me, but God knows when it'll turn up. Not until after the invasion, I suppose.'

'And that can't be for another four months at the earliest,' Rebecca observed. 'Not even Eisenhower is going to be crazy enough to start an invasion in the dead of winter. Ah, well, we all have our crosses to bear.'

'Nurse and Baby back yet?'

'Not so far as I know,' Kristin said.

Alison looked at her gold Omega lapel watch. 'Twelve. I wish she wouldn't keep him out so long in the cold.'

'She's a health freak. Still, it's way past sherry time.'

'I'll pour.' Alison went to the sideboard, filled three sherry glasses with Kristin's favourite Bristol Cream, handed them out. 'I put petrol in the car.'

'Well done.'

Alison sat beside her. 'And you'll never guess who I met?'

'As you say, I'll never guess.'

'Sub-Lieutenant James Goring, VC, DCM and bar.'

'Oh, terrific!' Rebecca cried.

'Do I know this person?' Kristin inquired.

Alison merely smiled. 'He looked so utterly handsome, in

his new uniform, and the stripe on his sleeve, and he was, as always, utterly charming. So remind me, who have we got coming to Christmas lunch, so far?' As she had organized the party, she knew very well who was coming, but it was a useful lead in.

Kristin put down her glass. 'I hope to God you are not trying to tell me what I suspect you are trying to tell me.'

'I am not trying to tell you anything, darling. I have invited Jamie Goring to Christmas lunch.'

'Wow!' Rebecca said. 'I can hardly wait to see him again.'

'My God!' Kristin commented.

'With his mother and father.'

'What?'

'And his fiancée.'

'What? That—'

'High-powered nursing sister. I'm dying to meet her. And I know that Duncan is too.'

'Hold on a moment,' Rebecca said, 'I'm way behind you. You saying that Jamie is engaged?' She looked at Kristin, eyebrows arched.

'That—'

'I haven't actually invited her yet. I am going to do so now.' Alison picked up the phone and at the same time turned to look at Kristin. 'And there is something I would like you to remember: If you are rude to her, I am going to be very rude to you, in front of everyone. And there is something else. I want Lucifer kept under control.'

Kristin went to the sideboard and refilled her glass.

'I think,' Rebecca said, 'that someone could be kind enough to put me in the picture.'

'I am as nervous as a kitten,' Emma confessed.

She had driven to the garage to join the Gorings, very smartly dressed in an ice-blue suit with a matching hat, high heels and kid gloves. Her cloth coat was in dark blue.

'You're not half as nervous as I am,' Jamie said. 'Looking at you.'

She blew a raspberry.

'I mean, is all that, well—'

'Going to be placed in your hands for the rest of your

life? Well, you know, the important parts of me have already been placed in your hands, but I'm quite prepared to surrender the rest so long as you always remember it's a two-way deal. Merry Chrstmas, Mrs Goring.'

'My dear, you are absolutely beautiful.'

'You are a flatterer, Mrs G. And you look lovely yourself.'

'We'll use my car,' Tim decided. 'It's a lot older than yours, Emma, but it's bigger.'

She and Jamie settled themselves in the back seat. 'There is something I should warn you,' he said. 'I hope you like dogs.'

'I adore dogs. Mummy and Daddy have always had dogs.'

'I hope they were big dogs. The Evershams have a very large dog. Well, actually he belongs to Kristin.'

'That figures. What is he?'

'A Pyrenean Mountain Dog.'

'Gorgeous. I can hardly wait to meet him.'

'She calls him Lucifer.'

'That also figures.'

'The point is, he's very boisterous, and she uses him, well, to overawe first-time visitors.'

'Ah.'

'Especially those she wishes to embarrass. For whatever reason.'

Emma squeezed his hand. 'And she has cultivated an inbuilt hostility to me. Don't worry about it. She didn't invite me. Lady Eversham did.'

'Yes. But—'

'Please relax, darling. There is no dog I cannot handle.'

They arrived ten minutes later, to find the Sunbeam, the Bentley, and the Bugatti, all parked outside the house. 'Seems the others are already here,' Jamie said, opening the door for her.

'Quite an assortment,' she commented.

'What does your dad drive?' Tim asked.

'Well, I hate to admit it, but it's a Rolls. He feels it goes with his image.'

The front door opened, and Duncan came out. 'Jamie! How good to see you. And looking so well.'

Jamie shook hands. 'Well, sir, it was a school, not a prison.'

'In my experience, there's often not too much difference. Mrs Goring . . . Mary! Welcome to Eversham House. It's been too long.' He kissed her on the cheek, and she giggled girlishly.

'It's an honour to be here, milord.'

'Duncan, please. Tim!' He shook hands. 'Good to see you. And this is Emma.' They gazed at each other. 'Am I allowed to kiss the bride, Jamie?'

'I'm not a bride yet, Lord Eversham.'

'The name is Duncan.' He kissed her lightly on the lips. 'A friend of yours is my secretary.'

'My oldest friend. Owing to one thing and another, we haven't seen too much of each other over the last couple of years.'

'I invited her to join us today, but she felt she should be with her parents. Seems they're not in the very best of health. But you know, she never told me quite how beautiful you are. Neither did you, Jamie.'

'Emma did say, last time we spoke, that you're a treat to work for,' Emma said.

'Well –' it was his turn to be embarrassed – 'Alison!'

Alison came out of the doorway, where she had been waiting. 'Jamie!' She embraced him. 'You look absolutely splendid, as always. Tim! Mary! You must be so proud of him. Emma! I have wanted to meet you for so very long.' She embraced her as well. 'Jamie, do you realize what a lucky man you are?'

'I do indeed, milady.'

'Alison, please.' She turned to face the doorway. 'I think you've all met Duncan's mother?'

Kristin swept towards them in a swirl of silk. 'Jamie! Your new uniform becomes you. Tim! Mary! And, of course . . . the formidable Sister Broughton.'

'I think, today, just Emma will be appropriate, milady.'

Kristin looked down her nose at her, then turned to the door. 'You haven't met Lucifer.'

'What?' Alison said. 'I told you . . .'

But she was too late. There was a rushing sound, and Lucifer, clearly just released from restraint, emerged in a burst of panting white fur. Mary gave a little shriek and retired into the arms of her husband. Even Jamie stepped back.

But Emma stepped forward. 'You are absolutely gorgeous. Oh, no,' she said, as he reached for her with his front paws. 'Down!' Her voice suddenly cracked like a steel whip. 'Behave!'

A look of utter bewilderment crossed Lucifer's face; he had never been spoken to like that in his life. He sank back on his haunches while he considered the situation. Emma stooped before him, held his massive head in her hands, and kissed him on the nose. 'You may kiss me back,' she suggested.

Lucifer licked her nose, carefully. Emma looked up at an utterly thunderstruck Kristin. 'He is an absolute sweetie, milady. But I think he could do with just a little discipline. Dogs do appreciate it, you know.'

There were a few moments of silence. Then Alison said, 'I think we should go inside and have a drink, and meet the others. Come along, Emma.' She tucked her arm through hers, and escorted her to the door. 'As of this moment,' she said in a low voice, 'you are my very best friend.'

'As Alison says, let's join the others,' Duncan invited. 'Come along, Mother.'

Kristin was still standing as if turned to stone, watching Lucifer padding obediently behind the two younger women, but very obviously following Emma. Now she slowly accompanied the Gorings into the house.

'Jimmy,' Alison said. 'I'd like you to meet Emma Broughton.'

'Oh, I say.' The admiral's eyes glowed. 'This is a pleasure, Miss . . . did you say Broughton?'

'That is my name, yes, sir,' Emma acknowledged.

'I was at school with a fellow named Broughton. Odd chap, with a funny name. Ah . . . Kenelm. That was it. Perhaps you've heard of him. Delivers babies for royalty and that sort of thing.'

'Sir Kenelm Broughton is my father, sir.'

'What? Good lord! Oh, I say, I do apologize.'

'Why should you? I think you summed him up both accurately and succinctly.'

'Well . . . and you're a friend of Alison's?' His tone suggested, who has been keeping you secret all of these years.

'She is now,' Alison told him. 'She is also Sub-Lieutenant Goring's fiancée.'

'Sub—?'

'Come in, Jamie,' Alison invited. 'I believe you do know Rear-Admiral Lonsdale?'

'We have met, yes, sir.'

Lonsdale peered at him. 'Goring! My God! Where have you been these last six months?'

'At Dartmouth, sir.'

'And now you're commissioned? I say, well done. Where are you assigned?'

'I have volunteered to return to MTBs, sir. And been accepted.'

'Brilliant! Brilliant! Did you know that, Duncan?'

'I did, sir, yes.'

'And you never told me. Still, welcome home, eh? Welcome home. Don't you agree, Mr Calman?'

'Oh, indeed, sir.' Richard, wearing the two stripes of a full lieutenant as well as the ribbon of the DSC, had been greeting Emma. 'Jamie is a most fortunate man,' he confided. 'All he touches turns to gold.'

'In that case, Mr Calman,' she said, 'Am I not the most fortunate of women? And this is . . . ?'

'Rebecca Strong.' Rebecca grasped her hand and pulled her forward for a kiss. 'And you are Emma, Jamie's fiancee.' She looked at Emma's empty left hand; although widowed now for more than two years, she still wore her enormous diamond solitaire engagement ring.

'I know,' Emma conceded. 'We haven't got round to buying the ring yet.'

'It's the fact that you're engaged that matters. And you couldn't have a nicer guy. Eh, Jamie?'

'Well . . .'

'The first time we met,' Rebecca confided, aware that everyone was listening, 'he took off all my clothes.'

'Here, I say,' Lonsdale protested.

'It was in the line of duty, sir,' Duncan explained.

'And the second time,' Rebecca continued, 'He did it again.'

'He must have become quite good at it,' Emma suggested, equably.

'Actually, I tell a lie. A nasty Nazi lout had already taken away my clothes. You must remember that, Jimmy. You were there. With Jamie.'

'Well . . .' Lonsdale flushed scarlet.

'And do you know,' Rebecca said, 'the admiral had a gun, and he shot the guy stone dead. All over me.'

'Well,' Lonsdale said again, 'what was a fellow to do?'

'You seem to have lived a most exciting life, Mrs Strong,' Emma commented. 'But I'm not quite sure how Jamie fits into this second adventure.'

'Well, you see, he was there too, when it happened, and he had to lend me his clothes for the trip back. It took four days.'

'I can see that you do know each other very well.' But she squeezed Jamie's hand as she spoke.

Alison decided it was time to call an end to the reminiscences before they got out of hand. She advanced into the centre of the room, and raised her glass. 'We shall now drink a toast,' she announced. 'To the happy couple. Jamie and Emma!'

She looked at her mother-in-law. 'Jamie and Emma,' Kristin echoed.

They drank. 'And now,' the admiral announced, 'I also have something to tell you.'

All heads turned towards him.

'I am leaving Portsmouth.'

'What?' The three officers and Kristin spoke together.

'I am being promoted to Vice-Admiral, and given a place on the Staff.'

'Congratulations, sir,' Duncan said. 'Although we shall, of course, be sorry to lose you.'

'Oh, I'm not going until after the invasion. But also, I am to get a K.'

'Jimmy!' Kristin cried.

'What's a K?' Rebecca asked.

'A knighthood,' Emma explained.

'Oh, Jimmy!' Rebecca screamed, and threw both arms round his neck to kiss him.

'So when are you getting married?' Lonsdale asked as, the shattered turkey having been removed, they contemplated their flaming plum puddings. The table was round, and Alison had, not without some malice aforethought, placed Jamie on her right, next to Rebecca, with Duncan on her other side, next to Mary. Richard was next to Mary, with Kristin on his right. Lonsdale was next to Kristin, with Emma on his right, and Tim was between Emma and herself.

Well,' Emma confessed. 'We would like to, right away. But there are problems.'

'Tell me about them.'

Emma looked at Jamie.

'Sir Kenelm has not quite got around to the idea of having me as a son-in-law,' Jamie said.

'Good heavens! Not approve, of an officer in my command? What possible reason can he have for that?'

It was Jamie's turn to look at Emma.

'I don't think Daddy knows that Jamie is in your command, Admiral.'

'Oh, call me Jimmy, please. Why doesn't he know that?'

'I suppose because I've never told him. I mean, I didn't know that you were a friend of his, until just now.'

'He was my fag at Marlborough,' Jimmy announced.

'Well,' Duncan commented. 'That should put a different complexion on things.'

'Unless the memory makes him hate your guts,' Kristin put in, and received a severe glance from Alison.

'You may leave the matter with me,' Jimmy declared, grandly.

'Have some more port,' Duncan poured.

Emma decided to strike while the iron was boiling. 'There is, of course, another problem.'

'Name it,' Jimmy said, more grandly yet.

'Well, even if Daddy agrees, there is the question of when, and how. I mean, Daddy and Mummy are stuck up in London, where all their friends live. But there is no way all of them would be allowed into the restricted zone, such as down here has become. While we are stuck in this zone, and of course there is no question of any of us getting leave anyway, to go up to London at this time. And then there is the question of whether it is right to have a big wedding, at such a time.'

'Absolutely,' Kristin said.

As Alison happened to agree with her on this one, she could only nod.

'So it seems that we should wait. But we don't want to wait. If all the rumours of what is going to happen next year are true, or even some of them, God knows where we are going to wind up. If and when the balloon goes up, we want to be married. But what do we do?' She regarded the admiral with enormous eyes.

'You are absolutely right, my dear, on every front,' Jimmy said, and proceeded to take command, as admirals are wont to do. 'All hell is going to break loose as soon as the weather improves. If you wish to get married, then you should do so without delay. And the solution is very simple. There is no law to prevent you getting married twice. I assume you are both over twenty-one?'

'Yes, we are.' Jamie and Emma answered together.

'Then you will get married now. We'll get a special licence, and that parson fellow, who Lucifer adores, in here to perform the ceremony. Just us, what?'

'Do you think he'll come?' Alison asked.

'He christened Baby Duncan didn't he?'

'Well, yes. But it cost him a cassock and a nervous twitch.'

'We'll protect him. Well, that's settled then.'

'And you'll explain it all to Daddy,' Emma checked.

'Of course he will,' Rebecca declared. 'He's an admiral.'

Lonsdale looked at his watch. '1400. We'd better get started.'

'With respect, sir,' Duncan said. 'There is a small residual problem.'

'Name it.'

'Today is Christmas Day.'

'Well, could there possibly be a better day for a wedding? No chance of the anniversary being forgotten, eh?'

'I agree, sir. An ideal day for a wedding. Providing one has a licence.'

'What? What? I said—'

'That we would procure a special licence. But Southampton Town Hall will be shut.'

'Good God! Well, then—'

'And tomorrow is Boxing Day, which is also a public holiday.'

'I never thought of you as a killjoy, Duncan.'

'I don't think I am, sir. But I do try to be a realist.'

'Well, then—'

'And we're all back on duty on Wednesday.'

'For God's sake . . .'

'You can sort it out,' Rebecca said, winningly. 'You're an admiral. And you're going to be a sir. Issue a few commands.'

'Well –' the admiral drank some port and squared his shoulders – 'very good. Kristin, you will procure a special licence for Petty Officer Goring and Sister Broughton as soon as anywhere opens after the holiday.'

'Me?'

'You. This operation is now a naval matter, under my command. Alison you will organize the wedding and the reception – it'll just be those of us here today – on a date to be given you as soon as possible. Sister Broughton you will arrange leave for that day and the next I should think.'

'Aye-aye, sir,' Emma said. 'May Second Officer Dunning come too?'

'Who?'

'My secretary,' Duncan explained.

'My best friend,' Emma put in. 'I'd like her to be my bridesmaid.'

'Of course you must have a bridesmaid. Duncan, you will organize a duty roster allowing yourself, Lieutenant Calman, and Sub-Lieutenant Goring simultaneous liberty. As well as Second Officer . . . what did you say her name was?'

'Dunning, sir.'

'Absolutely. This roster must not interfere with your patrols more than is necessary, but must be fitted into the next week. Mr Calman, as Mr Goring's immediate superior, you will be best man. Mr and Mrs Goring, you will be the guests of honour.'

Tim and Mary looked at each other in consternation.

'And I'll be maid of honour,' Rebecca announced. 'Oops! I meant, matron of honour.'

'Why you?' Kristin inquired.

'Because I am the most appropriate.' Rebecca gazed at her. 'Besides, you have all the fuss of getting the licence.'

Alison decided that it would be a good idea to defuse any possible crisis. 'And what role will you play, Admiral?' she asked.

'In the absence of her father,' Lonsdale announced grandiloquently, 'I will give away the bride.'

# MATTERS OF THE HEART

'I am giving you *437*,' Duncan said. 'I'm afraid you won't know any of the crew, with one exception. But I'm pretty damned sure they all know you, at least by reputation. And you will be serving under Lieutenant Calman, who, as you know, now commands C Flotilla in Commander Linton's squadron.'

'Aye-aye, sir,' Jamie said. 'May I ask what happened to Mr Owen?'

'He has transferred to a heavy cruiser. I don't think he found MTBs entirely congenial.'

'Yes, sir. And the exception?'

'Cook Wilson. Frankly, I think he is unhappy at sea if you are not on board.'

'I'm very flattered, sir.'

'Don't be. I imagine he is not alone in that sentiment. And Jamie, I am extremely happy to have you with us again. I just wish to make one point. Both you and Lieutenant Calman, but more especially you, have deservedly gained reputations as fighting seamen par excellence, and you should be proud of that, as is the entire command, myself included. However, I would like you always to remember that you have nothing to prove, to anyone. I know you will never shirk any duty, however hazardous. But I wish no wild adventures unless you are specifically commanded to it.' He smiled. 'I would very much like to have you standing there on the day Germany surrenders. And besides, you are soon going to be a married man, with added responsibilities. Understood?'

'Aye-aye, sir. And again, thank you, for making that possible.'

'I think you need to thank the admiral, for that. And my wife, for setting up the conditions in which it could happen. But I am sure you will do that on Wednesday.'

'I will, sir. May I ask a question?'

'Certainly.'

'Were there any repercussions following that Oleron business?'

Duncan grinned. 'We were successful, which is all that matters. Very good, Lieutenant. Yes?' he called, as there was a tap on his door.

Emma Dunning came in, her face flushed. 'A signal, sir. Sent down by Admiral Lonsdale.'

'What now?' Duncan unfolded the sheet of paper. 'Good Lord!' He looked up. 'On Christmas Day, *Duke of York*, supported by cruisers and destroyers, caught and sank *Scharnhorst* in the Arctic Sea.'

'*Scharnhorst*!' Jamie exclaimed.

'The very last major unit in the Nazi fleet capable of still putting to sea. I will give you ten minutes to reach your boat, Lieutenant, then I shall make this announcement over the harbour tannoy. Thank you, Miss Dunning. Carry on.'

'Congratulations,' Emma Dunning said. 'On every front.'

'Thank you. I'm still finding it difficult to believe.'

'Emma has invited me to be her bridesmaid, if you have no objection.'

'I think it's a splendid idea.' He glanced at the captain's door to make sure it was closed, then kissed her. 'Now I have to rush.'

He picked up his kitbag and hurried down the ramp on to the pontoon. Linton came on deck to greet him. 'Sub-Lieutenant! Welcome back, and to the squadron.'

'It's just great to be here, sir.'

'I'd like you to join me in the mess, this evening, for a drink.'

'Aye-aye, sir. And thank you.'

*432* was as usual moored alongside with *437* outside her. 'Permission to cross your deck, Petty Officer.'

'Yes, sir.' Wellard had also been promoted. 'May I say, welcome back, sir.'

'It is very good to be back.' Jamie stepped on board, and Richard emerged from the hatch.

'Sub-Lieutenant. Welcome to the flotilla.'

'Thank you, sir.' Jamie formally shook hands, although it was only three days since they had last seen each other.

'I know you'll want to get settled in and meet your crew, and I also know there is nothing I, or anyone else, can teach you about MTB strategy and tactics, so . . . shall we have a drink in the mess this evening?'

'Thank you, sir. Ah . . .'

He turned to face the dock as the tannoy blared into sound and Duncan made his announcement. There was a moment of almost stunned silence, then all the crews spontaneously burst into applause, their cheers reverberating around the harbour and scattering the seabirds. Richard shook Jamie's hand again, and then he stepped on board his own boat.

His own boat! He could hardly believe it, even now. He didn't suppose he would, until he had actually taken her to sea.

'Sir!' The warrant officer was waiting for him. 'Petty Officer Trumble, sir. May I say what an honour it is to serve under you?'

'You haven't actually done that, yet, Petty Officer. Then you may wish to revise your opinion.'

'Yes, sir. I doubt that, sir. The men are ready for inspection, sir.'

'Very good.' He accompanied the petty officer down the line of seamen, remembering the times he had had to do this with previous new commanders, greeting each man in turn. Wilson waited at the end, as always. 'Mr Wilson, good to see you again.'

'And to see you, sir.'

'You know you're a glutton for punishment.'

'I know I'm more likely to survive this war with you on the bridge, sir.'

Jamie grinned at him. 'It always pays to be optimistic. Carry on, Petty Officer.'

'Aye-aye, sir.'

Jamie's kitbag had already been taken down to his cabin. He followed it, but went first to the engine room, where he was joined by Fellows, the artificer. 'I don't suppose I've anything to tell you about this, sir,' he ventured.

'Not really.' Jamie bowed his head and walked round the Packard. The area was spotless, as it should be, the engine a gleam of powerful metal. 'Service?'

'Three years on a destroyer, sir.'

'And on MTBs?'

'Four months, sir.'

'It looks good. Carry on.'

'Sir.'

He went aft, and into his cabin. His cabin! He had never had a cabin of his own, even when yachting. He took off his cap, opened his tunic, loosened his tie, tested the bunk, and then sat at the desk. His own command! Something he would never have thought possible, four years ago. And what a tumultuous four years they had been. Apart from the war, without which none of this would have happened and he would have remained his father's mechanic, with nothing to look forward to save eventually inheriting the garage. Instead he had encountered Kristin, earned national fame and prestige, made a friend of the finest man he had ever known . . . and was now about to marry the woman of his dreams.

Often, when with Kristin, he had wondered where it would end. How it could end, without catastrophe. Now, at the age of twenty-two, as an officer with already a glittering career behind him, the future promised to be no less glittering. So, let the end stretch forever into his old age, with Emma at his side.

'We have a ceremony to perform,' Emma said, stoking the fire. She had elected to spend her one night's honeymoon in her parents' Eastleigh house. For the most part it had been empty now for a year, but she had visited it before the wedding ceremony, and although it could not be properly aired because of the cold – it was snowing at that moment – she had changed the bed linen and laid several fires, which she had lit earlier that day.

Jamie could only look on and admire her efficiency, even when full of champagne. He was still in something of a daze, sat on the bed. 'I thought we'd had the ceremony.'

'That ceremony. This is more important.' She opened her handbag, took out the packet of condoms she never seemed to be without, at least when meeting him, and tossed it into the flames.

'Hold on,' he said belatedly. 'I mean . . . you could become pregnant.'

She sat beside him. 'In one night? The odds on that happening are fairly astronomical. Anyway, don't you want me to become pregnant? Or have you so many children scattered about the place you feel one more would be over the top?'

He kissed her. 'I have no children scattered about the place.'

'That statement is usually accompanied by, 'to my knowledge'. What about this female you were shagging before you got around to me?'

'History.'

'I love history. And I have none, at least sexually. As you know.'

'What about all the bedpans or towel baths you've been involved with?'

'I suppose you could say that I learned an awful lot about men that I did not really want to know. There was not one who measured up to you, and I mean that literally.'

'I do know, my darling. I'm sure that's why you married me. And as far as I am concerned, my sex life began that day last year when you first came to Eversham's boat. The history of the world, my world, started on that day.'

'And you'd already won the VC. Do you think your pre-historic partner knows about us?'

'I would say she knows that we are now married.'

'Don't tell me it's in the papers? Or something?'

'Not yet.'

'Then you reckon she's clairvoyant?'

'Do you think we could can it? I really don't want the past, which is no longer relevant, cluttering up the present, or even more, the future.'

'Aye-aye, sir. Your wish is my command. I do love forceful sea captains. Now –' she looked at her watch – 'seven. Or should I say, 1900? You must be ravenous. I filled the icebox with stuff yesterday. Shall I fix us something?'

'After that lunch? I couldn't eat a thing, except you. But I'm dead keen on that.'

'Then I'd better take a few things off.'

\*   \*   \*

She lay with her head on his shoulder, her body nestling against his. 'How do you think it went?'

He hugged her. 'It always goes well. For me. And you sounded pretty content.'

'I'm talking about the wedding, dummo.'

'You have to admit that the Evershams know how to throw a party. I suppose that goes with unlimited wealth.'

'I'm sure that helps. But you know, for all that, they're such absolutely delightful people. I'll tell you a secret. On Christmas Day, I was scared stiff.'

'No one would have believed it.'

'I suppose you could put that down to being a public schoolgirl, as well as the daughter of someone like Daddy.'

'I can believe that. Even if I can't actually believe that he's given us his blessing.'

'Oh, you can thank the admiral for that. Isn't he an absolute sweetie?'

'Ah . . . I don't think that's how he regards himself, or wants to be regarded by any of his men.'

'That's fair enough. But even admirals can be sweeties. As for Lady Eversham – I mean, the dowager – well, she had been so unfailingly hostile whenever we met in the hospital last year, I did not know what to expect. But she turned out to be a sweetie as well.'

'To get to Kristin, you have to be loved by Lucifer. I think you must have accomplished that more quickly and comprehensively that anyone in history. But in any event, she really is dominated by Alison. In her own quiet way she rules the roost.'

'And she's such a sweetie, too. As for the American . . . did you really have to take off her clothes?'

'I was told to do that, by Duncan. She really was in a mess, sopping wet and half dead with cold . . . it was January, you see.'

'She's awfully good-looking.'

'Yes, she is. But she's also a dozen years older than me, and it was three years ago.'

'When I'll bet she was even better looking.' Her hand slid over his thighs, 'And remembering her is stirring your blood.'

'You're not getting set to be jealous?'

'No. I jut want to be part of you. All of you. Your every thought, every emotion.'

He slid his hand between her legs. 'You are. Now and always.'

'As that cute old preacher said, till death do us part.'

'And even after that, my darling girl.'

She raised herself on her elbow, suddenly serious. 'Jamie . . . you have achieved all the honour and glory any man can expect in a lifetime. As regards the Navy, your feet are now firmly set on the rungs of the top ladder. You could wind up an admiral. As regards glory . . . you can't really improve on the VC, you know.'

He kissed her on the nose. 'I believe it is possible to get a bar, even to that. Although I don't know anyone who ever has.'

'Or ever should even try. You must leave something for the others. What I'm trying to say is . . . I really would like us to be able to grow old together.'

'Do you know, those are almost exactly the same words Duncan used, when I reported for duty.'

'Oh, yes?'

'Oh, not in that sense, of course. But he, you, everyone, seems to feel that I have some foolhardy death wish. Would you believe that I have only ever carried out my orders, to the best of my ability?'

'Only you seem to have more ability than anyone else. So here's an order, from me. Come back to me, Jamie. Always come back to me.'

'Excuse me, sir,' said Second Officer Grace. 'But there is a lady here, wishing to see you. How she got into this area God alone knows.'

'Would she be an American lady?' Lonsdale asked.

'Yes, sir. I would say so from her accent.'

'Then she probably has a carte blanche to go wherever she wishes. Show her in, if you please, Nancy.'

'Yes, sir,' Miss Grace said, still doubtful. She opened the door. 'Rear-Admiral Lonsdale will see you now, Mrs Strong.'

'Thank you.' Rebecca entered the room in a swish of mink – the March wind was distinctly cold – and Miss Grace carefully closed the door. 'Must be fun to be protected by a dragon.'

'Rebecca!' Lonsdale came round the desk, holding out his arms, somewhat hesitantly. But she entered them willingly enough, kissed him on the mouth. 'I didn't think I'd see you again,' he gasped when he got his breath back.

'Well, that's up to you, I guess.' She released him and went to the window to look out at the harbour. 'Wow!'

He stood behind her. 'It is impressive, isn't it?'

'You can hardly see the water at all. How many ships are there?'

'I understand something in the nature of six thousand are to be used. They're not all in the Solent, of course.'

'I should hope not. Otherwise you'd be sitting on the edge of a vast cesspool.'

'What?'

'Well, say ten toilets to a ship, that's sixty thousand toilets, all being flushed maybe twenty times a day.'

'You say the most outrageous things.'

'You mean I say the obvious, and the true.'

'Well . . . actually, well over half the ships you see there are transports, and they're empty save for their crews. The troops won't be embarked until your man Eisenhower gives the word.'

'Yeah. He's aiming for May the eighth, or something. That's confidential.'

'But you know it.'

'Well, of course I do. I work for George Marshall.'

'Good God! I never knew that.'

'That's confidential too. I'm one of his troubleshooters. He reckons women with enough gumption can wriggle into the minds of men better than men can.'

'I'm sure he's right. Especially if they happen to be extraordinarily good-looking.'

'Why, Jimmy Lonsdale, what a charming thing to say.'

'I have said it before,' he reminded her.

'I remember.' Her ears were pink. But she was now looking down at the pontoons. 'Are those Duncan's lot?'

'Some of them. A third of the fleet are out all the time, sweeping the Channel.'

'That figures. So . . . would Jamie's be one of those?'

Lonsdale fetched the binoculars from his desk, focussed. 'As a matter of fact, yes. It's their day off.'

'So I'm lucky. Or are the crews all out wassailing, or at home in bed with their loved ones?'

Lonsdale focussed again, for several seconds. 'No. That squadron is not on Rest and Recuperation. It's on Standby. That is, ready to respond to an emergency.'

'Then this really is my lucky day. Have you any objection if I go down there?'

'You mean, on to the pontoons?'

'Sure. I haven't been on a pontoon since the day we got back from Norway.'

He looked at her mink and her high heels.

'And I've fallen in before, too. And been dragged out, dripping.'

'By Goring. I assume it's him you wish to see?'

'You got it. He did save my life, and I'm on my way back to the States, and well . . . with this show coming up . . . I assume those MTBs are going to be involved?'

'Very much so.'

'Well, there you go.'

'If it will set your mind at rest, on his record, Goring is just about indestructible.'

'But he's not immortal. None of us are.'

The admiral returned to his desk and sat down. 'Of course you have permission to go down to the pontoons, Rebecca. I'll just write you a note, shall I?'

Rebecca pulled up a chair and sat opposite him, crossing her knees. 'Now you're all in a huff.'

'Why should I be in a . . . huff, was it?'

'I'd like you to tell me.'

'Well—'

'Come on, Jimmy, spit it out.'

'I also saved your life once, remember? I would say, more urgently than Jamie Goring.'

'Absolutely. I also remember that once upon a time, two years ago, you and I had something going for each other. Like honeymooning in Sicily when this show is over.'

'Which you terminated, rather abruptly.'

'Guilty. Somehow I got the impression that you were a stuffed shirt.'

'Well, I suppose I am. I'm afraid it rather goes with the job, the Navy tradition.'

'But don't you see, it's just a veneer, laid over your true personality, as you say, by the Navy. You're not a stuffed shirt at all. You proved that at Christmas.'

'Ah, well,' Lonsdale said, somewhat uneasily. 'I'm afraid that was rather a surfeit of Eversham hospitality, and Duncan's excellent wine cellar.'

'Then we'll have to establish an excellent wine cellar of our own, won't we?'

He frowned. 'We?'

'Or have you gone right off the boil?'

'My dear girl . . . I don't know what to say.'

'Just invite me out to dinner tonight. Then we'll let things take their course, shall we?'

'Rebecca . . . well . . . I have always adored you. You know that.'

'More than Kristin?'

'Kristin! Oh, well . . . she's somewhat more terrifying than adorable.'

'And anyway, I have more money than she does. Just kidding. It's my Chinese sense of humour. I'm quite prepared to keep it under wraps when we're in company. I'm also quite prepared to adore you, too.'

'Rebecca . . .' He started to rise.

'Dinner,' she said. 'And afterwards. Right now how about writing me that pass, or whatever.'

'I actually should come with you.'

'No way. You'll terrify all those poor boys right out of their wits. I can manage on my own.'

'Sir!' said Petty Officer Wellard, urgently. 'There's a lady on the pontoon.'

'What?' Richard ran up the ladder on to the bridge. Rebecca's progress had been observed from the other boats, and every deck was crowded. 'Mrs Strong!'

'Hi! Permission to come on board.'

'Oh! Well—'

'I have a pass. From Rear-Admiral Lonsdale,' She waved it at him.

'Well, yes, but . . .'

He was looking at her shoes, as she now realized. 'Shit!'

'I beg your pardon.'

'Just an expression. I'm sure you must have heard it, you being a sailor and all. Ah, well.' She stood on one leg, somewhat precariously on the swaying pontoon, to take off her shoe. 'If I get frostbite, you'll have to rub my toes for me.'

She removed her other shoe, placing them neatly together on the wooden boards. By then Richard had come down to the deck to help her on board, while his men exchanged glances. 'Thank you,' she said. 'Stockings can get a bit slippy. Actually, I want to get on to the other boat.'

'You want to see Mr Goring.'

'You got it.'

'And the admiral has given you permission.'

'Sure he has. Jamie is my oldest friend in the Royal Navy.'

'Then please cross my deck, ma'am.'

'Ma'am?'

'I'm on duty, ma'am.'

'Wow!'

'But may I say how good it is to see you again.'

'You may say that as often as you wish, Lootenant.'

Richard winced, but she had reached the other side. 'Jamie!' she cried. 'Oops! I meant, Sub-Lootenant Goring.'

'Yes, ma'am.' Alerted by the commotion, Jamie had come on to the bridge.

'May I come on board?'

'Ah . . .'

Rebecca waved her note at him. 'I have Jimmy's permission. Ooops! There I go again. I have been granted permission to visit you by Rear-Admiral Lonsdale, Mr Goring.'

'Open that gangway,' Jamie commanded, and hurried down from the bridge to take her hand and assist her across the narrow gap between the two boats.

Rebecca squeezed his fingers, while the crew, having heard the word admiral, stood to attention. 'Do you think we could go below?' she whispered. 'I guess it wouldn't be Navy-correct to kiss you in front of these guys, and I'm pretty damned sure Jimmy is watching us through his glasses.'

'But to go below—'

'He can't expect me to stay on deck without shoes. My feet are freezing already.'

'Oh. Right.' He opened the cabin door for her. 'Where . . .'

But she was already descending the after companion, and he remembered that she was well acquainted with the interior of MTBs. He hurried behind her into his cabin. 'I'm really not sure—'

'That's my problem.' She had taken off her gloves, and now turned into his arms to kiss him. 'How's married life treating you?'

'Magnificently. As much as I've been able to see of it. Which is six nights, so far.'

'But you've been married two months.'

'It's a matter of Emma and me getting time off at the same time.'

'Say, that's real tough. You must be horny as hell.'

'Now, Mrs Strong . . .'

'Rebecca. Or I'll scream rape.'

'Rebecca. Please . . .'

She sat on the bunk, swinging her legs up. 'All I want you to do is massage my toes. They're freezing.'

'I don't really think—'

'For Christ's sake, the first time we met you massaged a lot more important bits of me than my toes.'

'I thought you were dying.'

'Oddly enough, so did I.'

'And you were unconscious.'

'So I was. Bu no woman stays unconscious for very long when her tits are being massaged. All I'm asking today is my toes. You wouldn't want me to lose a couple of them through frostbite, would you?'

He sat at the end of the bunk and cautiously began to rub her feet.

'If you know what memories this brings back,' she said dreamily. 'Not just you, but being in this cabin, the whole ambience of the boat . . .'

'Now, Rebecca, please.'

'I'm not going to seduce you, Jamie. I'm engaged.'

'What?'

'Fact. To Jimmy. You remember he was getting set up to propose to me in Malta, a couple of years ago. You were there.'

'Yes, I was.'

'And Kristin had followed you two thousand miles for a fuck. I got the idea you were pretty permanent. What happened?'

He sighed. 'I suppose nothing lasts forever. You mean she hasn't told you about it? I thought you and she were bosom buddies, in every possible way.'

Rebecca made a moue. 'Not quite every way. We never had sex. That's not to say I wasn't tempted. But I guess I realized that Kristin would never be content with just possessing my body. She'd want my soul as well. I guess you figured that out for yourself.'

'I suppose so. Maybe not quite so clearly.'

'And Emma provided the catalyst.'

'Again, not quite so clearly. I think I would have gone for Emma no matter what the circumstances. But I'll admit that it's always easier to end a relationship when you know that you have another relationship waiting for you.'

'So who doesn't think clearly? Does she know about Kristin?'

'No, she doesn't. And she won't, unless someone tells her.'

'Well, don't look at me. I'm not going to tell anyone.'

'But you think I'm wrong, to keep such a secret from my wife.'

'Hell, no, Jamie. There are secrets and there are secrets. Did you go on seeing Kristin after taking up with Emma?'

'No, I did not. I ended it then.'

'Then you have nothing to feel guilty about. You've got red blood in those veins, thank God. So you had an affair, before you met your lasting lady love. For Christ's sake, what man hasn't? Why tell her something that might just upset her friendship with the Evershams? What possible good could come from that?'

'You're a pragmatist.'

'That has been a basic principle of American philosophy

since the Founding Fathers, or we wouldn't be where we are
now. Gosh, I can actually feel my toes again.' She drew up
her legs, and then swung them on to the deck, and stood up.
'I'd better be going, or Jimmy will have the Shore Patrol,
or whatever you guys call it, out looking for me.' Jamie had
risen as well, and she hugged him and kissed him again.
'You have everything going for you, Jamie, and I'm so happy
about that. Before I die, I reckon you'll be an admiral, and
I'm looking forward to that. Oh, you'll be getting an invite
to my wedding. Ciao.'

'An amazing woman,' Duncan commented. 'I'm sorry I
missed her.'

'Oh, she's coming back in a couple of months. Apparently
her boss, this fellow Marshall who, as you know, is the
overall commander of the US Army, likes his secret under-
cover observers to report fairly regularly on relations between
the various generals. But she's hoping to be able to wind
that job up by the summer, if all goes well with the invasion,
of course. And then, well . . .'

'Well, my most hearty congratulations, sir.'

'I suspect there's a but in there.'

'Well—'

'I know. You've always thought that if I ever married it
would be to your mother. And I would like nothing better
than to have you as a stepson. But frankly . . . well, I gave
you some idea of the situation when Kristin and I got engaged
a couple of years ago. Before that ridiculous Malta jaunt of
hers.'

'Yes, sir, you did. And I entirely agreed with you. Much
as I would like to be your stepson, anyone marrying Mother
now . . . well, he'd be taking on a full-time job. Actually, you
know, sir, Father, who married her when she was fifteen,
discovered it was a full-time job even then, and didn't do at
all well at it. In fact, he was a complete failure.'

'Well, I'm very glad you understand the situation.'

'However, sir, I cannot help but wonder, well, Mrs Strong
is her best friend.'

'That does not appear to bother Rebecca. Apparently she
holds the point of view that all's fair in love and war.'

'Of course, sir. But . . . best friends generally look at life through similar glasses, so to speak.'

'That does not apply across the board. What about the saying, opposites attract? Anyway, Rebecca has spent the last three years undertaking high level diplomatic missions for the United States government. She at least knows what is acceptable behaviour and what is not.'

'Of course, sir. Are you going to inform Mother of the situation?'

'I suppose it would be the decent thing to do. Although God knows how she'll react.'

'Would you like me to do it for you?'

'Oh, I say, that would be very decent of you. But I don't want to cause trouble between you and your mother.'

'I believe shooting the messenger who bears bad news is no longer in fashion.'

'It's just that, I really need to be fully concentrated upon what is coming up. That is the real reason I asked you to have this chat.'

'Of course, sir.' Duncan agreed, reflecting that not even an admiral could be equally courageous on all fronts.

'Well, then, the situation is this. The invasion date is set for the eighth of May, and will take place in the Bay of the Seine. I know it sound ridiculous, as that is about as great a distance across the Channel that there is, north of Biscay. But the logistics have apparently been carefully worked out and the top brass seems to be confident that they can sustain an army over that distance of water. We have to hope they are right. That information is not to go beyond you and me.'

'Aye-aye, sir.'

'As far as is known, the Germans are unaware of the date, and certainly of the place, which is not surprising; Jerry is a very logical fellow, and Normandy is not a logical venue. It is believed that he is assuming we will cross at the most logical point, that is, Dover–Calais. However, he does know we are coming, at the first available moment, and it will not take a genius to work out when that will be, as wind, tide and weather have all got to be just right.' He gave a grim smile. 'Unlike at least one other operation we can think of, eh?

'Now, from a purely naval point of view, the Bay of the

Seine is not all that far from Calais, and while Jerry will not
risk any heavy units in the Channel, and in fact he does not
have any heavy units left to risk, he is certainly likely to
throw every other thing he has at us. We could be talking
about more than a hundred S-boats, and even a few destroyers,
who, if they manage to reach the invasion fleet could do an
awful lot of damage. We are expecting heavy casualties
anyway when we start putting men ashore. We certainly do
not wish to lose several thousand more by drowning to
suicidal enemy naval attacks. There will of course be several
of our heavy units with the fleet, but their main duty will
be to provide artillery cover with their big guns, not to spend
their time dodging torpedoes. Protecting them, and the entire
fleet, is our responsibility. We are bringing every available
MTB and destroyer to the south coast, and their, and our,
task is to keep the Channel clear.

'Now, for the moment, you will maintain your regular
patrols, and your rotation system. When the go-ahead is given
for the troops actually to embark, all liberty will be cancelled
and every boat you have will put to sea. Do you have any
questions?'

'No, sir. But I have a request.'

The admiral sighed. 'I knew it. Don't you think, Duncan,
that I would give anything to be going out with them?'

'I know you would, sir. But you have a duty to perform,
here. Even after all the squadrons have gone to sea, you
remain in command. You can direct your boats where they'll
do most good. But once all thirty-six of my boats put to sea,
I have absolutely nothing to do save twiddle my thumbs. I
was in at the beginning of this business, sir. Surely I have
the right to be in at the finish.'

'The war is not going to end the day after the invasion,
you know.'

'If we get a foothold on the continent, sir, and we all
assume that will happen, the Channel war will be virtually
over. That means the MTB war.'

Another sigh, then the admiral said, 'Very well, Duncan.
You may lead your ships to sea when the time comes. Just
remember that I have no desire to have two things for which
I have to beg your mother's forgiveness.'

# THE VORTEX

'That's all for today,' Commander Linton said over the VHF. 'Squadron will return to port.'

'And not a bloody thing to show for it,' Jamie grumbled, bringing *437* round in a wide circle to follow the other boats, becoming aware of the strength of the wind as he did so.

'Maybe they aren't there any more, sir,' Petty Officer Trumble suggested.

'I'm damned sure they are, Mr Trumble. They know what's looming as well as anyone. They're just waiting, preserving their strength. Crikey, that was a big one.'

A sudden twelve foot wave had reared in front of them, into which the boat had ploughed. Green water flooded the deck and even broke on the bridge windshield, scattering spray across the two oilskin-clad men.

Jamie hastily throttled back and used the intercom. 'Everything all right down there, Fellows?'

'All correct, sir.'

'Carry on.'

'Tell you what, sir,' Trumble said, 'I'm not sorry we don't have to spend the night at sea.'

Duncan surveyed his commanders, assembled in the mess hall, having to shout above the howling of the wind outside. 'I have received a directive from Rear-Admiral Lonsdale, on orders from Admiral Ramsay. The MTB fleet will stand down from extraordinary activity, and resume normal patrols, until further notice.'

There was a rustle of discontent.

'I know you are disappointed, gentlemen,' Duncan went on, 'And the decision has nothing to do with any of your recent duties, which have been carried out with all the drive and efficiency anyone could wish. It is simply a result of the weather. This storm is apparently going to last for at least three days, which will take us to the tenth of May. As you know, the set date for our return to the continent was the eighth, because of the ideal conjunction of tides and moon, and dawn. In three days' time that option will be gone. And so there can be no prospect of such conditions returning until the first week of June. So that's it. I'm afraid Jerry will probably be able to work this out for himself. So he also will probably resume his normal activities of convoy raiding etc etc. Thank you, gentlemen.'

'Hello,' Jamie said into the telephone. 'Hello! Frobisher Ward?'

'Yes, sir,' said the unfamiliar voice.

'I'd like to speak with Sister Goring, please.'

'I'm afraid she's not here, sir.'

'When do you expect her back?'

'I'm not absolutely certain, sir. May I ask who's calling, please?'

'This is still her ward, isn't it?'

'Yes, sir, it is.'

'Hm.' He looked at his watch. 1700. 'Look, when she comes back, will you tell her that Jamie called?'

'Jamie,' the voice said, doubtfully. Then added, in a higher tone, 'Jamie! Mr Goring!'

'That's right.'

'Oh, Mr Goring, of course I'll give her the message. She's with Dr Clifton. But she shouldn't be too long.'

'There's nothing wrong, is there?'

'Oh, no sir. At least, I don't think so. Where can she reach you?'

'There's the problem. This is a call phone. However . . . will you tell her that I have tonight off. As it would take me at least two hours to get home by bus, I will wait here, in Portsmouth, for that time. That is, until seven o'clock tonight. I will be at the Officers' Mess, Portsmouth Dockyard. Tell her if she cannot make it by then to pick me up, I will take a bus home, and should get home about nine.'

'Yes, sir. I'm sure she'll get to you if she can.'

'I'm sure she will too, nurse. Thank you.'

He hung up, put on his greatcoat, and left the mess, trudging through the pouring rain to the gate in the fence, where there was an SP post. 'Good evening, Petty Officer.'

'Mr Goring, sir!' Everyone in the Naval establishment at Portsmouth knew, or knew of, Jamie Goring.

'I would like you to do me a favour.'

'Of course, sir.'

'I'm expecting my wife to pick me up some time in the next couple of hours. She won't have a pass, but I would like you to let her in. She will be driving a small, dark-blue Hillman. I will be waiting for her in the mess.'

'Yes, sir. Will do.'

Jamie returned to the mess, hung up his coat, toyed with the idea of having a drink, which he desperately felt like, but decided against it; his moments with Emma were so widely separated he wished to savour every second of each one. So he selected a magazine, and sat in an armchair to read it, while unable to keep his eyes off the clock over the bar.

Various officers came in, and greeted him, but most of the others were not quite sure what to make of an enlisted man risen to their status, quite apart from the outstanding display of ribbons on the breast of his tunic. But then Richard appeared. 'Jamie! Not going home?'

'I hope so, sir. If I'm picked up.'

'Emma?'

'Hopefully.'

'Lucky lad.'

He spoke somewhat sombrely, and Jamie remembered that this so likeable colonial had no home in England, and when not on call used a room here in the mess. He ventured, 'You'll find the right woman, soon enough, sir.'

'To find the right woman, Jamie, one has to look for her. And I never seem to have the time for that. Still, this lot could be over by the end of the year. Will you stay in when this is done?'

'Frankly, I haven't yet decided.'

'As is your wont, eh? Total concentration on the job in hand, until it's done.'

'It's always seemed to me a good idea, sir, when the other bloke is shooting at you.'

'Absolutely. And you've proved your point often enough.'

'But you're considering staying on, sir.'

'Actually, I had selected the Navy as a career even before the shooting started. So, yes, I'll be staying on.'

'This looks like a serious confab,' Emma Dunning said. She had removed her coat and hat and still looked somewhat drenched.

'Emma,' Richard said. Since they had stood together at Jamie's wedding, he counted her as a friend as well as a fellow officer. 'Join us.'

'I would like to, yes. I'd also like a drink. It's bloody awful, out there.'

Richard signalled a steward. 'Three whiskies, please.'

Emma sat down. 'Not going . . . well . . . home, Jamie?'

'I'm hoping Emma will pick me up.'

'You've spoken with her?'

'Not for a while. We've, I mean the flotilla, been sort of tied up the last couple of weeks.'

'Ah!'

He frowned. 'Are you trying to tell me something?'

'Well . . . I think if there is anything, she should tell you herself.'

Richard signed for the drinks, watching the pair of them with interest.

'We have to be able to see each other first. But I'd like to know . . . she's not ill, is she?'

'Why should she be ill?'

'Well, when I contacted the hospital just now, she wasn't available. Closeted with Dr Clifton, the nurse said.'

'Ah.'

'Come on, Emma. Out with it.'

'Well . . . oh, here she is,' Emma said in relief.

Both Richard and Jamie stood up as a somewhat bedraggled Emma Goring joined them. 'Darling.'

As the mess was quite full, Jamie kissed her lightly on the mouth. 'As always, you look good enough to eat.'

'Gravy and all. Richard!'

'You certainly look good enough to kiss,' Richard said, and did so.

'Hi!' Emma Dunning said. 'We were just talking about you.'

'Oh, yes?'

'But we hadn't actually got around to saying anything yet.'

'I have a distinct feeling that something is going on that I know nothing about,' Jamie said. 'Was it something to do with this mysterious meeting you were having this afternoon with Clifton?'

'Well.' Emma sat down. 'He is my boss. But as it happened, it was important, yes. He wanted to confirm something I have pretty well been sure about for the past month.'

'Emma!' Emma Dunning cried. 'Oh, best congratulations.'

Jamie looked from one to the other, feeling suddenly very hot. 'You mean . . .'

'I'm afraid so. Daddy.'

'Oh, my dearest girl!' He looked accusingly at the Wren officer. 'And you have known all along.'

'No, I did not,' Emma Dunning protested. 'Emma told me that she felt it was there, but she had to wait on the tests, and she didn't want to tell you till she was sure.'

'Well,' Richard said, 'as Emma said, best congratulations.' He signalled the steward. 'We'll have a bottle of champagne, Peter.'

'Right away, Mr Calman.'

'I'm not sure we should,' Emma said.

'A glass of bubbly can't possibly harm the little fellow.'

'It's not that, but as Jamie has liberty we have somewhere to go and a lot to do.'

'But can we still do that?' Jamie asked.

'Of course we can. Anyway, he'll have to get used to it.'

'One glass,' Richard said, pouring. 'Here's to . . . ?'

'We'll decide when we see what it is. But I do promise it won't be Kenelm.'

Richard and Emma Dunning watched them leave, hand in hand. 'You ever been in love, Emma?' Richard asked. 'I mean, so in love you can almost see it coming out of their ears.'

'Oh, yes,' Emma said. 'But it was a few years back. And I got over it, when I discovered what a louse he was. You?'

'Never met the right girl,' Richard confessed.

'Well,' Emma said, finishing her glass. 'I suppose I should—'

'We have this bottle to finish,' Richard pointed out. 'And then . . . well, they do a good pork chop in the canteen here. And it would save you getting wet all over again.'

'Gentlemen!' Rear-Admiral Lonsdale himself had come down to address his officers, assembled in the mess. 'I'm sure you'll be pleased to know that General Eisenhower has made his decision: we go tonight.'

There was a moment of stunned silence, and several heads turned to look at the window. The June afternoon was bright, and there was no rain, but they could hear the wind.

'I know it doesn't sound so good,' the Admiral said. 'But is it that bad? You were on patrol today, Commander Howorth. How was it?'

'Lumpy, sir. But it seemed to be dropping.'

'That's exactly it. This front is travelling through very fast, and the Met Office has promised us a window of two, perhaps three, days of reasonable weather. There is apparently a very deep low in Biscay, and moving this way. But if we don't go now, it means July, and the tides and timing will by then be all against us. So the general has decided to take the risk. If we can put sufficient men and materiel ashore in the next three days, we can secure a bridgehead and hopefully keep it supplied until we can develop our strength. That is the theory of the thing, anyway. For us, it's a case of holding the Channel above the crossing area, that is, between The Isle of Wight and Le Havre. I will now hand you over to Captain Eversham.'

Duncan stepped forward. 'As of this moment, all liberty is cancelled for the foreseeable future. As you have all been on standby for the past week, you should all have full complements. Any crew who are ashore for whatever reason must be recalled immediately, or you will sail without them. The same goes, unfortunately, for boats who have crew members absent in hospital and are awaiting replacements. They too will have to manage without them for the duration of this operation.

'Now, you will immediately, in the order I shall give you, top up with fuel as we may have to keep the sea for a considerable time. Having reached our position, we will heave-to under power. When the tide turns, we will of course have to reverse our courses while maintaining our positions. Now, when it comes to engaging the enemy, I will discuss our tactics in a moment. But following an engagement, each squadron leader will determine, according to his situation, when a boat or boats should return to Portsmouth for replenishment of torpedoes and other ammunition. We at least know that we will be operating within an hour or two of our base. In the event of a general engagement, which will probably involve the expenditure of all our torpedoes, it will be a case of returning to the nearest port for replenishment. As I have said, these will be available all along the south coast.

'Now, I don't want to discourage anyone –' he paused to grin at them – 'but Admiral Lonsdale has given me permission personally to lead the fleet.'

There was a moment's silence, then there was a storm of applause. Lonsdale beamed as if it had all been his idea.

Duncan waited for the noise to subside. 'That being so, I shall sail with Commander Linton's Number One Squadron.' Another grin. 'Don't look so apprehensive, Bob. I shall exercise overall command of the fleet, not interfere with the running of your ship. However, that being so, Number One Squadron will be the first to leave, in one hour's time. This is to say, we shall be the first to fuel. My intention is to take up station in mid-Channel and await developments, or –' he glanced at Lonsdale – 'further orders. Commander Howorth, Number Two Squadron will follow second, and will take station on my starboard quarter, closer to the French coast. We will of course all be subject to radar observation, but the RAF and the USAAF are doing their best to neutralize these at this moment. However, you may well come under visual observation. According to our information, there are S-boats stationed in Le Havre, and these may well come out. However, as the Germans are apparently under the impression that the crossing, when it comes, will be in the Pas de Calais, it is considered that the main concentration of S-boats will be in the Dieppe, Boulogne, Calais area, that is, up-Channel of our positions, so that to get to the invasion fleet they will have to come through us.

'Commander Lucas, Number Three will be third out, and

will take station, on our port quarter, to act as a reserve. Your duties will be to deal with any enemy who gets through our position and prevent it from proceeding to the Bay of the Seine. But in the case of a general engagement, it will move up to support the attack.

'In the case of a general engagement, that is, if the enemy come down the channel in force, it is my intention to charge them, with two objectives. One is to break them up, the other is to use our superior speed, once we have gone through them, to turn and close on their rear, where they have proved vulnerable in the past. This being so, the initial attack will be carried out using your six-pounders and machine guns. Your torpedoes should only be used if you have a clear target. This is because when we approach from the rear, your chances of discovering such a target will be enhanced. But as I have said, this must be left to your individual situations and judgement.' He paused to look around their tense faces. 'Any questions?'

'What about Cherbourg, sir?' someone asked. 'Aren't there likely to be S-boats stationed there?'

'That is certainly possible, Mr Barnes, but Cherbourg is below the invasion beaches, and is not including in our jurisdiction. The Navy is detaching some destroyers to watch that flank. Thank you, gentlemen. Number One Squadron will now prepare for sea.'

The officers filed from the room into the lobby, Jamie casting a longing glance at the telephone booths against the far wall. There was no way of letting Emma know what was happening. On the other hand they had no date for this week – as she was only three months pregnant she was continuing to work for the next couple of months – and he could at least feel sure that when it came to her delivery she would be in the hands of the nation's premier gynaecologist.

Richard walked beside him, having seen the look. 'You'll be back in three days, Jamie. That's before she'll know you've gone.'

'Of course,' Jamie agreed. 'I'm being childish. It's just that . . . for the first time in my life I'm feeling vulnerable.'

'The pitfalls of being about to become a father,' Richard observed.

'Hm,' Jamie commented. 'And I suppose it's rougher on your Emma. She'll know exactly when we've gone, and where, and why.'

'Yes,' Richard agreed.

'Are things serious? Or shouldn't I ask that?'

'You're welcome. As to how serious they may become . . . we'll leave that until after this show is over. As the captain said, this could, and should, be the last big one, for us.'

The last big one, Jamie thought, as he helmed *437* out of the harbour, taking up his usual station on Richard's starboard quarter. C Flotilla was third in line, the three boats of A Flotilla, with Duncan on board, were already a mile ahead.

He wondered what he *would* do, when it was over. The last five years had been the happiest of his life, certainly when at sea. But now, when ashore as well. He wished they could last forever. But would they be as enjoyable if there was no enemy to be fought, no critical situations to be faced and overcome?

He actually had no idea what a heavily armed MTB could be used for in time of peace, certainly in home waters. Perhaps they could be sent overseas to undertake local peace-keeping duties. He wasn't keen on that idea, certainly if it involved a separation from Emma. So . . . transfer to a bigger ship? Become a tiny cog in a vast machine instead of master of his own world, however small? And as a war hero with no war to fight he would become an antique the moment Germany surrendered.

As Richard had wisely said, all things to be considered . . . once this show was over.

'Not too bad,' Linton observed, as they emerged into the Channel swell. 'Force Five, I would say.' As they had only fifty-odd miles to go to their position, they were travelling at half-speed and with the wind south-west and therefore behind them, the movement was easy.

'And no rain, at least for the moment,' Duncan agreed.

'Do you think they'll really come at us in force, sir?'

'I'd be surprised if they don't. You're not bothered?'

'With you beside me, sir?'

'You've done pretty well on your own, these last couple of years.'

'Um. There is something I've always wanted to ask you, sir.'

'Now's as good a time as any. You may not have another chance.'

'You've never felt that . . . well, that I deserted you, that day in the Adriatic?'

'Good Lord, no. You obeyed my orders: fire your torpedoes and then get out. As you did. For all anyone knows, yours may have been the ones that hit and crippled *Napoli*. And what else could you do? The way that rain and mist closed in, you couldn't possibly see what was happening to the rest of us, so you couldn't possibly offer any assistance. And it was that weather that saved me and what was left of my crew.'

'Thank you, sir. That takes a great load off my mind.' He looked at his watch. '2000. I'd say we're on station.'

Even with the low cloud cover, it was still full daylight. Duncan used the binoculars and could just make out the gleam of Beachy Head to the north, about thirty miles away, he estimated, which placed them in mid-Channel. 'Very good, Mr Linton. Throttle back and have your petty officer use the lamp and signal the squadron to do the same, and heave to under power. What time does the tide turn?'

'2200.'

'Very good. Then have you crew eat their dinner.'

'And you, sir?'

'I will eat with the crew, Mr Linton.'

Jamie looked down the table as his men tucked into their meal. His men! He still couldn't quite get used to sitting here at the head, being treated with due deference. Of course he could reflect that they would have done that anyway, even had he still been their petty officer, simply because of his awesome service record. But as petty officer, he had not been ultimately responsible for their lives. Even on the crazy jaunt into the Coureau d'Oleron, the responsibility for what they were doing had rested on Duncan's shoulders.

As indeed did the responsibility for what might be going

to happen tonight. A responsibility that had never seemed to bother Duncan in the least. And therefore could not be allowed to bother him, in the least.

'What will happen, sir,' ventured Ordinary Seaman Hapgood, 'if we sit here all night, and Jerry never shows.'

'Well, then, Hapgood, we'll all go home to bed.'

The meal over, he went up on to the bridge to look at the evening. It was well past nine, and the dusk was closing in. The distant land had disappeared, and there was nothing but the sea and the twelve little ships, engines growling at slow ahead to maintain their position. The clouds were still low, and while he thought he could hear the distant rumble of aircraft, he could see nothing above him. It was hard to believe there was a war on at all, much less that in a few hours this whole area was going to explode into unprecedented violence.

Trumble joined him. 'I must apologize for young Hapgood, sir. I'm afraid he's a little tense.'

'As are we all, Mr Trumble. He has nothing to be ashamed about.'

'Thank you, sir.' The petty officer peered into the gloom. 'The flagship is signalling.'

Jamie levelled his glasses and read the Morse flashes. 'Fleet will reverse course to face tide.' He increased speed and turned the boat, in unison with all the other boats. Once in position, he checked his alignment with his neighbour, then throttled right back, and looked at his watch. '2200. Have the men turn in for a couple of hours. All we need is a watch of two, to keep an eye on the flagship for other signals. Course will be reversed again at 0400.'

'Aye-aye, sir. And yourself?'

'I think one of us should remain on the bridge. You may take your pick.'

'I'll take now, sir, if I may.'

'Very good. I'll be up at 0200.

To his surprise, he slept heavily, and awoke with a start, having dreamed of Emma. He found it difficult actually to envisage her as a mother, even if he could have no doubt that, with her so positive personality, she would be a successful one. He had only removed his shoes, tunic and tie, so as to be able to respond immediately to any summons. Now he dressed himself and went up to the bridge.

'No change, sir,' Trumble said. 'Save . . .' He cocked his head. Now the drone of aircraft overhead was very loud.

'It's happening all right,' Jamie agreed. 'Very good, Petty Officer. Stand down.'

He was wearing gloves, as although it was 6 June the pre-dawn was chill; his cheeks were cold. He slapped his hands together as he looked around him at the darkness, and the vague shapes of the other boats. All seemed to be still on station. He thumbed the intercom to the engine room.

'Fellows.'

'All well, Fellows?'

'Oh, yes, sir.'

'Have you had a sleep?'

'A couple of hours, sir.'

'Enough?'

'Oh, yes, sir. I'm fine.'

'Well, remember, when things start to happen, they will happen very quickly and may involve violent changes of speed.'

'Aye-aye, sir. Just as long as things do happen.'

'Absolutely. Carry on.'

He felt that spirit animated all of his crew, and indeed, all the crews of the entire squadron. No skippers could ask for better men to lead.

The next hour drifted by, and at 0300 he was alerted by a growing noise from in front of him. They were still facing down-Channel to front the tide and he could see nothing, but the huge growl told him that the armada was on its way! It was not quite an hour later, as the flagship signalled the next course reversal and the first streaks of dawn were in the sky, that they were overwhelmed as the south-east lit up to the explosion of a thousands guns, hazy in the morning mist.

Men appeared on deck, as did Trumble. 'Action stations, sir?'

'Not yet, Mr Trumble. Have the men breakfast and then wear their life jackets and steel helmets, and check both the guns and the tubes.'

'Aye-aye, sir.' He hurried below.

Now that he could see, Jamie looked at the Flotilla Leader. Richard was on his bridge, using binoculars to study the east – the horizon remained hazy – and also to keep an eye on the flagship. Around them the other boats were moving to and fro, their skippers equally looking to the east. The tension was almost tangible, so that it was almost an anti-climax when, just after sunrise, the light started winking from the flagship. 'Enemy in sight. Estimated fifty. Distance twenty miles. Squadron will attack in flotillas. Good hunting!'

Jamie rang the bell for action stations, and his men took up their positions. He continued to study *433* and Richard now looked at him, gave the thumbs up sign, and then pointed straight ahead.

'Aye-aye, sir,' Jamie muttered, and eased the throttle forward, timing his speed to that of the Leader, which settled on fifteen hundred revolutions, or something over twenty knots, a speed that was not uncomfortable for those on deck, especially with the wind and sea at their backs.

Trumble joined him. 'All weaponry ready for use, sir.'

'Well done, Petty Officer. Now, if I know Mr Calman, we're going to go in hard. Tell Leading Seaman Horton to stay alert; the moment I see a worthwhile target I intend to fire. I will give you no further orders, so you will fire the gun at will, whenever you see something you can hit.' He grinned. 'I mean, of course, an enemy vessel.'

'Understood, sir.'

'Very good. Carry on, Mr Trumble.'

Trumble left the bridge, and Jamie thumbed the intercom. 'Going into action now, Fellows. If all is well down there, come up as soon as the firing starts to assist Cook Wilson in the mess, and also to receive any radio calls.'

'Aye-aye, sir.'

Jamie looked right and left. The little fleet made a splendid sight. One Squadron was spread out virtually abreast, maintaining the same fast but not excessive speed, ensigns streaming in the self-created wind, which was greater than the following breeze. Farther off to starboard Two Squadron was just coming into line, a little behind the right of One.

Astern, Three Squadron was taking up its long-stop position. And in front of them was the somewhat awe-inspiring sight of the fifty-odd S-boats, massed somewhat closer together, their combined bow waves, emerging from the morning mist, seeming to form a continuous line of white surf. It occurred to him that the German commander had the same idea as Duncan's, that of busting through the opposition. But he wouldn't be turning back, and he realized that if the enemy orders were to attack the invasion fleet, he would also be seeking to retain his torpedoes until he reached his prime objective. That meant he would be intending to shoot his way through with his twenty-millimetre cannon. Against six-pounders! By God, he thought, with a surge of exhilaration, we actually have the advantage.

The scene in the still misty dawn reminded Jamie of pictures he had seen of two cavalry forces charging each other in the olden days. But here, both the opposing sides were operating at a speed and with armaments far exceeding anything ever dreamed of by an erstwhile cavalry commander.

A ripple of red ran along the German rank as the two fleets closed. To his right there was an explosion and a quick glance told him that one of B Flotilla's boats had been struck, either by a lucky shot or several together, because she was burning. Shit! he thought. But there was nothing he could do about her. In front of him two S-boats were slightly diverging to pass one to each side, guns continuing to spit fire. The glass on his windshield shattered, and he felt another of those dull thuds.

Damnation, he thought. Not again. From behind him there came a thud and a moan. He turned to see one of the pom-pom gunners lying on the deck. The other was still rotating his gun and firing. 'Wilson,' Jamie shouted down the hatch, 'OS Canning is down.'

Both Wilson and Fellows came up to get to the stricken man, while Jamie realized that they were through the melee and in open water. As expected, the Germans were continuing on their way, but *433* was already turning to go after them. Jamie could not see *432* but he spun the wheel to follow his Leader, and discovered that his left arm wouldn't function. But the boat came round quickly enough, to streak after *433*, as indeed, most of the squadron was doing. He did not think they were all there, but there were also half a dozen S-boats on fire to either side.

'You've been hit,' Wilson said, standing at his shoulder.

Jamie looked down. Blood was seeping from his left sleeve, just below the shoulder, and dribbling down his arm, although as with his previous wound he felt no immediate pain. His left arm again, he though in disgust. Probably broken again. 'Have you seen to Canning?' he asked.

'Ordinary Seaman Canning is dead, sir.'

Jamie has a strong sense of déjà vu. But he now knew the long-term damage that could be caused by excessive blood loss.

'If you'd hand over the helm and come below,' Wilson was saying.

'Fix me up, right here,' Jamie commanded.

Wilson gulped. 'Yes, sir. But when the shock wears off . . .'

'You can give me some brandy.'

'Aye-aye, sir.' He apparently summoned Fellows, and the two men started cutting away Jamie's sleeve – with difficulty as he did not let go of the helm. *432* was now back in line, and with their greater speed all the MTBs were closing the enemy, who were trying to ignore the shells with which they were being peppered. Trumble was still firing away, and the crew gave a cheer as the S-boat directly in front of them, some three miles distant, suddenly gave off a puff of smoke.

But she was by no means mortally wounded, or even incapacitated, although she had lost speed, and realizing that he was bound to be overtaken, her skipper had pulled out of the line and was turning back, at least to see if he could not dispose of his pursuer. And he still had not fired his torpedoes. But neither had *437*, and the S-boat was still turning, directly ahead of her. 'Fire one,' Jamie said into the tannoy. 'Fire two.'

The torpedoes hissed away from their tubes, and Jamie throttled back as he waited for a result. Which was everything he could have wished, as there came one of those terrifying explosions from in front of him.

\*     \*     \*

'There goes Jamie,' Duncan said admiringly. 'That boy operates on a different level to us ordinary mortals.'

'And we missed with both ours,' Linton said in disgust.

'Someone has to.' Duncan called down the hatch, 'Telegrapher, make to One Squadron, return to base for replenishment, then proceed to the Bay of the Seine. Then make to Two Squadron, are you still armed, if so follow enemy and attack. If not, do the same as One. Then make to Three Squadron. Disorganized enemy closing. Engage and advise fleet admiral.' He turned to Linton. 'We will continue the pursuit, Mr Linton.'

'We have no torpedoes, sir.'

'We still have shells for the six-pounder, and besides, I wish to keep overall command of the battle.'

'Ay-aye, sir,' the commander agreed, and then gasped as there came an enormous explosion.

'Signal from flagship, sir,' Wilson said. 'Return to base for replenishment.'

'Return to base,' Jamie said in disgust. 'We still have the six-pounder.'

'And then rejoin action in the Bay of the Seine,' Wilson continued imperturbably. And then looked past his skipper. 'Holy, Jesus Christ!'

As Jamie turned his head, the sound of the explosion reached them. Then he saw the huge plume of water rising perhaps a hundred yards in front of *432*, and looking over his shoulder could just make out the shape of the ship emerging from the mist. It was a large ship, either an outsize destroyer or a cruiser, and it was only about four miles away, unnoticed once the MTBs had turned back to pursue the S-boats. And visibility was improving all the time. Even with their speed the squadron, now entirely lacking torpedoes, would need half an hour to get out of range, and in that time . . . he saw several more flashes of light, and as if mesmerized turned his head to watch the great spouts of water where the shells landed, and in horror as there was an explosion from a few boats over and another great column of smoke.

'Shit!' Wilson said. 'He'll sink us all.'

Jamie thumbed the tannoy. 'Stand by to go about,' he said. 'I'll be using full speed. But you'll stay at your tubes, Mr Horton.'

The leading seaman turned his head to stare at the bridge in amazement, and Wilson said, urgently, 'Jamie! We've no fish.'

Jamie thrust the throttle forward. 'If our tubes are manned, Joe, the bugger won't know that. If he takes evasive action, the squadron will have a chance to get away.'

Wilson sucked air into his lungs. The cruiser seemed to be leaping at them, her sides spitting red from every gun she possessed. But she was also, as Jamie had hoped, turning away to avoid the expected torpedoes, and in her instinct for self-preservation, had forgotten about the rest of the squadron.

Oh, what a target, he thought. If I had just one left . . . and then he realized that his racing boat, still virtually filled with petrol, was a torpedo in herself.

'My God!' Linton said, fighting the helm as the boat surged to and fro in the wake of the explosion. 'That's a cruiser!'

'Or a bloody big destroyer,' Duncan said. 'And she's got us under her guns. Mr Todd, make to all ships: scatter and make for home.'

'Aye-aye, sir.'

'And then check below to make sure we're not making water.'

'Aye-aye, sir.'

The sub-lieutenant hurried below.

'My God!' Linton gasped, his voice hoarse. 'That was *452*! Matthews!'

The last survivor from the Adriatic, Duncan thought. And he was not going to be the last to be lost. He looked back at the looming warship, and gasped himself. 'Holy Jesus Christ!' He grabbed the binoculars. '*437*!'

Linton also looked back, *432* now again under control. 'He's lost steering!'

'No he has not,' Duncan snapped. 'He's attacking the bugger.'

'But . . . he's no fish left. He can't have.'

'But he's still manning his tubes, so Jerry won't know that. And by God, the bugger has turned away.'

'And he's stopped shooting. At least at us. Are we following him, sir?'

Duncan considered, but only for a moment. His every instinct was to charge behind his best friend. But lacking torpedoes he could accomplish nothing more than Jamie was doing, and his prime responsibility was to the command. He sighed, 'No, Mr Linton. Let's get out of here. Maybe, as he always says, he'll get lucky.'

'That crazy kid . . .' Linton concentrated on the helm, but his head jerked as there was a blinding flash of light; the rumble of the explosion reached them a few seconds later.

'That crazy kid,' Duncan muttered.

Sir Kenelm Broughton pulled his Silver Cloud into parking before the station, got out, and walked round the car to open the door for his daughter. Not a tall man, in his late forties, he exuded personality and pride in his position, enhanced by his Savile Row suit. Facially, he was very like Emma, and this morning he was looking more concerned than usual. 'Are you going to be all right?' he asked.

Emma got out. No longer in uniform, she wore a black dress, loose enough to disguise the slight swelling at her waist, with matching black accessories, hat, gloves and shoes. She looked warm, but then it was a warm July day. 'I'm all right, Daddy. Really.'

But she could not suppress a shudder as she looked at the waiting hearse. The driver and his assistant bowed to her. Behind the hearse there was a truck, with a marine driver. He saluted.

They went up to the platform together, the stationmaster touching his cap, and watched the train pulling into the station. I am all right, she told herself, even if she could not overcome a sense of unreality at what had happened, was happening. It was not as if she had been unprepared for the news. She had always known that a man like Jamie lived, certainly his service life, to the limits of what that service required. She remembered what he had said to her on that first day at the boatyard, that he had got his medals for doing the right thing at the right time. Jamie had never doubted what was the right thing. As he had not doubted that day in the Channel.

But as she was a human being, she had hoped. Just survive that last battle, and the entire future was theirs.

As it was six weeks since the dread news had arrived, she had all but recovered, accepted the reality that that brief but glorious part of her life had ended with his, that the only thing that now mattered was her baby. His baby. Now, suddenly, the reality of what had happened, was being thrown back into her face, to be accepted all over again.

The hissing stopped, the doors opened. Duncan stepped from his compartment, came to them. 'Emma!' He embraced her. 'Sir Kenelm!' They shook hands, then turned to look at the train.

The six marines and their sergeant, accompanied by the bugler, all wearing full dress uniforms, had disembarked and were waiting by the doors to the guards' van, rifles slung. Now they took hold of the coffin and carried it across the platform and down the steps to the open hearse. The sergeant saluted. 'Whenever you are ready, sir.'

'Very good, sergeant. Carry on.'

The coffin was placed in the hearse, the doors closed, and the hearse moved off. Duncan, Emma and Kenelm got into the Rolls, Duncan and Emma sitting in the back seat, and followed, the truck carrying the marines behind.

'Is it possible to open the coffin before the service?' Emma asked.

'I don't think that would be a good idea,' Duncan said.

'Aren't I allowed to look at him for a last time?'

Duncan held her glove. 'Emma, when a body is washed up on a beach after having been in the water for six weeks, it is not identifiable.'

She gazed at him. 'Then how do you know it's Jamie?'

He felt in his pocket, placed the ribbons in her glove. 'These were taken from his tunic. Only one naval officer wearing the Victoria Cross, was lost at sea during the invasion.' He closed her fingers over the ribbons. 'Emma, you do understand how sorry I, the entire command, is about this?'

She continued to stare at him. Then she squeezed his fingers back. 'I do know, Duncan. And thank you.'

The little church was packed. Emma sat in the front row between her father and Mary Goring. Vice-Admiral Sir James Lonsdale, KCB, DSO, gave the address.

'Sub-Lieutenant James Goring,' he said, 'Victoria Cross and bar, Distinguished Conduct Medal and bar, Jamie to his friends and colleagues, had a brief career in the Navy, but one which is unparalleled for its utter devotion to duty. Time and again he carried out assignments beyond those normally required of any serving officer or man, always without hesitation, and always, I may say, with total success. He understood his talents, and he also understood that before him lay a glittering career. But his final act, in sacrificing without hesitation his command, his crew, and himself, to save the entire squadron from almost certain destruction, will be remembered forever in the annals of this great service.'

The reports of the rifles echoed away into the distance, followed by the strains of the Last Post. Emma turned away; it was time to greet the other mourners.

She embraced Mary, and then Tim. Both were in tears. So was Alison, who whispered, 'You're coming to lunch. With Mary and Tim. And you, of course, Sir Kenelm.' He was at Emma's shoulder, watchfully.

Kristin was also weeping. 'I loved that boy like a son,' she said, as she kissed her. 'He was so like a brother to Duncan.'

Lady Rebecca Lonsdale gave her a huge hug. 'Jimmy and I would love to see you, any time.'

Richard and Emma Dunning stood together, Emma proudly wearing her engagement ring. 'Oh, my darling,' she said. 'Oh, my darling.'

Richard squeezed her hands.

'You don't know me,' Linton said. 'I was Jamie's CO. I never new a finer man. Lieutenant Todd, my executive officer.'

'Ma'am.' Todd held her glove.

Probert looked absolutely shattered; Emma gave him a hug, then faced someone she had never seen before, a somewhat nondescript man, nondescriptly dressed, certainly in the midst of all the uniforms. 'Name's Harold Lawton, Mrs Goring. It was my privilege to accompany your husband on an operation a year ago. I would like to say I have never known a finer man, or a finer seaman.'

'Thank you,' she said. Then her father escorted her towards the waiting Rolls, together with the Gorings; the Evershams and the Lonsdales followed, towards the Bentley, but Kristin hung back to walk beside the naval officers. 'I don't think I know you,' she remarked.

'Lieutenant Todd, milady. I'm Commander Linton's exec.'

'How exciting. Do you have a first name?'

'Jason, milady.'

'Good heavens! You mean you have an *Argos?*'

'I'm afraid not. Although I hope to have one, one day.'

'I'm sure you shall,' she agreed. 'Jason. I like that. You must come to lunch. Jason.'